PACKING SERIOUS MAGICAL MOJO

TWISTED SISTERS MIDLIFE MAELSTROM BOOK 1

BRENDA TRIM

This book is dedicated to my sisters, Becky, Belinda, Bridget, Barbra, and Beth. You guys have had my back, and supported me throughout life and helped me through the worst moments, as well as, the best. I couldn't have asked for better sisters and friends in my life. I look forward to our next big adventure together! Love you all to the moon and back.

GLOSSARY OF THE SIX TWISTED SISTERS & THEIR HUSBANDS

Dreya – Her nickname is Dre and she is the oldest sister of the Six Twisted Sisters. She is also the third of the Smith children. Her power is telekinesis.

Dakota – Her nickname is Kota and she is the second oldest sister of the Six Twisted Sisters. She is also the fourth child of the Smith children. Her Frenchies are named: Daisy, Willow and Scout and her power is materialization.

Dahlia – Her nickname is Lia and she is the third oldest sister of the Six Twisted Sisters. She is also the sixth child of the Smith Children, Her Frenchies are named: Oscar and Zoe and her power is scent induced premonitions.

Danielle – Her nickname is Dani and she is the fourth oldest sister of the Six Twisted Sisters. She is also the seventh child of the Smith children. Her Frenchie is named Frida and her power is psychometry.

Deandra – Her nickname is Dea and she is the fifth oldest sister of the Six Twisted Sisters. She is also the ninth child of the Smith children. Her powers are empathy and the ability to see spirits on every plane.

Delphine – Her nickname is Phi and she is the sixth oldest sister of the Six Twisted Sisters. She is also the youngest child; of the Smith children. She has the power to freeze objects.

Steve – Dreya's Husband

Jeff – Dakota's Husband

Leo – Dahlia's Late Husband

Hugo – Danielle's Second Husband

Mike – Danielle's First Husband

Maleko – Deandra's Husband

Tucker – Delphine's Husband

CHAPTER 1

DANIELLE

I was standing on the lawn of Willowberry Plantation House. The sprawling property was located just outside of New Orleans. One that my five sisters and I just purchased. A silhouette caught my eye close to what used to be the slave quarters. I took a step closer and noticed the stacks of beehives.

Shaking my head at my superstition, I told myself I knew better. I was born and raised in NOLA. We were no strangers to the supernatural. I believed in ghosts, vampires, witches, and voodoo queens. It didn't matter that I had no proof. My mom saw the ghost of her grandfather when she was a kid. When she was little, Deandra used to say she saw the specter of a woman wearing a floppy pink hat, as well. That was enough for me.

I focused on the next step in the dream I shared with my sisters. I never thought this day would happen. We started our business after losing our mother to cancer. It was a way to ensure life didn't get in the way and force us to drift apart. I couldn't imagine losing touch with the five women I loved most in life, my sisters.

Mom was the glue that held us all together, so without her, it seemed logical we would all drift apart. To avoid that and remain close like I knew she would want, I talked my sisters into joining me in a party planning venture. Our four brothers were business-minded but didn't have an ounce of creativity and had no desire to be part of our venture, which is how we became the Six Twisted Sisters rather than Kay's Talented Ten.

STS started small with a party for one of our brother's grandchildren and grew to the point where we now needed a venue of our own. I dreamed of one day owning one of the beautiful old plantation homes in the area, but never thought my sisters would go for it, let alone put in money of their own.

"I can't believe this is finally ours." I smiled and held my hands out as I twirled in a circle. "We are living the dream, Lia."

Perhaps that had been a ghost. It would be just like our mom to come back and share this day with us. I went on tiptoes, searching the spot I thought I'd seen the apparition.

My older sister, Dahlia, snorted, making me look her way. She was a few years older than me. We'd reached the middle of our lives, but she didn't look forty-five. I hoped that meant I didn't look forty-two. "The only thing missing is the pool and the hot cabana boy."

I chuckled. "We brought Fred, the gardener instead. And, look, he's even sweaty."

Lia lifted one brow and thrust her hands on her hips. "And happily married. That does not count. At least we don't have to live here with the others. No way would we hear the end of the amount of work from Kota and Dre." Dahlia was absolutely right about that. Our two oldest sisters hadn't read the inspection report.

I winced. Dahlia wasn't wrong. Dreya was the oldest of us six and Dakota was just under her. They put in their share of money and trusted Lia and me when we assured them that we could handle fixing the house and getting it ready to host events. When they find out how bad the house really was, they'd want to kill us for buying this place.

I wasn't sure what they expected, but you couldn't get a plantation this big for under a million-five in this area. We got it for half that *because* of the problems. "Thank God for Phi, she's already making a list for us of the first issues we need to tackle. We've got this, sis."

Lia nodded and headed toward the car that was packed so full you couldn't see the interior color. "Let's go play reverse Jenga and get all this stuff out before the tires pop under the pressure."

Standing on tiptoe, Lia stood around five feet, six inches, and was able to grab the zipper for the bag strapped to the top of her SUV. With a yank and a pull, black vinyl parted and spilled pillows, towels, and blankets on top of her.

A laugh escaped me before I could stop it. Before I knew it we were both laughing as the cargo bag continued to spew its guts at us. I had to cross my legs as I bent over at the waist.

No one could make me laugh like my sisters and I loved it despite the consequences. When we were together, we devolved into laughter that ended with one or more of us dashing to the bathroom. None of us had great bladder control after having our kids. Mine went to shit after I had twins.

We could hear Dea chuckling as she got out of the car. Her laugh was the loudest and most infectious of us all. It warmed my heart when I heard it. "What are y'all laughing about?"

"Lia played Jenga a little too well. Now we'll have to wash everything before we can sleep tonight." I hugged Phi as she got out of the car next.

Kota slammed Dre's car door and hurried toward the house. "Do not make me laugh."

That of course made us all devolve into another fit of giggles as we each grabbed up towels and pillows and headed to the house. I had the key and Dakota would be dancing a jig outside while cursing me to hell and back.

Kota was shifting from one flip flop to another with sweat running down her perfect makeup by the time we reached her. "Hurry the eff up. I gotta go."

I chuckled and set my burden on the porch, praying the wood held all of us at once. I already had the key in one hand and inserted it in the lock and twisted. Dakota was through the door like a shot. "We don't have any TP!"

"Or water," Lia yelled over my shoulder. "We forgot to have it put into our name. She's gonna kill us."

Dreya rolled her eyes. "Do not take a dump in the bathroom, Kota! Or you will be fishing it out."

Phi set her pile in the parlor to the right of the entrance and had her phone in her hand. "I'll get the water, electricity and internet turned on. Tucker is on his way with the first load." Once again, Delphine saved the day.

She was super organized and one of the reasons we were so successful. Each of us had a different talent and helped the business run smoothly. I liked to call myself the queen bee, but not because I was more valuable than the others. It was to get under Dakota and Dreya's skin. They were the two oldest and most outspoken of the six of us. I'm sure it bugged the others, but they kept it to themselves. For me, I wanted to feel needed. The truth was, since my divorce from

Hugo, I had been floundering and worried I would end up alone.

The only reason Dahlia was moving into the plantation with me was that her husband Leo died a few years back. He was killed at work by some angry kids in the foster system. Maybe she needed me as much as I needed her. I couldn't imagine what I would do in her shoes. Losing Leo then mom had to be awful.

I stopped that runaway train before it led me to thoughts that would make me cry, like the fact that our mom wasn't here to see us celebrate this achievement. "Steve is on his way to your place Lia, to pick up the laser engraver and supplies. He has the boys with him, so between the five cars, they should be able to get all of our products along with the machine over here and into the barn," Dreya called out as she returned with another load.

Dreya and Dahlia are the workhorses of the bunch. They dove right in and got to work no matter what we were doing. I jumped and dumped the stuff. I looked around at the faded and peeling wallpaper. The musty smell was likely from the mold they found in the attic. Or perhaps it was the broken sump pump in the basement.

My heart squeezed as I walked out of the house to go back to the car. I paused and looked at the wrap-around porch and our investment. The front deck was one of Lia's favorite things about the place. That and what she called the perfect spot to put a gazebo under some willow trees in our yard.

The holes in the flooring were laughing at me. They seemed much bigger now that we owned the place. Rotten wood, check. Mold, check. Broken window, check. I had poured every penny I'd squeezed from my crappy ex-husband into this house. My sisters had each put everything they had into the place as well. Laughter rang out through the massive house, making me smile despite the crushing weight of the project we had just taken on. That right there was the reason this was going to work. Moments like this were priceless, and part of the lesson our mom tried to teach us for years. It wasn't until she was gone that I understood why she wanted the ten of us to be close. You could always count on your family to have your back. At least I could. That was the legacy I inherited from my mom. She didn't leave behind a house for us to fight over or jewelry. She left us love and laughter.

With a smile on my face, I continued while listening to my sisters through the open door. I stopped short when something blue darted out of the corner of my eye. My heart started racing and my breath caught in my throat.

My heart plummeted when I turned and all I saw was the beehives. They were my favorite part of the plantation and one of the reasons I wanted to buy the place. I loved honey bees.

Deandra's arm wrapped around my shoulders as her infectious laughter died down. "Whatcha looking at, sis? Your bees?"

"Our bees." I considered telling Dea about the ghost I swore I kept seeing, then decided against it. There was no doubt she would believe me. She had personal experience seeing them.

Hell, all of my sisters believed in them. We'd grown up with stories, but that didn't mean they wouldn't be freaked the hell out. The only one I was certain wouldn't run away screaming was Lia. She loved the paranormal, particularly witches, as much as our mom had.

Dea wrinkled her nose. "You're the bee whisperer. I'll eat the honey, but that's about it."

I laughed as we paused by the trunk of Lia's overflowing

car. "I'm afraid to touch anything. Lia had to contort her body to get this stuff in here."

"Don't be such a baby. I'll hand boxes to you," Dea said with a sigh.

I smiled at her even though she couldn't see me. She knew me so well. I was a hard worker like all of my sisters. I'd be right there with Lia repairing walls and striping the wallpaper and painting. However, tweaking my back while unloading the car wasn't my idea of fun.

"Thanks, Dea. Or, not." I grunted as she added a third box. I took off before she could add another.

I was perfectly balanced with the packages, so when one disappeared, I practically fell into Dahlia. "You looked like you could use help."

I lifted one eyebrow. "Is that the box with your BOB?'

Dahlia made a pfft noise. "I had to sell my vibrators plus my house. How else do you think we got such a reasonable monthly payment on a house with fifteen bathrooms and almost double that number of bedrooms?"

I chuckled as I followed Lia up the stairs to the side of the porch. Not many appreciated Lia's sense of humor like us. We passed the detached kitchen and headed up the side of the house. It was amazing how having my sister with me made me see the holes in the porch differently. Instead of lamenting my decision to pressure my sisters, I was busy creating stories for those who had lounged there on a hot summer day two hundred years ago.

"We made the right choice, didn't we?" I hadn't meant to blurt that out. My mouth had a tendency to get away from me.

Dahlia stopped, set her box down and gave me a side hug. "I don't know how to explain it, but this is where we are supposed to be. Everything in our life has led us here. Me losing Leo, you divorcing his royal highness, even losing mom. None of us would have taken the risk without the loss. We know better than most know how imperative it is to live life to the fullest and enjoy the little moments."

I nodded in agreement. "Keep that in mind when we are in the hot attic cleaning out the mold and sealing the wood."

Lia chuckled and picked up her box. "Can we sleep in the ladies' parlor tonight? I'm not ready to be in a room alone yet. I swear there's something here."

I glanced over my shoulder wondering if she'd seen the ghost. "Did you see something, too?"

"What do you mean, too? I haven't seen anything. It's more a feeling that I can't explain."

"Don't tell me you guys bought us a haunted house," Dakota said as we entered the house. "We can't afford for this to fail, we're extended as far as possible."

"Lia and I gave up our homes to make this work. Our kids don't have a home to return to during spring break next month." I shouldn't have risen to the bait.

Dakota meant well, but I was irritated. Mostly because I worried this would ruin us. I'd quit my nursing job and Dahlia gave notice at social services. Between the parties, tours, and personalized gifts we planned to offer online, there was no choice. And that was the biggest risk for us. If this failed, Dahlia and I were out of a job while the rest still had theirs.

Dahlia set her box down and took mine from me. "They're coming here and going to work their tails off. I've already warned mine."

I took the branch and kept myself out of the muck. The six of us got on each other's nerves at times which should mean this wouldn't work. It was because we had each other to vent with when we were upset that kept us from really blowing up with one another. That was what would make it work.

"I know I haven't thanked you guys yet, but it means a lot to me that you have sacrificed so much for us to achieve this dream." It helped keep things calm when Dakota showed insight like this.

She was the most outspoken of all of us and never hesitated to say what she thought. I both loved and hated that about her. I kept my mouth shut about far too much in life which is why I just went through my second divorce. It hit me that I envied Dakota's ability to avoid the hardest of the work and say what she thought, as well.

I hugged her then went back out for more. Another two loads and the cars were all empty. Dahlia's clothing and mine were all in the ladies' parlor along with the air mattresses we'd be sleeping on tonight.

My back started bitching at me the moment I laid my eyes on the plastic beast that refused to be contained. "Let's take a look around. It doesn't look like the previous owner moved anything out since our last walk-through, I want to take an inventory to see if we will need trash removal."

Phi held up her iPad. "I'll take notes as we go through. I bet there is stuff we can refurbish and sell. Who knows, in an old place like this we might find some real treasures." Delphine was the most organized of the six of us.

She was smart enough to be a surgeon. Could have been if she wanted. Instead, she decided to become a professor in biological sciences. She and her husband, Tucker, bought a hundred-year-old house and refinished the entire thing from top to bottom, so she would know better than me.

The layout was nothing like I was used to in my old house. The entrance was massive with a beautiful crystal chandelier and twin staircases that branched off to the two wings of the house. Beneath the section where the two met and became one wide staircase was a wide hall.

The aisle leading from the front door was long and there

were a few doors on each side as you proceeded into the house. The first rooms on each side were the parlors. One side was for women and the other for men. They would serve as changing rooms for weddings.

The dining room and an area that was used as staging for the servants before they served a meal were next. The library was across from that, along with an office. We would keep the library and restore it.

We didn't have plans for the office or servants' prep area. That is what excited me. I loved planning differently-themed parties down to the last little detail and I would enjoy doing the same with this house.

It was hard to be patient when I wanted it done now so we could start making money. "They could have cleaned the chandelier for us," I grumbled as we reached an area that had been renovated in the back to be a kitchen. When this plantation was built, the kitchen was built in a separate building to avoid a fire burning down the entire house if one started.

Lucky for us the detached kitchen had been updated with modern appliances and would be the perfect location for caterers to prepare. The iron stairs were solid and clean as we climbed.

"These stairs weren't made for people as big as me," Dakota complained.

Deandra started laughing. "This house will never survive us."

By the time we got to the second floor we were all laughing so hard, I had to go low with my legs crossed. As I balanced on my hands and tried to stop, I swear a ghost appeared at the end of the hallway. It was a blue woman clad in a dress with a wide skirt, high neckline, and fitted top with poofy sleeves. The woman's hair was twisted on top of her head and her face was pinched.

Dahlia turned wide, frightened eyes my way. Deandra

wiped her eyes and opened the first door. "Where's the bathroom?"

Lia pointed further down the hall. "Third door on the left." Dea ran past everyone and into the bathroom. We heard the sound of her peeing a second later. She hadn't bothered shutting the door. I would question that, but as sisters, we often didn't bother closing ourselves in. The second Deandra moved, the ghost-woman vanished.

Delphine shook her head with a smile. "Are we leaving this floor open for wedding parties?"

"Yeah. That's the plan. The place is big enough, we could live in the other wing, but we're good with the third floor." It was likely an attic at one point, but whoever updated the house with electricity and air conditioning had converted it into a space with three rooms and a bathroom.

"I love this old brass bed." I went on my tiptoes and looked into the room Dakota was standing outside.

"It's gorgeous. Looks like we will have a few things to work with. That'll save some money." Dreya was the oldest and like a mother figure to us. She was the first to find a solution to saving money. She was also the only one that had stories about the rest of us when we were kids she shared.

"Wow, I didn't realize how many beehives were out there," Delphine remarked from the end of the hall.

Dakota scowled. "What are we going to do with so many beehives? How do we even take care of them?"

Deandra joined us holding a roll of toilet paper. "Maleko and I looked into that, actually. We will need to make sure the structures remain in good condition and have proper ventilation. Bees also need a way in and out that we can block when needed. It also said something about woodlice and termites."

I shivered as I listened. There was a cold spot where we were standing, yet there was no vent spewing cold air down on us. This was where the ghost had been standing. Was she still there?

Delphine shrugged her shoulders. "We can sell the honey if we open a gift shop in the old carriage house."

I was overcome with excitement. "We have to have a gift shop. Tourists love their souvenirs. And homegrown honey will be a literal gold mine."

Dreya nodded in agreement. "You're right about that. We can engrave jars with bride and groom names for weddings and sell it to them as personalized tokens for them to give out."

I saw a person round the corner from the slave's quarters and I turned and ran for the stairs. My five sisters were running after me and calling my name. I couldn't tell from the window if it was a ghost, but I wanted to make sure it wasn't anyone messing with our property.

I was across the lawn before I was winded. I paused in the middle of the beehives and looked around. The air was sweet from the honey in the nearby drawers. "I thought I saw someone out here," I told them when they all caught up with me.

The six of us were standing in a circle searching our property for anyone that shouldn't be there. The only people on the property was us. Fred the gardener had already left. All of a sudden the bees went into a flurry as if someone had agitated their hives. I dropped to my knees and so did my sisters. Keeping my hands over my head, I watched as they buzzed above our heads.

Kota grunted. "I'm not made to do squats."

"I'm more worried about us being stung. What are they doing? It smells like lavender now." I wished I had an answer for Dreya.

Sniffing the air, I smelled the same thing she did. "I don't recall there being any lavender bushes on the plantation." My skin tingled from the energy produced by the bees. It almost felt like it was vibrating through my blood. Looking at my sisters I was sure that they felt the same thing. I pointed to the left and commando crawled that way, staying low to the ground.

"I'm not sure what that was," Lia said and rubbed her arms as the bees settled and went back to their hives. "But at least we know the bees are healthy and active. Now, let's talk names. Are we keeping Willowberry Plantation? Or changing it?"

Laughter bubbled up as we helped each other stand up and discuss name ideas for our venue. We talked and continued the moving process. It would take time and some loud discussions for the six of us to come to an agreement on the name, so I steered us to important tasks while we processed.

We had some shelves to put together in the converted barn, where we planned to have our workshop. It had been a major selling point for us. We just needed the electricity and structure updated to accommodate our laser and other supplies.

My heart lightened, and a smile broke across my face. This was going to work. We finally had our own venue for weddings and other parties.

CHAPTER 2

DAHLIA

"*A*re you asleep, Dani?" My whisper sounded like I was belting out an audition for American Idol. At least that was how it seemed in this massive house.

I loved the place. It had a distinct haunted vibe to it that suited me just fine. I know Danielle worried she had overextended us and pushed the others and me to invest in something that won't work. But I believe in her. This is what we are supposed to be doing and where we are supposed to be.

"Yes, why are you whispering?" Despite her question, her voice was hushed as well.

I rolled over and stared at the decorative tiles on the ceiling. "This house makes more noises than the littles after eating a bowl of chili." I loved my French bulldogs' snores, farts and all.

Dani chuckled and rolled over to face me. Plastic groaned, overwhelming the wind outside and snores of the three French bulldogs sleeping on the air mattresses with us.

14

"Doesn't smell much better, either. At least Oscar stopped barking at the ghosts."

I turned onto my side and ran my hand over Oscar then Zoe. "I didn't think he would ever stop barking. It might be cute if he sounded like a velociraptor. That noise is one of my favorite things about Zoe and Frida."

"We could get a jump on taking this wallpaper down if you want. I can't sleep. I keep thinking there are ghosts everywhere. What if this place really is haunted? What will we do?"

My heart started racing when I considered it. My hands on Oscar and Zoe became rougher as my thoughts raced in a million different directions. "Then we deal with it. This is our house now. Besides, we knew it was going to be a lot of work but we have a ton of people to help us. That was one of many things mama gave us."

Dani sighed and sat up, making Frida bounce on the air mattress and let out a yelp. "Sorry, love." She soothed her Frenchie. "What do you think mama would say if she could see us now?"

I chuckled and took care sitting up, so I didn't send my puppies into the air. "She'd tell us we are insane and that we spent far too much money on this place. If she were with us, she would have negotiated the price down a lot more than we did after getting the report with mold. But I know she would be proud of us and tell us exactly how to get that awful bird pattern off the walls."

I was up and crossing to turn on the light. Oscar burrowed under my pillow while Zoe curled next to him. Those two had been my loyal companions for several years now. When Leo died, I had the kids until my youngest left for college last fall. I'd have been a mess without my fur babies and sisters.

Dani shifted her Frenchie Frida to the bed with Oscar

and Zoe before grabbing the scrapers and clothes steamer. "I'll steam while you scrape. By morning we should have this room cleared. That way we can get to painting."

I rolled my eyes. "We need sleep somewhere in that schedule, sis."

The steam started shooting out of the handle she aimed at the wall. "Nah, I bought a case of those passion fruit energy drinks. And two flats of tall-boys for me." I had to have my Pepsi like most people needed their coffee or tea.

Dani was addicted to Pepsi while I ran on energy drinks. "No time like the present to crack one open. Keep steaming, I'll be right back."

The kitchen that we would use was on this floor of the house and down the hall. I grabbed my cell phone and turned on the flashlight. I shivered as I passed through a particularly cold spot. My breath caught, then came out in white puffs when I exhaled.

I shone the light around me without stopping. It was one thing to know there were ghosts and another to come face to face with them. I was in the kitchen and grabbing our stainless-steel cups then scooping ice into them. I grabbed a tall-boy and an energy drink and raced back to Dani.

She took her cup and I poured her drink into it before doing mine. After a sip, I picked up the flat metal instrument and started on the birds. "What era is this bird-covered monstrosity from?"

Dani was in a groove as she ran the steamer up and down the wall. "I'd guess the nineteen-sixties. We should put up wallpaper with a monstera leaf pattern or maybe a geometric pattern."

I shook my head back and forth. "No freaking way. I liked the idea of doing an abstract geometric design using two-inch pieces of trim. It'll look nicer and not overwhelm the room."

I jumped and dropped the scraper when something crashed on one of the floors above us. Dani reached down slowly and flipped off the steamer. "That wasn't a ghost. We should check it out."

I gaped at my sister. "Are you kidding me? Have you forgotten the first rule in horror movies? Never go searching for whatever makes loud, scary noises."

Dani blew a raspberry at me. "We aren't in a horror film. If anything was after us, Oscar would be barking up a storm instead of sleeping like a baby."

I nodded my head and ran my sweaty palms down my fuzzy skeleton pajamas that Dani made for us for our first night in the plantation. The tops said *home sweet haunted home*. "Good point. We might as well go find out what it was."

Dani might want to know what happened, but she wasn't about to lead the way. She grabbed my arm and shoved me in front of her. "You're the better fighter."

I snorted. "Yeah, I brawl often. You have me mistaken for Wonder Woman. I can see why. I do resemble her. Albeit a much fluffier version."

She chuckled and loosened her grip on my arm. The stairs creaked loudly under our bare feet. "It's a good thing our business is all about parties. We would not make good assassins."

I wasn't sure whether to laugh or give in to the shock. "Aside from being loud, there is the moral consideration to that chosen profession. We weren't built for killing."

"I don't see anything here. Let's go to the attic." Dani was already to the stairs leading to the third floor, having poked her head in the rooms along the way.

There was another wing that we could check. The noise sounded like it had been right above us, not on the other side of the house. The third floor was mustier than the lower levels given its proximity to the attic where our mold problem was.

We stuck our heads into the rooms where Steve and Jeff had moved our beds and personal items and saw nothing amiss. Dani continued to the skinny door at the end of the hall before I could turn to get back to work. I sighed and followed her to the small space left for storage.

The second she opened the panel, I would have sworn we were about to enter an antique store. They all have the same old musty dusty smell to them and that's what came at us from our attic storage.

"Wow, this is bigger than I thought it would be." Dani waved the flashlight from her cell phone all around us. I yanked the cord when her light illuminated it. There was so much to examine when we went through the place before buying that I scarcely recalled it all.

"Holy crap. Look at all this stuff. Why would they leave so much here?" All thoughts of the noises in the night were forgotten as we surveyed the treasures. It was hard to believe what we were seeing because we would never leave the chairs and dressers behind. Not to mention whatever else there was. After all, it was impossible to tell what was in the cardboard boxes with a glance.

"There's enough here to furnish the entire house. And it might be the original furniture. We will have to ask Phi and Tucker to refurbish some of these items." Dani was in her element.

She was so good at taking something old and slightly worn down and making it even better. She was also the brain behind the parties we threw. All of us tossed ideas into the mix, but none of us put it together quite like Dani could.

Delphine and Deandra came the closest to what Dani did for us. We each brought a different skill to the business that none of the others did which is one reason we worked so well together.

"We should bring some stuff downstairs and show it to them when they get here in a few hours," I suggested.

"Good idea. Moving stuff will let us see what we are dealing with in here, as well."

We immediately got to work with Dani sorting through the items and indicating what we should take down with us. I carried the smaller chairs and two big mirrors while she continued combing through stuff.

We'd turned the lights on as we moved through the house, so it wasn't dark. After depositing the items in the parlor across from where we were sleeping, I schlepped myself back up to the third floor, wishing I hadn't had bread pudding with dinner.

When I got to the second floor, I noticed Dani had carried several items from the floor above. I left them to go up and help her. When I walked in, she was sitting on a cedar trunk holding an old leather-bound book.

"What did you find?" I peered over her shoulder and worried the paper was going to crumble every time she turned a page.

"This is some kind of journal. Inside the hope chest, there are pictures from the original owners of the plantation. We should take them down and hang them where visitors can see them."

I looked around. Despite what had already been removed the room was still full of stuff. "Great idea. I love seeing the history of the place. There may be information in that diary about the history of Willowberry Plantation House."

Before the others had left for the night, we'd decided to stick with the original name, rather than come up with a new one. The history was part of the appeal. Together we carried the trunk and the rest of the things she'd picked out then we sat and started going through pictures.

I found some old frames in the corner of the attic. They were good as new after some polish. We were hanging a fifth picture when Deandra walked through the door.

"Good morning, sestras! How long have you been up and working? Two or three hours?" Dea used the Russian term for sisters that we adopted after watching a popular television series together. It always made me smile when I recalled watching the show during Phi's mastectomy recovery and cancer treatment. It had been a scary, trying time for us, but we bonded as a group and grew closer to one another.

Dani and I gaped at Deandra, unable to believe our eyes. "How are you here before any of the others?"

Dea cocked her head to the side and dropped her purse. "Didn't we say we'd start at six this morning?"

I checked my watch. "Yes, we did and it's only five-fifty. You're early. You're never early."

Dani snorted and smiled. "You would have been late to your wedding if we hadn't hurried you along. You have to come and see what we found in the attic last night."

Deandra was laughing as she walked our way which made Dani and I both start giggling with her. She was always upbeat and positive. I didn't know how she did it given the mistakes she made early in life. There were drugs, the wrong guys, and babies at seventeen. Yet, she had pulled it together and graduated from college, and married a wonderful man.

"Oh, those are great pictures. Do we know the names of who is in the pictures? You could engrave a plaque to go under each one, Lia."

I nodded my head, already ahead of her. "We haven't found the names, yet, but we have journals and will look for descriptions so we can identify the people."

Delphine arrived next, followed by Dakota and Dreya.

Each loved what we had found and Kota managed to rearrange the grouping of frames to make it a statement piece. She'd arranged them in the shape of a hexagon and made it look like a mini-hive of photos. Kota was the interior decorator of the bunch.

We walked into the kitchen to make some breakfast. Dakota and Dreya reminded us to eat on a regular basis, otherwise, I'm sure Dani and I would have kept working.

Delphine pulled out her tablet. "We need to talk about what other staff we need to hire on a full or part-time basis. Running a plantation like this is difficult. The first thing I think will be to get Fred some help. The grounds are too big for one man alone," Phi suggested as I handed her a mug and her tea-making supplies.

Dreya pursed her lips. "We need to watch our budget until we are up and running. Dani and Lia have to feed themselves and we have a lot of improvements to do to the place." Like a mother hen, Dre kept us grounded and looked out for each of us. She and Phi had a big picture take on things which helped when the rest of them had blinders on while prepping for an event.

Dakota grabbed some muffins out of the fridge that she'd picked up from one of the big box stores. "Our husbands can help with some renovations which will save money. And the kids will help when they're home."

Dani held a hand over her mouth as she chewed a bite of apple cinnamon muffin. "Lia and I found a ton of old furniture that we can use to save money on furnishing such a big place. Some of it will need to be refinished, if you and Tucker are up for it, Phi. I think we need to discuss how we are going to do the bedrooms on the second floor and the parlors down here."

"We need to set the parlors up for space where people can do hair and makeup comfortably as a group. I think the furniture from your homes will be perfect in there. It will give both a television, a chair and a couple of sofas. The armoires you had, Dani could be used to hold mirrors and folding tables where implements can be laid out," Dakota replied.

I enjoyed listening to the plans. I was creative in many ways. Decorating and arranging things was not my forte, so I left that to the experts. Dani nodded in agreement. "I found a full-length mirror in the attic I was going to put in the women's room down here, but that is better suited for one of the bedrooms. That's where clothes will be changed anyway."

"I told you it was fun to have rooms on separate floors for dressing and hair and makeup. You guys gave me a hard time saying we wouldn't have any fun together while we got ready." Deandra was referring to her wedding. She wasn't wrong. We originally balked at the idea. That was before realizing how much fun it was.

Dakota squealed as she chewed her food. "We will need a bar in every room. It was the mimosas that made that so much fun. We already have the decanters engraved with the types of alcohol."

Dani lifted her arm and pointed out the window. "Fred's here." She was rushing out the back door before any of us could ask why that was important.

The rest of us set our stuff down and followed her out. We had a pack mentality. We didn't let anyone use the restroom alone in a public place, and we never forced someone to face a situation alone if we were there to do anything about it. I was certain my sisters would travel across the country to help me prepare for an event if needed.

"Hello, Smith sisters. How was your first night in Willow-berry Plantation?" No one corrected Fred that we each had married names. We would always be the Smith sisters, no matter what else changed in our lives.

"It was productive." Dani rocked on the heels of her bare feet, likely regretting not slipping on her shoes. I know I was. "I wanted to ask you where the lavender bushes are on the property. We're going to be selling the honey and I think adding a sprig of it to the top would add a nice touch."

Fred's head jerked back. "What are you talking about? There is no lavender here."

Dani looked at Phi then turned back to Fred. "There has to be. The honey is lavender honey. We smelled it after the bees swarmed yesterday and Delphine and I added some to our tea last night."

The gardener lost his dark coloring and turned his head slowly to look at the beehives twenty feet from where we were standing. He shocked us all by crossing himself. "It's the magic of the plantation. You six have awakened it. I don't know enough to tell you what this switch means, but it takes powerful magic to alter a substance like that."

I looked at Fred sideways and shivered. First, we saw ghosts and now he was telling us there was magic in the plantation. I knew there was something more here, but magic didn't exist. Did it?

Deandra put her hands on her hips and spun in a slow circle. "We need to look into the history of this place and find every document we can. There has to be information about the lore out there if Fred is aware of it, right, Fred?"

The gardener agreed while I watched the reaction of the others closely. I know Dani worried the others would be freaked out and might want to sell, so when Dreya started talking about adding magical tours and even haunted tours at night, I realized I'd been right all along. We were exactly where we were meant to be.

CHAPTER 3

DANIELLE

I walked into the parlor and slumped on the couch that used to be in my living room. After Hugo left me for a younger, firmer woman, I had wanted to burn everything he'd ever touched. Dreya saved me from making a big mistake by having it all professionally cleaned instead. While Dakota had pointed out that he couldn't have gotten too many cooties on the leather.

My entire body ached. Lia and I had been up all-night cleaning, clearing wallpaper, and hanging pictures. I don't know why I bothered because Kota came in and rearranged everything and it was exactly what I wanted. Now we just needed to know who the pictures were of and Lia could engrave plaques underneath them.

Dakota paused in fixing the Pampas grass and pointed to the chest. "You should look through those journals while I fix lunch. I want to know more about the original owners. Now that Fred mentioned magic, it makes sense. What those bees did yesterday wasn't normal."

With a groan, I heaved my butt off the couch and crouched by the hope chest. "You're right about that, I've never seen anything like it in my life."

Crap, now that I was halfway down, there would be no getting up. I wasn't that old. I was only forty-two years old, so my body bitching at me had nothing to do with my middle-aged mom bod and everything to do with how out of shape I was at the moment.

Tucker, Phi's husband, poked his head in the door. "Where do you want this armoire?" Steve grunted somewhere behind the wall. Steve was married to Dreya and a bit of a smartass at times. He was the first brother-in-law to join this crazy family and we loved him to pieces despite that personality trait.

Dakota waved her arm to the corner we had cleared in the parlor. "Against the green wall. But be careful. I just painted that section so we could move that down here."

She had gone up to the attic while we got the rest of the wallpaper off and searched the goodies. She found two stunning pieces amongst the collection and had declared one would go in each of the parlors.

The guys deposited their burden and Dakota told them where to move the second one in the room across from where we were now. I took my book and found the other four sisters covered in dirt and paper bits. The walls used to be covered in trees and ducks in the men's room.

"I can't believe you guys got all that wallpaper off already. Do you think we can get this place ready by spring break? I was asked if we can do a baby shower that week." I cringed when I saw the looks, they all shot me. I had a tendency to expect too much and underestimate how long something would take.

25

Dreya was shaking her head back and forth, yet Deandra was the one that stepped forward. "There is not a chance in hell that will happen. I have the night shift at the hospital tonight."

Delphine wiped her dirty forehead with the back of her arm. "And, I only have this week off. I'm only teaching part-time, but I still have to go in three days a week for classes."

Dreya helped her husband run his business and Dakota was a stay-at-home mom. All of Dakota's kids were out of the house, so she would be with Lia and me daily, but she wasn't the best worker. There were times I wanted to scream because she was sitting there on her phone. I never did. Like my sisters, I avoided conflict like the plague.

Besides, it's not healthy to work all day and night without taking care of yourself. All Kota is doing is setting firm limits and ensuring she is healthy. My inner critic had taken on the voice of my mother since she died which was a good thing. She was one of the few people I listened to.

I picked up my tumbler from the coffee table and took a drink. Ugh. The tall-boy was flat and watered down. I'd need a new one. *You should be drinking water, not soda.* My inner critic could shut the hell up. My liver and kidneys would revolt if I put something so pure in them at this point. I sweated brown and that was fine with me.

Dakota brought in a tray filled with sandwiches and Tucker was behind her with chips, sodas, and water. Deandra returned at that moment with clean hands and sat on the sofa from Lia's house, which was next to me.

Dea picked up a bottle of citrus tea and cracked it open. "After we paint in here, we can move onto the design you and Lia decided for the other room. When we finish that, Dakota can finish decorating and arranging the room. That way we will have one space completely done to sit and visit."

I chuckled and shook my head. "Sit and visit? There'll be none of that for a long time, sis." Deandra's laughter filled the room, making me smile.

"Look, I found some more journals in this armoire." Delphine carried five similar leather-bound books and set them on the coffee table, changing the subject and ending our laughter. "Hopefully, we will learn some good information from these. Dreya's idea of a haunted tour will likely make us the most money, but we need stories to tell. Oh, those look delicious, I love fresh mozzarella on sandwiches. I'm going to go wash my hands."

Lia and Dre filed in laughing about something and Dakota brought some paper plates and napkins. "We will be sharing these stories with our tour guides. I made a terrible guide the one summer I tried it. Thanks for making this Kota. We won't starve with you around." Lia winked at me to let me know she wasn't upset that I rarely thought to stop and feed her.

She and I were the same in that respect. We continued working until we got lightheaded before stopping for sustenance. I set the journal I had in my lap and picked up a sandwich. "So far there isn't anything juicy in this journal. It had to have been a guy writing it. He's talking about how many crops they planted and what they are expecting at harvest time."

I hadn't realized how hungry I was until I started eating. It was a good thing I wasn't trying to impress anyone because I shoved half the sandwich in my face, chewing with my mouth open. "Oh, my gawd, this is so good."

Deandra laughed. "What did you say? I couldn't hear you with the half-masticated cheese rolling around in your wide-open trap."

That started everyone laughing as Dre referenced one of

Sandra Bullock's funnier movies. Lia brushed off her hands and reached for one of the books in front of her. "Oh wow. This is from a woman. And, oh my she was a dirty thinker. I don't know why I thought they were chaste hundreds of years ago."

Dre leaned forward and read over Lia's shoulder. "You weren't kidding. This is dirtier than mom's romance novels. This woman was talking about how lonely she was when her husband went out to work the plantation with the slaves and she found herself dreaming about one of the slaves assigned to the house."

Lia flipped a few pages then held the book up. "She finally cornered the guy and convinced him to hike up her skirts and do her in the parlor next to the stone fireplace."

We all stood up and looked through the double doors at the fireplace in the parlor across from where we were eating. I finished my chips and balled up the bag. "Can you imagine the stories these walls hold? The history and emotions embedded in them have got to be powerful."

"I bet it adds to the magic of the plantation," Lia said.

We shuffled away from the door. I grabbed a drink while Lia continued reading. "Oh shit. Her husband found out what happened. He dragged the slave outside and chained him to a post in the yard where he beat him with a leather strip. The woman's hands were shaking when she wrote this. It says she was afraid for her life."

Dakota picked up Frida and held her close to her chest. She had three Frenchies of her own at home. "Did the slave live? I bet he died and is haunting this place."

Lia chewed her lower lip and scanned the pages, turning several of them before she stopped. She shook her head from side to side. "It says here that he killed the slave and left him outside her window as a reminder."

Delphine had a book in her hand and tapped a page. "This book talks about her wanting to use the devil's powers. She says her lover visited her in her dreams and told her to avenge his death. Can you imagine?"

I shook my head and rubbed the ache in my chest. "What does she mean by using the devil's powers? Did she kill her husband? Life was hard enough back then. A situation like this would have made it that much worse. It's not like she could have owned the property, right? She would have lost everything, including her home."

Deandra's sudden scream got everyone's attention and made my heart start racing in my chest. Oscar started barking and Zoe hurried to Lia where she hovered close. My head moved like it sat on a swivel stick and stopped when I saw the bluish figure of a woman dressed as she had done when she lived a hundred years ago.

"Is that a fucking ghost?" Dakota's voice broke the stunned silence and made the woman disappear.

Lia dropped the book to the table and she and Dreya approached the location where the woman had been standing. Dre shivered. "It's cold right here. You guys, we just bought a haunted freaking house."

Delphine gasped. "And you two have to live here. You can always come to stay with Tucker, the kids, and I."

Phi was the baby of the family and always the first to offer her help. If I admitted how frightened I was at the moment and how badly I wanted to take her up on the offer it felt like the first step down the road to failure.

I smiled at Phi and met Dahlia's gaze. Lia shook her head imperceptibly. "I'm not gonna lie, that is freaky as hell. However, Lia and I managed just fine last night and will be fine. We can't let ghosts scare us out of our home. Besides, we need to know what potential guests might face."

"I think I saw her yesterday," Dea blurted. "I wasn't sure. It was when we were up on the second floor. What if she's the wife and is mad that we're reading about her business?"

Lia shrugged her shoulders and sat down on one of the sofas. "If she is the woman that wrote these journals she is here because she has unfinished business. Perhaps, we can help her resolve it and move on."

I rolled my eyes. "You're the social worker. That'll be your task, sis."

Dreya sighed and sat next to Lia. "At least we wouldn't be lying if we billed the place as a haunted plantation."

Deandra scoffed. "We need to lie and say it isn't haunted. I'd never get married in a place with ghosts! Would you want your granddaughter's baby shower held here?"

Dre smiled. "Sure, my son would love it."

Delphine picked up her tablet. "I'm going to start documenting stories to share with tour guides when the time comes. That angle will be lucrative for us."

I drank the rest of the Pepsi I'd opened and set my cup down. "I never *actually* believed mom when she talked about seeing her grandfather's ghost as a child. Did you guys?"

Dakota set Frida down. "Not for a minute. I thought it was one of those things she embellished. I wish I could tell her I believed her now."

"I miss her more every day," Deandra added.

Lia's eyes watered and she sniffed. "Dani and I were talking about what she would say to us about this venue."

Dre laughed. "She'd tell us we were crazy for paying so much money for this place."

Emotion burned in my throat making my laugh hurt like a bitch. "That's exactly what we said. Now that we have it she would tell us not to give up, that we could do it. She believed we were capable of anything."

Dakota nodded. "She would have these rooms painted

already. And she'd have a list of people waiting for their party here."

"Yeah, but she would give them the venue for free. She gave too much and went without a lot because of it. I hated that for her." It was one of the things I both admired about her and didn't like. She had ten children and she still fed others and did for people without asking for anything in return.

"What if she's a ghost and can come to visit us? That would be nice." Zoe jumped up into Dakota's lap and curled in a ball.

Delphine shivered and clutched her tablet to her chest. "It would be nice if ghosts could talk. If not, I don't want to see her hovering in a room with us. That would be too painful of a reminder that she was gone."

Dreya gestured to the location the woman had been. "Mom might not be a ghost, but she's still with us. How else do you think we were able to find this place and get the deal we did? I believe she is watching out for us and making sure we have what we need. She spent fifty years of her life caring for us, she isn't going to stop now."

The ache in my heart intensified and illuminated the cracks. My life had gone to shit and I was certain my mother knew it would. She knew my first husband was an asshat and told me I shouldn't marry him. I didn't listen and ended up leaving him when his abuse got to be too much.

Now, I found myself with marriage number two on the rocks after Hugo left me. Part of me hoped we could work it out, while the rest was ready for it to be over. I didn't want to be with someone that didn't want to spend time with me. The truth is that Hugo and I had drifted apart over the years. He lived his life and I had lived mine. It was time I stopped worrying if things would work out between us and focus on me.

One thing that drew me to Willowberry was the energy of the place. It felt like home to me, despite the fact that it was haunted. It was the next big adventure in my life. I was willing to do whatever it took to make this venture work for the six of us because my mama didn't raise a quitter.

CHAPTER 4

DANIELLE

I was exhausted after a long day of painting, moving furniture, and putting up the design in the parlor where Lia and I were now sitting. We had our trusty air mattresses set up in the middle of the room again.

Neither of us wanted to sleep in the rooms on the third floor yet. Knowing there was a ghost haunting these halls was frightening, to say the least. And, I couldn't stop thinking about Fred's expression when he'd said the plantation had magic.

I shivered and wrapped the fluffy blanket around me. Frida curled up closer to me in the process. "Do you think Fred is right about magic being real?"

Dahlia paused with her hands dangling on the edge of the large shipping trunk she'd been going through. Her bleached white-blonde hair fell over her forehead, reminding me I needed to cut and color it again for her. "Honestly, the world seems topsy turvy ever since we moved into Willowberry.

Mom was right, ghosts are real. Magic? Nah, my gut says there is no way. Although having grown up here, you know as well as I do that stuff has happened around town that no one can explain. We don't need to worry about it just yet. That ghost is more important. We need to deal with her or every night will be a battle against the plastic beasts trying to swallow us whole."

I laughed at her apt description of what we were using as a bed again tonight. "You're right about that. My neck is sore from the work we did. I don't look forward to a night of twister to stay above the folds."

Dahlia chuckled and picked up a really old book from the chest. "I don't think the journals we found were from the original owners. This trunk dates at least a hundred years before the other one we found."

I got up and joined her on the floor with a groan. "After we finish the renovations, I'm joining you on your morning workouts. The pain from using muscles I didn't know existed is horrendous."

"I'll hold you to that," Lia promised. "Do we know the name of the family that built this plantation? Was it the Carltons?"

I'd been trying to think back to what the realtor told me all day. It wasn't until she said the last name that it clicked. "Yes! Jesus, getting old sucks. I have been trying to remember what Stacy told me about the place all freaking day. It was William Henry Carlton and his wife Mary Alice Carlton."

Dahlia nodded as she scanned the pages in front of her. "This is the book documenting the purchase of the land. He bought more land than we just did for a couple of thousand dollars. And had his slaves build this house for him."

There were mostly clothes and candleholders in the trunk. I found another book at the bottom that documented more expenses. "There's nothing in here from the wife. What part of the attic did you find this trunk in?"

Something told me we would have some pretty juicy stories about the original owners, just as we did the ones who had followed. I'd always been fascinated by the history of places. It was one of the things I loved about living in a city like New Orleans, with such a varied background. There was something new to learn every time I turned around.

"It was in a corner behind some fantastic old paintings, likely of the original owners. The guy had a tall top hat and tails on his coat, along with a cravat and tie. The woman's hair was pinned under an elaborate hat and her dress was big in the back with ruffles flowing down from the shelf over her butt. It was like half of a hoop skirt. Very fancy. They obviously had money."

"Let's go look around and see if we can find anything from the wife. Women are more likely to have kept records of a personal nature." The sounds I made as I pushed myself to my hands and knees then to my feet made Oscar start growling while Frida came over and butted her head against my leg. "I'm just sore, Frida."

Lia made similar noises and her two puppies jumped off the air mattress with a bounce, then followed us as we climbed to the third floor. I could already see the changes we were making, improving the house.

Aside from the completed parlor, we had put a nice rug in the hallway. Dreya had painted one side a popular shade of green. Dakota and I had purchased enough scent devices. The house smelled more like a flower shop than a musty mop bucket.

Delphine and Tucker had gone Mr. Clean on the stairs and landings and the area was now sans cobwebs and dust. "This place is coming together little by little."

Dahlia nodded as she followed my gaze. "It's amazing

how much cleaning changes things. Without all of us and the guys, we wouldn't be nearly as far into this as we are right now. We already have one room completely done. Steve made good progress on the barn. The shelves are up and he got Lacey all set up and vented. We might not have unpacked our pots and pans, but we can etch a tumbler if we need to."

We both laughed at that. When Lia had purchased the laser engraver it was like steroids for our crafting and our parties. As fast as rabbits made babies, we added new products and gifts which in turn had us all thinking bigger.

"We have the priorities sorted out then. Steve knows we have to be able to fill orders as we get them. Our clients expect our stellar service." I smiled as I thought about how much our customers loved us. They came back again and again for various reasons.

"We should get that CNC machine we've been wanting. Or maybe a UV printer. The things we could do with either of them. Talk about magic." Dahlia had been angling for both machines for a while now, but it hadn't been in the budget.

Guilt swamped over me for how heavily I had pushed buying Willowberry on my sisters. I'd been the one to find it. Our dream was to own a place like this, but we never believed it would be possible, so it hadn't been all that difficult to get them on board.

"Stop, sis. I'd rather be here than have either. We will get there eventually."

I narrowed my eyes at my sister. "Last I checked you couldn't read minds. Perhaps there is something to Fred's theory the plantation has magic."

Dahlia snorted as she opened the door made for brownies. Seriously, who made portals this small? I was shocked Tucker and Steve had managed to get the armoires through it.

"I know you better than I know myself, Dani. I know you

are putting pressure on yourself about making this work and that you feel responsible for buying this place. But we all agreed. You aren't in this alone. We will succeed or fail together, just like mama would have wanted. And I don't regret leaving my career for a second. Or selling the house." Lia shrugged her shoulders at me. Or maybe she was just trying to squeeze through the doorway.

"The place was where Leo and I lived and it weighed on me far more than offered me comfort. As long as I lived there, I would never be able to move forward. I owe you for nudging me and getting me free of my grief and pain. I finally feel like I might be able to live again. The trunk was over here." Lia pointed to a section off to her right.

My heart ached for my big sister as she ducked behind a tall dresser. I knew she was avoiding the topic and that was alright. She was making progress. This was the first time she didn't pretend like life was a box of chocolates and nothing was wrong.

A large painting greeted me as soon as I stepped around the furniture. "Wow, you weren't kidding about the hats. I am so glad that fashion died out long before we were born. I'm not a hat person."

"I know, right? I could never dress up like that, either. I can't even go back to business casual at this point. Give me my yoga pants and t-shirts any day."

With my hands on my hips, I scanned the area while the dogs ran around the clutter. "I think you're right. This is the furthest back. It has to be from the original owners. I bet we could mark the transition between various owners by working our way out of this corner."

Lia's eyes brightened. "I have no doubt that we can. Let's stick to this section for now until the others come back. Phi will be able to organize discoveries and keep track of them, so we know what we have."

I nodded and got to work rifling through the various drawers, trunks, and boxes. I completely lost track of time as I found an old parasol that was still in great shape. We could make a box frame for it and put it on display.

Having found some women's items, I stuck to the trunk and dresser and kept searching for a journal of some kind. I couldn't explain the drive to understand what the original owner's wife experienced, just that I felt it imperative to know. And it seemed Dahlia felt the same way.

After what felt like hours, Dahlia shouted. "I found something."

I straightened and set the old-fashioned ankle boot down. "Is it a journal?"

Lia set the book on the top of the tall dresser that blocked off this section and flipped it open to the middle of the book. She was about to turn to the front when a word caught my eye.

I snatched her wrist. "Wait, a minute. It says here she used a spell. She's talking about magic."

Dahlia and I silently read over the pages then I had to reread. It was difficult to follow given the different use of the English language. We had slang terms in our day and age and so did they.

"She was a witch who cast a spell on her husband. Did I read that right?" I looked to Lia for confirmation.

Lia pursed her lips and nodded her head. "Her anger is clear as is the desire to curse her husband and the land on which his precious plantation stood. Let's read why she was mad and what happened after."

"But the curse only affected male owners," I pointed out. Praying that meant we were exempt from any curse because we were women.

We turned to the page before. My eyes went wide and cold fingers skittered down my spine when I read how Mary

Alice had discovered her husband had impregnated one of their slaves after he had forced her to give up a child from her affair with one of the slaves. Apparently, he had forced the child to act as Mary Alice's slave while he was going to elevate his child's status. That would piss me off, too.

"I get why she was so pissed about him cheating on her," I observed. Hugo had done it to me and I still couldn't get over the betrayal. "I wonder what she did. I could have used some magic on Hugo."

Dahlia chuckled. "You could make his penis shrivel up and fall off. Or turn him into a pig. Although, that last one might be too close to home for him. You don't really think she cursed this land, do you? I mean, magic isn't real."

Lia was turning the pages as she spoke. I was saved from responding by the words on the page. In moments we were both engrossed in what she documented over the next couple dozen pages. When she moved on to talk about the way a slave was flirting with her, we stopped reading and stared at each other for a silent second.

I ran a hand down my face. "I can't believe she actually cursed this land. And to her own detriment, it seemed. When they started losing money and the pregnant woman met with an unfortunate accident, I was sure she was going to undo the spell."

Dahlia took a deep breath and shook her head. "I'm not sure I believe it. However, thoughts have power and I could feel a warning tickle the back of my mind as I read the words."

The silence in the attic was broken by the loudest clap of thunder I'd ever heard. Instinctively, I ducked and put my hands over my ears. Lia did the same and we huddled there until the room was lit from the lightning that started up outside. There was one small window to the left of us but it lit up the entire room like the middle of the day.

Oscar started barking and Zoe and Frida ran from the room like their tails were on fire. Lia jerked her chin to the door and I nodded then walked in my hunched-over position.

We hadn't made it halfway there when Oscar jumped into the air to attack a water droplet. "What's he doing?"

Dahlia rolled her eyes. "He's got a thing with water. You know how he attacks the sprinkler like it's a tasty steak."

My blood froze in my veins. "Wait, water? There should be no water."

We turned as one and started cursing at the same time. It was raining outside and leaking through the roof above us. "What do we do? All this stuff will be ruined. Not to mention our house has a major problem."

Dahlia scooped up Oscar. "I'll get some buckets and bowls and be back. You call Delphine and ask her to find some roofers. We will need someone to look at this and give us at least a temporary fix."

She was gone and I was right behind her. How she moved so fast carrying forty pounds of a dog still trying to get at the evil water droplets bent on the destruction of everything we owned was beyond me.

I snatched the phone and hit Phi's contact then told her what was happening as soon as she answered. After hanging up, I grabbed some of the five-gallon buckets we kept to use when we went to the flower mart to purchase fresh-cut stems for events and raced back inside the house.

Dahlia was already there, positioning buckets beneath the worst drips. I put mine to good use and went back for more. I could only carry so many at one time. After two trips, we stood there panting and looking around at the containers spread all over the place.

"We can't leave this and go to sleep. We're going to have to empty these and make sure new leaks don't spring up." My gut churned and my heart was racing. My mind immediately went to the journal that we'd left on the dresser. This place was cursed. *Now you know why the price was too good to be true.*

"You're right about that. I'm going to grab blankets and pillows ." Lia put the year she was on the track team to good use as she jumped hurdles on her way out the door.

I sighed and picked a spot on the floor that was dry. She returned a second later and we leaned against one another as we listened to the rain pound down on the roof. "Perhaps this place really is cursed. What are the chances of this happening so soon after buying the place, otherwise?"

Dahlia's jaw cracked as she yawned before responding. "We're women. Even if this place is cursed, it shouldn't affect us. We will have to wait and see if more crap happens. If it does, we might need to seek out an exorcist or something."

I lightly slapped her shoulder. "You're mixing up your paranormal phenomenon. Those are priests that banish demons from possessing a person."

She shrugged her shoulders. "Alright, we need to find Marie Laveau. Isn't she like the voodoo queen of magic or something?"

My eyes felt heavy as I thought about what she'd asked. "Ummm." My mind went blank and my eyes closed. I'd only rest them for a minute.

A loud noise jerked me awake and my eyes flew open. "What's happening?"

"Morning sleepyhead."

I blinked and tilted my head. Damn my neck was stiff. "Dreya? When did you get here? How bad is the water damage?"

Dahlia was no longer sitting next to me. Perhaps, she went to bed. My body ached and was stiff as I stood up. It felt like I had been sitting there for hours, but that couldn't be right.

"It stopped raining an hour ago, but despite having fallen asleep, you and Lia managed to keep the worst at bay. I'm drying what slipped past the buckets," Dre replied.

I jerked my head around. "It's morning? How is that possible? I just closed my eyes for a minute."

"That minute turned into several hours, girl." Dakota walked in with an arm full of clean and dry towels. "The roofers are here. We should all be out there."

Footsteps echoed above us. It sounded like whoever was on the roof might come crashing through any second. I was moving like a sloth as we left the attic and went outside.

I looked up and the moisture dried in my mouth at the guy on our roof. Another one walked over the peak of the other side and was pointing at something and talking to his partner.

"Who is that?" My god, I had never seen better looking men. Although, it was the one with the black hair and red flannel that had my engine revving.

"That's Noah and Lucas from Shadowtail Construction. They had great reviews on Yelp and came highly recommended. Plus, they were the only ones that had an hour free to stop by this morning. This wasn't a matter that could wait," Delphine replied.

Dahlia nodded. "Our luck has changed, sis. The only ones able to respond on such short notice are literal eye candy. It might not be so bad to need the roof worked on."

The one with dark brown hair and the blue flannel descended the fifty-foot ladder leaning against the side of the house. The other was right behind him and I was engrossed in watching them approach us.

I lifted a hand to my face to make sure I wasn't drooling. Seriously, the one with dark hair gave new meaning to luscious lips. Speaking of lips, I wonder if his were soft and if his kisses would make my toes curl. There was something undeniably feral about the guy. About both of them that I couldn't explain.

"Well, how bad is it?" Phi asked.

Luscious Lips twisted his mouth to one side and he shook his head. "Before I get to that, I should meet the rest of the group. I'm Noah." He held a hand out to me. "And this is my partner and best friend, Lucas."

My heart skipped a beat when his warm fingers wrapped around mine. "Nice to meet you. I'm Dani, Danielle."

"I'm Dakota, the second oldest sister."

"And, I'm Dreya, the oldest of the girls in the family."

"Six sisters. And you bought this place together? I never thought I'd see the day this place sold," Lucas replied with an easy smile. "I've always liked this old plantation."

Dahlia returned his smile and took a step toward him, then stopped. "We're excited to be at this stage of our venture, but we need to know if our dream is going to die a sudden, unexplained death, or if we can salvage it."

Noah dropped his shoulders and ran a hand through his messy black hair. "The bad news is that the entire roof needs to be replaced."

My jaw dropped to my chest as my heart cracked. While he was nice to look at, Noah couldn't make the loss any better. "Is there any good news?"

Lucas rocked on his heels and his smile widened. "Actually, yes. Delphine told us that the six of you run an event planning business. My daughter is getting ma...married. With your assistance, I'd like to have that wedding here in a few weeks and we will knock down the cost of the roof."

I was back to being a guppy with the mouth opening and closing. Dreya didn't have that problem. "That's the best news we've had since we discovered the leak in the roof. It's a deal. What do we need to do to protect the house until you guys can get started?"

Noah gestured to their truck. "We will get some tarps up there, for now, I think we have some ceramic tiles that will work perfectly for this place, or if you prefer we can do a more traditional shingle. If we go with the latter, we will need to place an order. We have some nice rust-colored tiles from a job that fell through and there should be enough."

I inclined my head and looked from the covered porch on the first floor to the balcony on the second. Both wrapped around the house and were painted a light-yellow color while the roof was dark gray.

"That color isn't going to look great with the yellow of the house now." I should have known Dakota would say something. She was the best of us at design stuff.

"We need to paint the house anyway, so we just pick another color," I reasoned. "That can be worked out later. Right now, I have to say thank you for coming so quickly and being able to get right on the job."

I got lost in the smile Noah gave me while the others discussed ideas and how long it would take. I could look into Noah's green eyes all day long. It wasn't until he and Lucas were walking away, that I realized I had been creepy staring.

"God bless it, I am still exhausted. Do I have time for a nap before we get back into the mess?" Hopefully, they chalked my gaping up to being tired and not turned on by our contractor.

Dani clapped a hand on my shoulder. "Not a chance, sis. There's too much to get done."

Of course, there was. I gave her a dirty look and headed back inside to figure out if we were cursed or not. Last night I was convinced we were. Now, I wasn't so sure. Someone with bad luck wouldn't be given a new roof for half the cost like we were. Sure, we had to host a wedding far sooner than we would be ready for, but that is what we did.

44

CHAPTER 5

DAHLIA

"*A*re you ready to hurl? These paint fumes are doing a number on me," I told Dani as we rolled the walls in the library. I loved the library and its floor-to-ceiling built-in bookcases. They covered three of the four walls and had one of those attached ladders to reach the top shelves.

Dani glanced over from the bookshelf she was sanding. "This filter keeps the worst of it at bay. Although my arm feels like it's going to fall off. We can take a break. I'm finished sanding for now."

I laid the paint roller in the tray and took off the latex gloves. I tossed them in the bucket we were using for trash and squeaked when I straightened my spine. There was a woman glaring at me right outside the door.

"What...oh my God. Is it her?" Dani moved closer to me as she spoke out the side of her mouth.

The woman had her hair pinned up, but she didn't have a hat on and her dress contained a bustle in the back. "I have no idea. Hi, my name is Dahlia and this is my sister Danielle. Are you Mary Alice? Do you have unfinished business we can help you with?"

The ghost cocked her head and nodded. "I need the magic to release me. I've been trapped here."

My heart started racing and I clutched Dani's hand. She was shaking. "She can speak. What the hell do we do?"

I stood there speechless as the ghost flickered in front of us. "We aren't witches, how the heck should I know? I'm beginning to think there really is magic in the world." And my brain struggled to comprehend that concept.

"What do we need to do to help release you?" Dani moved closer to the ghost, making me want to scream.

"You need to break the spell. It is keeping me here." The spirit of Mary Alice wasn't asking for much.

Break whatever enchantment was trapping her in the house. Yeah sure, no problem. We could do that before lunch. "Exactly how are we supposed to do that? We saw your journal and the ingredients you mentioned using to cast the spell. Do we need to find toad's hair and dragon scales?"

Dani shot me a wide-eyed stare. "Where would we even find those things? I bet it's easier to find Marie Laveau than dragon scales. They don't exist, Lia. It makes no sense."

"But talking ghosts does? Maybe we're hallucinating because of the fumes." It had to be something like that. I pinched my arm to see if perhaps I had fallen asleep while painting. Nope. Not only did that hurt, but my skin was already turning purple.

"You have magic, you need to help me." The ghost flickered several times like a light going out until she disappeared as quietly as she had appeared.

I turned to Dani. "Did that really just happen?"

Her head bobbed up and down. "Mary Alice is haunting

our halls and wants to be set free. Oh, and she thinks we have magic."

I snorted and shook my head. "We aren't in Kansas anymore, Toto."

Dani chuckled and went to the door to check out the hall. "Wait until we tell the other sestras about Mary Alice. They're handling it well. I think as long as they don't have to live here, they don't care. And Dre is pretty happy about already having a job."

I sighed and picked up the roller. "Speaking of, we need to get busy. This place is nowhere near ready to host an event."

Dani grabbed a sponge from a bucket of water and started wiping the shelves down to get the dust from sanding off every surface. When I looked back at the wall I had primed I wanted to kick my ass.

"How do you feel about textured walls?"

Dani had replaced the filtered mask back over her nose and mouth, making her look like she'd traveled back from the future. "Why?"

I gestured to the wall. "Because neither of us was thinking when I picked up the paint roller and started priming the walls while you were sanding."

"Shit!" She hurried over and dropped her head. "We are going to need to do a light sanding on that once it dries."

I nodded in agreement. My arms hurt and I had wasted precious resources I didn't have on priming that damn wall. "Yep, my thoughts exactly. I'll help with the cleaning and staining."

The filtered masks were big and bulky but kept the fine sawdust from choking us while working so close to it. I took the unit next to the one Dani was cleaning. "So, what do you think of Noah and Lucas?"

Dani's question wasn't a surprise. I could tell earlier that

47

Noah had piqued my baby sister's interest. I would never tell her or tease her about it because she had enough issues where men were concerned.

After two failed marriages, she was struggling to find her footing. I suspected she felt like it was her fault when that wasn't the case at all. Her first was abusive and her second was an asshole in my opinion. Dani felt differently. Bottom line is he screwed the wrong woman and my sister left his sorry ass. Dani needed to figure out what direction she wanted to go with Leo and if a hot guy helped her decide, I was all for it.

"I think they are blessings mom sent our way. Seriously, the timing couldn't have been better. And they're fun to ogle. Lucas's ass fills out a pair of jeans just right. His wife is a lucky lady."

I wasn't going to admit so much. The words just flew out of my mouth. Great, now my cheeks were blazing. Hopefully, the mask hid the worst of the red. *Get your groove on, Lia. It's about time you moved on and started living again.* My inner voice needed to keep her thoughts silent. She'd spent half the day reminding me of how many years it had been since I'd had sex. Long enough that cobwebs might be a real concern.

"Ho, ho, ho. Dahlia Smith, you little hussy. I had no idea you had such lurid thoughts running through your head. I assumed you were practicing to join a nunnery."

I rolled my eyes at Dani. "Har, har. What about you, and the googly eyes you were giving Noah?"

A thin line of pink appeared above the top edge of Dani's mask. "I was not giving him any eyes. I admit he's good-looking, but so was Hugo. Men aren't in the cards for me, sis. Besides, my focus right now is on myself. I need to work on myself before I consider anything else. I want to know why this has happened to me and what role I play in the mess my life has become."

"I'm proud of you. I don't say it often enough, but you are an example I hope to live up to someday." Dani was the one that took our mother's love and belief and pushed it further. Without her encouraging us, we would all be in the same boring boat as before.

"I'm not sure why. I don't have anything to show for my life except a rundown house that I'm hoping to restore to its former glory."

"You know that saying you used to say to your kids? The one you want to paint in one of the guest rooms?"

She nodded as she continued wiping the shelves. "The one about flying?"

I ran my sponge over a shelf, clearing the fine dust. "'What if I fall? Oh, but my darling, what if you fly?' You have lived that and inspired us to do the same. And guess what? You're flying, sis."

She turned tear-filled brown eyes my way as she brushed her dark blonde hair off her forehead. "It doesn't feel like I'm flying. More like I am falling. I feel like a failure."

I dropped my sponge into the bucket and wrapped my arms around her. "That's because all you see are the mistakes you have made. I'm not saying you are responsible for Hugo's decisions. However, I know it takes two to tango and things fell apart because of things both of you did or didn't do. That doesn't mean you have failed at anything. Life is too damn short to get sucked into perceived failures. Look at your role, see what you did wrong, learn from it and move the hell on with your life. There is so much more you have done right and excelled at and you aren't seeing any of that."

She stepped out of my embrace and nodded. "I could say the same thing about you, you know. You've mourned Leo long enough. Now, enough Hallmark Channel crap. We need to get these shelves stained tonight, so Phi or Dre can sand that wall tomorrow."

I nodded and picked up the sponge. Wipe, rinse, repeat. We set into a rhythm as Miley Cyrus sang about a party in the USA in the background. "We need to get a new painting playlist. I feel like we've listened to this so much I won't be able to use it while I run anymore."

Dani chuckled. "We could always rock the heavy metal hair bands."

I shook my head back and forth. "Anything but that. Remember how big our hair used to be then?"

Dani's laughter increased in volume. "Dakota's stood up like a perfect fan on top of her head."

I climbed the ladder and wiped the upper shelves. "I was so jealous. She got mom's thick hair while I got dad's thin stuff."

"You also got dad's hairy eyebrows!"

I waggled said eyebrows. "I've plucked and waxed these babies into submission. My poor son though has them worse than I did."

"My kids are grateful they escaped the worst of that particular gene. Hey, so what do you think we need to have done before your boyfriend's daughter gets married here."

I flicked dirty water from my sponge on her and shook my head. "Uh uh. You are not going to start calling him that. If you do, I promise to do the same to you. Then we will both be in hell with our sisters asking us a million and one questions."

She held up her hands with her palms out. "Alright. I won't say anything. Seriously though. I don't know if we will have the main kitchen renovated. That space will not work for caterers as it is now."

"You're right about that. We need to order a new oven and warming drawers. Steve can install them when they arrive. I know we were going to wait. Now, we have no choice."

"I think we should have one of the brothers come and do subway tile, or maybe glass tile as a backsplash, too." Dani and Dakota had the vision for how the house should look and what should be done to it, not me. I appreciated that they never made a decision without consulting us though.

I considered how I felt about it and ended up shrugging my shoulders. I wasn't like Delphine or Deandra who were both able to imagine what they were describing. I needed to see something before I could really say if I was going to like it. "I'm good with either. I can say I prefer glass tiles in a kitchen. Are we going with the grays in there?"

Dani made a noise in the back of her throat as I finished cleaning the shelves. The first ones were dry and ready for some stain. I would apply and she would follow behind and wipe it down.

"Dakota wants to stick with gray, but I was thinking black and white would look classy."

I snapped on gloves and handed her a pair before opening the can of stain and dunking the sponge brush inside it. "Then we should talk to the others and ask them to vote. I'm a worker bee. I have no talent for decorating homes. Give me a sign you want made, and I can come up with three designs for you. Although, we need to tell Dakota she can't put as many holes in the walls here as she did at her house. I'm not sure the house would remain standing."

Dani ran the rag over the surface where I had already applied the stain. "How the heck does she fit so much stuff in small spaces and make it look good? I counted a dozen knick-knacks on top of or underneath a three-foot-long sofa table when I was there the other day."

I laughed because I knew the table she was talking about. It was magazine-worthy and fit her house perfectly. If I had tried to cram that much into the same space it would look like it was in desperate need of being cleaned because a schizophrenic had paid me a visit.

"She has a gift. There's no other way to say it. While it's too much stuff in one place for me, she pulls it off. And she made the women's room look elegant despite having used my furniture in there."

Dani was laughing as she crossed to open the window. The smell of stain was ten times worse than paint. Her laughter died off and was replaced by a gasp. She'd ducked to the ground and was pointing out the window.

I went to my hands and knees and used one hand to crawl toward her. No way was I getting stain on the polished wood floors. "What is it?" I was careful to keep my voice low.

"There's someone out there by the beehives."

"It's probably just kids. Remember what Stacy said? They liked to come around here and smoke pot. Let's scare them away."

Dani nodded her head. I crawled to the shelves and dropped the brush in the can then grabbed the dry paint roller. With Dani right behind me, we ran out the back door and headed toward the beehives and slave quarters.

"Who's there? This is private property," I called out.

"We've called the police. You'd better get the hell off our land," Dani added.

A slender figure dressed in black darted out from behind my favorite willow tree. I took off in that direction, firing obscenities at the trespasser. My lungs started burning a few seconds into my run which was odd because I was in better shape than that.

I had to slow down to a walk. I couldn't catch my breath. I glanced over my shoulder to see Dani hunched over and bracing herself on her knees. There was a current in the air around us. It was almost like the moments before a thunderstorm struck.

"Are you okay?" I wouldn't leave Dani if she needed me. She nodded and waved me away. "I'll catch up."

I didn't waste another second as I continued toward the beehives which is where the person was. I couldn't make out any distinguishing characteristics and that pissed me off. *Why are you chasing someone that's prowling around your property? You could get killed.*

That thought brought me up short. I watched her disappear behind the slave quarters at the same time Dani came up to me huffing and puffing. The air cleared just then and it was suddenly easier to breathe.

We both started running then and were knocked on our ass when we made it to the corner of the old row of houses. The wind was knocked out of me and I lay there blinking stars out of my eyes while wondering what had happened. It felt like I'd run into a brick wall.

"What the hell just happened? Did we run into the house?"

I turned my head to Dani with one brow lifted to my hairline. "You're between me and the building. How could that have happened? C'mon, we need to find this asshole."

My attempt to rise was pathetic. I'm pretty sure turtles had an easier time getting off their backs than I did. Once we were up and around the structure, there was nothing there. The night was relatively clear and we could see for a distance.

"I don't think chasing them into the trees way out there is a good idea. Talk about a horror movie faux pas."

I slung my arm around Dani's shoulders, unable to shake the prickly energy surrounding us. It was worse behind the slave house. "I couldn't agree more. Let's take our ninja moves and knock out some more staining before we crash."

"Now you three come running?" I followed Dani's gaze and saw our three Frenchies running toward us. Surprisingly, Oscar wasn't barking his head off. Ever since Lucas had told him earlier that day to knock it off, my little guy had been more subdued. It had to be the energy of this place. It was becoming more and more probable that Willowberry Plantation was indeed cursed.

What did it say about me that the idea excited me? I looked forward to unraveling the mystery. It was official. I needed my head examined.

CHAPTER 6

DANIELLE

*D*elphine nudged my elbow as we were taking trash from the main house. She gestured to the roof where Lucas and Noah were busy working on repairing our leaks. "We should see if Lucas has an exact date for the wedding. We'll need to start making signs and wine glasses, or we will never have enough time with everything else."

After our would-be burglar the night before, Lia and I finished the staining and had moved to the rooms upstairs. When we encountered junk in room after room, we decided to call it quits and lay down. However, neither of us slept very well after our ghostly visitor.

The bags under my eyes were the size of carry-on luggage and dark purple. I did not want to see Noah looking like something the cat dragged in after a long night of prowling the alleys. Fortunately, I learned long ago to suck it up and deal.

"That's a good idea Phi. Lia was asking about it last night.

I know she'd appreciate some notice to get prepared." I shifted the bag of trash to my other hand and smoothed the fly-away hair. My heart raced when my hand got stuck in the short ponytail, I'd pulled it into.

The guys in question climbed down from the ladder as if they'd heard our conversation. The idea was ridiculous, of course, but I couldn't fathom another reason for them to stop what they were doing.

There was no salvaging my haphazard hair, so I yanked the holder out of my locks and shook the shoulder-length tangles out. "Good morning, Noah, Lucas. It's good to see you again so soon." Did I sound too eager? God, I hoped not. I was not a teenager mooning over a cute guy in biology class.

Noah smiled at me and it transformed his entire face. He went from good-looking to a Greek god. Seriously, it should be criminal for anyone to be that attractive. How was this possible without photoshop? "We rearranged our other clients to make sure we could get to you faster."

Dahlia waggled her brows at me from behind Noah and Lucas. It took effort not to roll my eyes at her. Delphine saved me from responding as I willed Lia to keep her antics to herself. I didn't want my sisters to discover my newest obsession. They'd undoubtedly have an opinion about my interest.

"We wanted to see if you had a date for the wedding. We need to prioritize what gets done. The first-floor rooms will be ready and picture-perfect for wedding preparations. The bigger kitchen in that building there," Phi pointed to the detached building, "needs to be updated and we have yet to find the right contractor. Plus, we need time to create the custom signs and other accoutrements your daughter might want. Lia runs the laser engraver and as you can imagine has a pretty full schedule."

Lucas turned and tracked Dahlia's every move as she and Dre continued to the dumpster we'd had delivered earlier in the morning. "It's going to be five weeks from this Saturday. I warned my daughter that Willowberry is a work in progress. She was just happy to have a plantation for her ceremony. She's always been drawn to these old homes. The pack does the food for these events and they can work in whatever kitchen you have available. Do we need to find tables and chairs? Flowers? My daughter has been working on all of those details, as we were going to have it on our land, so we can shift gears and look for companies to deliver here."

I smiled at him. "It would be best if we met with your daughter and her fiancé with you to discuss details. To save you time and money, we have tables and chairs for up to three hundred. Dreya's husband should have moved them into one of the barns on the property. As for flowers, we typically do them. We have connections at the flower mart. She can pick out what she wants, or simply tell us and we can handle it unless she already has someone picked out."

Lucas's smile vanished and his head swiveled to the parking lot at the same time Noah's did. The effect was eerie and made the hair on the back of my neck stand on end. What was happening now? I hoped our ghost hadn't made an untimely appearance. That isn't the word we wanted to spread.

I followed their gaze and couldn't believe my eyes. A group of people climbed out of a large SUV and was heading our way. There was a tall guy, almost as attractive as Noah with four women.

Dahlia and Dreya approached the group. I hurried to join them as the dark-haired woman at the front raised her hand. "Hello. We're here to see the Willowberry Plantation." She had infused her voice with so much fake excitement it was obvious she was nervous. Her wide smile only accentuated it.

57

She had to have noticed we weren't ready for guests, or perhaps she didn't know how to back out of her request now. To set me even more on edge Noah and Lucas drifted toward us without saying a word. Tension rode high in their shoulders and their expressions were more serious than I thought the situation warranted.

Another woman with long brown hair pulled into a ponytail and perfect makeup bounced forward in her heels and perfectly coordinated outfit. "I found your plantation on the internet and we fell in love and had to see it. We're dying to hear about the history of the place."

I made a mental note to remove the sign situated by the road. It was faded, but the panel hanging below the main one said 'tours daily.' Deandra had updated the website for the plantation this morning to reflect we would be open soon, but apparently not soon enough.

My sisters shot me wide, terrified eyes that begged me to handle this situation. I looked into features that so resembled my own, thinking how the hell I'd been elected queen bee. I liked the role when it didn't involve talking to people.

I stepped forward with my hand extended. "Hi, I'm Dani. These are my sisters, Dahlia, Dakota, Deandra, Dreya, and Delphine. And we are so excited you stopped by, but we just purchased the place and aren't ready for tours or parties. I'm so sorry you came all this way."

The first woman that had spoken shook my hand. There was a shock of static electricity the moment we touched. A sense of dizziness came over me for a split second and I wondered what that was about. Too many weird things had been happening lately and I didn't understand any of them.

"I'm Phoebe. Boy, your mom must have really liked the letter D. This is my best friend, Stella, my uh, boyfriend Aidoneus and my cousins, Selene and Layla. I appreciate the fact that you guys aren't ready for a formal tour which suits me so much better." I had to force my eyes to remain in my skull when the woman pulled a platinum credit card out. "I'm willing to pay for the cost of the roof that's being worked on. I really want to see the plantation."

Shock won out and my eyes went wide at the same time my sisters all smacked me. I knew what they were thinking. The problem was we were getting a deal on the roof for hosting a wedding. Not that it mattered. We could afford to redo the kitchen with that kind of money.

"Um, that's an offer we can't afford to refuse. Sure, we are happy to give you a tour. However, we know little about the house. We just signed papers this week." I wasn't sure about telling them that a ghost lived in the house with us.

Dahlia stepped forward and adjusted the hat she wore when we did the grueling three-day, sixty-mile walk for breast cancer. "Let's start in the main house. We may have just bought the place, but we already have our first booking."

"What are your plans for the place?" Stella asked as we walked toward the back of the house.

"That's the old carriage house over there and the kitchen is behind us. We will be updating that area soon so caterers have a place to work out of." I pointed out the buildings before holding the back door open. "We run a party planning business and bought this to expand our operations. This is our first venue."

Noah caught my eye. He and Lucas had remained close to us and inclined their heads. I wasn't sure what that meant until he shifted his eyes to Aidoneus and back to me. It was sweet of him to let me know he was there if we needed him. I nodded and focused on what Kota was telling them.

"Many of our clients will still want the Six Twisted Sisters to do their shindigs for them at their houses, but we will be pushing for them to use the plantation."

Dea smiled as she looked over her shoulder. "We've done

weddings, birthdays, baby showers, retirements, anniversaries, engagements, bridal showers, and bachelorette parties. Basically, any event you can dream up, we can plan for you."

"We do everything from decorations to food to gifts. All of our events have unique designs and personalized touches throughout," Phi added.

Phoebe chuckled. "Your business is called the Six Twisted Sisters? I love it. Do you guys travel? I couldn't give my daughter her sweet sixteen last year because her father and I were going through an ugly divorce."

Delphine turned around, her red hair flying around her face as she lifted an iPad. "For the right price, we'd be happy to travel. Where are you from?"

"I live in Camden, Maine now. I'm here on, uh business, but give me a card and we can plan something. I've needed to make this up to Nina for almost a year now."

Phoebe's boyfriend wrapped an arm around her shoulders. "She understands, Queenie. You need to stop being hard on yourself." Talk about a Greek god. He had the sexy smolder down.

"He's right," Dre interjected. "Kids understand more than we give them credit for. However, throwing a special party for her is something she will never forget."

I nodded. "Like, Phi mentioned, we customize our décor with our laser engraver. We can add customization on even the littlest details. It's what sets us apart from the competition."

Stella laughed. "That and the fact that you are six sisters doing this together. I've never heard of such a unique company. Two or three sisters, sure, but never six."

My mood brightened at the mention of how incredible it was to work with my sisters. We had our ups and downs, but I wouldn't trade it for the world. We walked Phoebe and her entourage through the first floor and shared what we'd learned about the plantation in the past few days.

I pointed out the images of the original owners. "Willowberry was built by William Henry Carlton as a present for his wife. She loved being close to nature and wanted to raise bees and make her own honey while he wanted to capitalize on the tobacco trade. It is said that Mary Alice was a witch and she cursed this land so that all who owned the land would be cursed to failure. Apparently, she had an affair with a slave and gave birth to that slave's child and her husband forced that baby to be Mary Alice's slave while he was ready to elevate the status of his child with a different slave."

I prayed Mary Alice herself didn't decide to pay us a visit. My sisters still didn't know the ghost had spoken with Lia and me last night. I didn't want them to find out in the middle of a tour for a VIP guest.

Phoebe inclined her head as she took in the house. "And yet you six bought the place. This couldn't have been cheap. I imagine you put everything you have collectively into the business. That's impressive."

Delphine held her iPad to her chest. "We have a solid business plan and countless happy customers to attest to our abilities."

Phoebe lifted a hand with her palm out. "I meant no offense. And I'm certain enough of your abilities to hire you for Nina's party. I'm surprised you would take the risk."

Aidoneus nodded. "I'm sure most people around here wouldn't touch the place. Creoles tend to be a superstitious bunch."

Dahlia snorted. "Tell us about it. We had a hard time finding someone to come out and retrofit one of the buildings for storage. Luckily, Noah and Lucas are able to help with that, as well." They had? That was news to me. I threw my sister a questioning look. She imperceptibly shook her head from side to side. We would talk about that later.

I kept getting tiny shocks as we showed the rooms and the furniture we'd discovered in the attic. My heart kept skipping beats as we walked. I was certain our resident specter was going to make an appearance.

I wasn't surprised when Phoebe yelped a few minutes later. I cursed our luck, giving more credence to the idea this land was cursed. Mary Alice had arrived to make this a legitimate haunted tour.

She wore her gown with the bustle in the back and all the ruffles flowing down the skirt. Her scowl said it all. She didn't like us showing the world her home. Well, too damn bad. We bought the place and had to make money to pay for it.

"Are you alright? Was it a spider? My husband is in the process of spraying the house," Dreya interjected. God bless her, she was always a step ahead of the rest of us. If we were lucky, Phoebe would brush off what she'd seen.

Phoebe was clutching her chest. "I bet a place like this gets a lot of bugs. I'd love to see the property. And Mary's beehives if they're still around." I had a hard time believing she bought this excuse.

I smiled. This was my favorite part of the plantation. "Some of the hives remain here. They recently started producing lavender honey which will become a staple in our gift shop when it opens."

"You will have many wi, uh women who will want the honey. You should consider shipping," Selene blurted. Her cheeks pinkened as she explained her reasoning. "Lavender is a true adaptogen. Not to mention a universal healing herb. Lavender goes into your system right where you need it to help your mind, body, and spirit find balance."

Fascinated, I moved closer to Selene. "I've tried

researching mystical properties of the stuff but couldn't find anything. I'd love to hear more about what you know."

"I'd be happy to share any information I know. I'm actually hoping you can help me, too. You haven't happened to see a necromancer around here, have you?"

My head whipped back as Phoebe clamped a hand on Selene's shoulder. What was the woman talking about? I swear ever since we purchased Willowberry, we'd had one crazy experience after another.

"I must have missed my morning coffee and am still dreaming. First, the money was too good to be true and now you're asking about necromancers. Whatever the hell that is." Dakota shook her head and replied as she pinched her arm. "Nope, not dreaming."

Dahlia tried to cover for Kota and kept her from saying what we were all thinking, that these people were batshit crazy. In the end, it didn't matter. We needed that money she'd promised for the tour. It would help us get so many things done in a timely manner.

Lia chewed her lower lip for a second. "I saw someone last night. I haven't said anything before, but I swear I saw a person dressed in black near the slave's quarters out back." What? No! She wasn't supposed to spill the beans.

Dreya's eyes went wide. "Why didn't you mention something?" I rubbed my temples where my head started throbbing.

Phoebe broke in before anyone could say anything else. "Can you take me there? I'd like to look around."

Dreya looked over her shoulder at their car then turned back around. I knew she was debating tossing them out. I wasn't worried because she was too practical for that. "Sure. The beehives are on the way there."

I decided to give them a little more. They seemed to believe in the crazy. "The bees acted strangely our first day here and the gardener that came with the property indicated it was the magic of the land. None of us believe it, but there have been several things we can't explain."

I stopped by the rows and rows of beehives. I loved the square bee houses with their drawers dripping in golden goodness. It was made even better by the strong scent of lavender in the air. I inhaled deeply and let it calm my jittery nerves.

When I refocused, I found Phoebe looking at us in an odd way. It was as if she knew we were hiding Mary Alice's ghost from them. I was caught completely off-guard by her question. "Are you guys Fae, or something? I sense something here that's connected to you six."

My jaw went slack and my heart raced so fast I thought I would pass out. My palms started sweating a second later. Dani looked like a guppy with her mouth opening and closing.

Our big sister came to the rescue. Dreya had always been a caretaker of sorts for us younger girls. I was as thankful for that now as ever. She faced Phoebe with her arms crossed. "Not at all. The most special thing about us was our mother."

Phoebe was shaking her head in denial of what Dreya was saying. "I sensed magic in the land and thought perhaps that's why you chose it. I'm new to magic, so I could be wrong."

Stella waved her hands, clearly trying to calm the situation down. "It could be that you never knew about your heritage. That happens in families where the magic is diluted over the generations. At least that's what I've read."

Aidoneus put his hand on Phoebe's shoulder. "There is definitely Fae in your family line. It's faint but there, nonetheless."

I narrowed my eyes and glared at the guy. He might be good-looking enough to be a Greek god, but he was crossing a line. I didn't need to look at my sisters to know they were with me on this.

"Here me out. Each of you has different skills. Some of you are good with animals and others with plants. That is a skill inherent with the Fae.

Dakota crossed her arms over her chest. "We'll take that payment now. You can leave and take your crazy with you." I couldn't have said it better.

CHAPTER 7

DANIELLE

*P*hoebe waved her hands and stepped in front of Aidoneus. "I know this must be shocking, but I've seen too much during this tour to ignore it as I had planned. If Aidoneus says you have Fae in your family then you do. He is the son of Hades, who is the god of the Underworld."

That guy was an *actual* Greek god. What the hell? How was that even possible? Had he lied to this nice woman? I had no doubt Phoebe was a genuinely nice person. She paid us far more than necessary for a tour. I just didn't get why she believed this guy was the son of Hades.

Hades?! Wasn't he evil? For all Aidoneus had said about us, I didn't think he was a bad guy, just delusional. Perhaps they were escaped, psych patients. My head swirled with the possibilities.

Dakota was the most outspoken of us and true to who she was, she dove right in with these people. "Alright, I'll bite. If you're a god, do you have a spell that paints walls? There are dozens of rooms in that place, not to mention all the outbuildings. And I don't want to paint them."

I scowled at Dakota. "Don't be such a shit, Kota. These people are obviously out of their minds."

Dre scoffed. "We wasted our morning showing them around and haven't been paid yet. I knew it was too good to be true. This is bullshit."

Phi jumped in with us. "Why are we even debating this? Let's escort them out of here and get back to work."

Dea shoved her finger in the middle of the huddle we had created. "No one is going anywhere until we get our money. We gave them a tour, they owe us. Crazy or not, Phoebe had a platinum card. Get the card reader out, sis."

Our discussion was interrupted when Phoebe whistled loud enough to hurt my eardrums. "Sorry, I'm prepared to show you my magic, if you'll allow it."

I lifted one eyebrow and looked at my sisters then nodded. We'd give her a chance. "That's the only way we will stop arguing about the truth of this stuff. Although, I have to tell you we don't believe in magic."

Phoebe shrugged her shoulders. "I get that. I didn't either until nine months ago when I was tossed in the deep end." She took several deep breaths and nothing happened.

I shifted from foot to foot. Dakota leaned in and whisper-yelled in my ear. "This is bullshit."

Dreya had her arms crossed and her big boobs pushed up to her scowling face. "She's a phony. That card is probably a fake."

"Nothing's happening because magic doesn't exist," Deandra said to Aidoneus and Stella. Layla and Selene stood by quietly.

Phoebe's eyes popped open suddenly and she spoke in

Latin. I recognized enough from my nursing school education. *"Et vade et revelare."*

Electricity coursed from the ground up through my body the moment her words about revealing something left her lips. Dahlia's wide eyes met mine, and I reached for her. Dreya grabbed my other hand and Dakota grabbed her at the same time as all hell broke loose.

Dahlia grabbed Deandra and Dea grabbed Phi. The six of us huddled close and held on for dear life while the bees that had been flying in and out of their hives flew into a frenzy like our first day here. Only this time we couldn't duck and avoid them. They came right for us.

The wind created by them flying around us blew our hair around our faces. I screamed and squeezed my sister's hands. I hadn't been this terrified since our mother died a few years before.

All I could hear or see was the buzzing of the bees. Next came the stings. Millions of them. Pain coursed through my veins and my body went rigid. My heart raced and I couldn't breathe. When I managed to catch a breath, all I smelled was lavender and honey. I doubted I would ever like the smell again.

Dreya tugged us and tried to get us out of the maelstrom, but it didn't work. We couldn't go anywhere. We were surrounded by a teal light. "What the hell is happening?"

I wanted to answer Dre, but I couldn't find my voice. I'd been stung everywhere it seemed. My eyes felt swollen and my entire body burned from the venom. Dahlia jerked her chin to the right. I wondered if the venom was playing a trick on me when I saw dozens of ghosts. Men, women, and children. Some were dressed like Mary Alice and others were in rags.

The bees built energy around us that was so intense I felt it all the way to my bones. It was impossible to do anything but wrap our arms around each other and hold on. "I'm sorry. This is all my fault." I needed to tell them how terrible I felt before we went into shock. Nausea churned in my stomach adding to my discomfort.

Dakota shook her head. "Shut the fuck up. It's not your fault. That bitch does have magic. She and her boyfriend did this."

I saw Phoebe trying to get to us through the teal barrier. She bounced off and said something. All I heard was the buzzing of the bees. It was a sound that would haunt my nightmares.

Her boyfriend shouted something back to her and I was able to catch pieces of what he said. Deandra gestured to him with her chin. "Did the god just say she unleashed the magic in the land? How the heck do they put it back? They need to stop this shit. It's worse than drinking on an empty stomach."

Dreya nodded her head as much as possible with the bees surrounding us. "He mentioned the curse too. I don't think they know what the hell they're doing. We're screwed."

Tears built in my eyes and emotion burned my throat. My sisters were the best friends I had. They'd been there for me through thick and thin, always at my back. The only thought that kept running through my head with each new bee sting was we were going to die right here like this and it wasn't fair.

I shook my head and tried to calm my heart. "Let's try to get out of here, again." Determined, I held my sisters tight and we moved as one. Between one step and the next, the teal light vanished and the bees returned to their hives.

I hissed and dropped their hands. My arms were covered in welts. I couldn't imagine what my face looked like. Phoebe and Aidoneus rushed toward us and stopped short, each wearing matching grimaces.

"Are you guys alright? I am so sorry. I have no idea what went wrong."

"The magic in the land surged forth and blocked us out. Not even I could broach the barrier. It seems the land has claimed the six of you and that is why it was localized around you guys," Aidoneus explained.

"I didn't believe magic existed," Deandra muttered. "But there's no denying what just happened. Damn, you'd be fun at a party."

Trust Dea to find the silver lining in the situation. Her laughter started a chain reaction like it always did and within seconds we were all laughing. It hurt and felt good all at the same time. I hadn't been sure I'd ever laugh again. I couldn't look at the hives, though. I might never be able to.

My laughter died and my breath left me like I'd been punched in the gut. My hand went into the air and all I could do was point at the person walking out from behind the slave quarters.

Dakota had no problem speaking. "What the fuck is that?"

"God bless it," Dahlia whispered.

An honest-to-god zombie was stumbling toward us on shaky legs. She was a black woman and was likely beautiful when she was alive. Her skin had chunks missing and the bone showed through in parts. I think she could have been a mixed breed because her flesh was light brown, maybe. It was an ashy color, so it was difficult to tell.

The woman tried to say something. And her jaw dropped to her chest. My nausea worsened when it hung from a thread. I couldn't tell if she was trying to talk because I refused to look that closely. One view of her rotted tongue wagging was enough.

"Figere quid habet debilitatem," Phoebe chanted. My heart skipped a beat hearing her say another spell. I braced myself for another disaster.

Thankfully, the bees remained close to their hives and didn't attack again. The zombie stumbled as the light hit her in the chest. I gasped when the creature's jaw lifted and went back into position. Her cheeks filled out and skin grew over missing parts. Hair sprouted from the newly formed scalp.

In a matter of seconds, her skin plumped and she looked like a regular person. Only her clothes gave away what she was before she was hit with Phoebe's magic. That was the only explanation for what we'd just witnessed.

"What is happening, miss? Why are you dressed so oddly? Where is everyone?" The woman wasn't from a decade I'd ever lived in. Her heavy creole accent was one clue. So was the clothing she wore and how she kept her head downcast as she spoke.

"What is she? She looked like a zombie a second ago." My arms were now itching where I had countless stings. The itching hurt, but I couldn't stop.

"Phoebe raised a ghoul when she cast her spell," Selene replied, looking at Phoebe with horror on her face.

There was a story there. Her cousin seemed beyond upset that she raised a ghoul. I shook my head. Ghosts, ghouls, magical bees. Those didn't exist in our world until Willowberry. I wasn't sure how much more I could take.

"Selene." Phoebe walked to her cousin like she was walking over ice that was cracking under her weight. She stopped when her cousin threw up a hand. "It was an accident. I would never have done the spell if I'd known this would happen." Phoebe sounded broken up about what she'd done. That was good to hear because raising someone from the dead was as serious as it got.

Selene and Phoebe darted forward when the zombie moved toward us. Phoebe asked, "Who are you?"

"I'm Camilla. Mary Alice's slave." The ghoul clamped her newly replenished lips closed.

I sucked in a breath. I hadn't heard her right, had I? We hadn't gotten to the part where Mary Alice had an affair of her own. It intrigued me. "You're her daughter."

The ghoul looked up and down. I wasn't sure if it was a nod or not. "I am. Not that she was ever a mother to me."

Noah and Lucas came running which made everyone jump. I clutched my chest as my heart pounded. The sight before me registered. I cocked my head. The guy I had the hots for and his friend had claws on the ends of their hands and fur covering their arms.

I screamed and jumped away from the pair, Lia did the same. I scrubbed a hand over my eyes. My mind went blank as I tried to figure out what was going on.

"What the actual?" Dahlia shook her head. "There has to be a gas leak causing hallucinations. None of this makes any sense."

Dea pinched Lia. "We aren't dreaming. But I have no idea what's up with your new boyfriend. And I think she turned us into witches, too."

Lia snarled. "Shut the hell up, Dea." I wasn't sure if she was telling Dea to knock it off about Lucas or the witch comment. I was up in the air about what would upset me more.

The fur and claws vanished and Noah walked toward me imploring me with his sexy green eyes. "We sensed the magic and assumed you were in trouble." He lifted my hand and scanned my arm. "What happened?"

His touch was soothing and gentle. Part of me wanted to recoil while the rest wanted to bask in his closeness. "She did." I pointed to Phoebe. "She's a witch, he's a god. I have no idea what the other three are. What are you?"

Noah let go of my hand and one corner of his mouth lifted in a half-grin. "I'm a shifter. I shift into a wolf."

Dahlia picked up Lucas's hand and turned it over. "Do you turn into a wolf, too?"

Lucas turned his palm and wrapped his fingers around Lia's. "Yes, I do. Noah and I belong to the same pack."

"Oh. That must be why Oscar listened to you and stopped barking." Dahlia's response said it all. What else could we say? Despite how much I wanted to deny what we were seeing, there was no way. They'd had fur a second ago and it disappeared before our very eyes.

Lucas smiled at Lia and continued holding her hand as he jerked his chin at Camilla. "Who raised the ghoul?"

Phoebe raised her hand like she was waiting to be called on in school. "It was an accident. We came here looking for a necromancer to help a ghoul of our own, and in my attempt to find a magical signature to follow, I let loose more than I bargained for."

Phoebe shifted her focus to Deandra. "I'm honestly not sure if I turned you into witches. My gut says no, but I didn't realize I had done it with Stella, so it is possible."

Lucas nodded. "You did something to the Six Twisted Sisters, but I can't tell if it's magical. They feel and smell different now, though. You came to the right place in your search. Plantations can be a good place to look for a necromancer. You have to be sneaky because there isn't much cover out here. They're wily and will evade you if you return when they come, which is at night. I recommend one of the haunted ghost tours in the French Quarter. One or two can be found doing one every night. No need for staking out a location and praying to come across one."

Phoebe sagged against Aidoneus. "Thank you so much. We will do that. In the meantime, do you want to come with me, Camilla? I can fix you and ensure a demon can't possess you."

73

Camilla shook her head from side to side. "I can't leave the plantation."

The look Phoebe shot us was worse than when my kids ask for something they know I'll say no to. Big, puppy dog eyes always killed me. "Would you keep her safe until I can return to tether her soul to her body? Then she will be free to leave and go wherever she wants."

I gaped at my sisters. They all shrugged their shoulders. It was Dahlia that finally stepped forward. "What kind of danger will this bring? And what do we do for her? We know nothing about her kind."

"Demons could be attracted to her. They might not sense her out here, but it is a possibility, so keep her on the property and close to you at night. Make sure she has lots of meat, she'll need it. Keep in mind that she is vulnerable until Phoebe gives her a soul," Selene explained.

"But she isn't going to attack you guys," Stella clarified. "In fact, she will do her best to help and protect you."

I looked at Camilla who was shaking and moving closer to my sisters and me. It was almost as if she could sense we were the owners of the plantation now. "I don't think she's going anywhere. We have plenty of space."

I was jealous of the way Aidoneus looked at Phoebe as he twined his fingers with hers. Phoebe held up her credit card. "If you give me the payment app you use, I will enter the amount."

Delphine considered it for a second then shrugged and gave the iPad to Phoebe after she opened it to the app. Phi's eyes went round as saucers as she watched Phoebe enter the transaction and scan her card.

After handing it back to Delphine, we exchanged phone numbers and said goodbye. My sisters and I stood there stunned.

"How much did she pay us?" Dreya asked. "Was it a lot?"

Phi nodded her head. "You could say that. She gave us seventy-five thousand dollars."

"Holy shit balls," Dakota blurted.

"We can make some real progress with this place," I said, finally feeling like Dahlia was right. We were exactly where we were supposed to be. The curse on the land couldn't be affecting us. It never would have allowed such good fortune to fall on us if it did.

Magic is real. Shifters, ghouls, ghosts and so much more exist. My mind was whirling with too much information and I had no idea where to begin.

CHAPTER 8

DANIELLE

*D*akota sank onto one of the couches from Dahlia's house. "Buying this place transported us to an alternate reality. There is no other explanation for what just happened."

Dreya took a seat next to Kota and braced her elbows on her knees. "I'm not sure what shocks me more. The fact that the men traipsing around on our roof turn into animals or that Phoebe gave us so much money. Did it hit our account, Phi? It seems too good to be real."

Delphine picked up the tablet she had set on the table and typed on the screen. A smile spread over her face as she looked up. "It's already in our account. I agree, Dre, I worried the charge would be rejected as it was processed. She could become a lucrative client for us. She's already expressed an interest in us throwing her daughter a sweet sixteen."

Deandra snorted. "She comes with a whole lotta crazy. I mean, look what happened to us. I'm covered in welts from countless bee stings and my skin still feels like they're buzzing around me."

I rubbed my arms, experiencing the exact thing she was describing. I had been since they swarmed us and started attacking. "What was that teal light? And the bubble we couldn't get past? Was it really magic?"

There was no holding any of it back from them any longer. With Phoebe's donation, we would be able to get a good head start on the house renovations. Worst case scenario is we'd end up fixing it and selling. Although my stomach twisted at the thought of walking away now.

I'd invested myself in this process and convinced my sisters to join me. We had to see it through. I hadn't understood Lia's earlier conviction about us being where we were meant to be, but now I did.

"I was certain magic didn't exist a couple of hours ago. Now, it's staring us in the face. Literally." Lia pointed to the zombie, no ghoul, standing in the doorway to the men's parlor. "You can come in, Camilla. You don't have to hover back there."

Deandra jumped to her feet. "Actually, we should get you some better clothes. Yours have been eaten by bugs and don't exactly blend in with the current style."

Camilla lowered her face, her hair and face caked with dirt. Pink stains appeared on her cheeks as she shook her head. "I don't have anything more. Sorry, ma'am. I'll clean myself before I start on the chores you have for me."

I looked at Dreya and Dakota then Lia and Phi. All of them had pursed their lips and were shaking their heads. Dreya stood up and crossed the room to join Dea and Camille. "You are not our slave, Camilla. No one owns slaves anymore. The world has changed since you were alive."

Dreya paused and shook her head. "I can't believe I am having this conversation with a woman that looked like a zombie half an hour ago. This is nuts. But that doesn't change the fact that you are a free woman, Camilla."

Camilla lifted wide eyes and a trembling lower lip. "I can't be a free woman. What would I do? I have nowhere to go, no money, and I can't get a job as a colored."

Dahlia joined them and placed a palm on the woman's shoulder. "You always have a place here, but not as a slave. We would love your help getting to know the stories of the plantation and would pay you for your efforts. It's going to be an adjustment, but life is different now and we want to make sure you understand from the beginning that we do not own you and you are not obligated to do anything for us. We will help you regardless."

"I have been a slave my entire life. We used to dream of being free. None of us ever thought it possible."

Dakota and I got up, as well. It was awkward to be the only one still sitting down. "Let's get you cleaned up," Kota told the woman. "We can show you how a shower works, so you can wash off all the dirt. You'll feel better when you're clean. I know I would."

I nodded in agreement. "And I will grab you some of my clothes that I think might fit. Or perhaps we should have you try Lia's first."

Lia shrugged her shoulders. "We can give her two sets to try on."

Camilla looked around as we headed to the back stairs. "The house has changed from when Mary Alice and Master Carlton built the place."

I chuckled. "I imagine it looks completely different to you. It's been a few hundred years and several of the owners have updated the house. There is electricity, which means lights that come on with the flick of a switch." I demonstrated on the hall light. "And indoor plumbing, running water."

"Is it witchcraft? That's powerful magic." Before we could respond, Camilla tilted her head as we turned toward the back of the house. "Why do you use the servant's stairs and not the ones at the front of the house?"

Deandra started laughing which was precarious as we ascended the metal spiral. Her chuckle always made us join her. It had the same effect on Camilla who seemed surprised by her reaction.

Deandra and I were hobbling toward the bathroom by the time we reached the second floor which made the others laugh even harder. "Deandra's mirth is infectious and we have weak bladders," I heard Lia explain with amusement clear in her voice. "Inevitably someone pees themselves thanks to the babies we had and our good friend peri-menopause."

"Full-blown menopause for some of us," Dreya interjected.

It was difficult to wait as Dea used the toilet. I was taking her place the second she stood up and flushed. To my relief, I managed to hold it until I sat down. I was washing my hands when Camilla was led into the bathroom.

The former servant stood there wringing her hands and trembling.

"I can't go in here. Magic is the work of the devil."

Dakota placed a hand on Camilla's shoulder. "Look, I know this is a lot to take in and most of it is unbelievable. I'm having a hard time myself, but this here is not something that should frighten you."

I shut off the water and dried my hands, then gestured to the bathtub. "This is a shower. There is nothing magical in this room. Centuries ago, engineers figured out how to make water run through pipes and come out the faucet."

"That sounds interesting, but I can boil the water to take a warm bath," Camilla offered.

79

Dea shook her head as she laughed. This time it wasn't her infectious giggle, so no one joined her. "Different engineers created the hot water heater, so it comes right out of the tap. C'mere and feel it."

I had pulled back the plastic curtain and twisted the tap. Camilla entered the room, looking around. Her fear sobered me and brought to light how traumatic this was for the woman. As upset as I was, what I experienced didn't compare to this woman who was brought back from the dead.

Dea held her hand beneath the water while Camilla watched. "It's perfectly safe. No magic or evil powers at work here."

Camilla looked at each of us. I decided to stick my hand under to show her I was unhurt. Phi scooted past us and followed suit before she pulled up the tab to start the shower. The ghoul gasped and jumped back, knocking into Dakota and Dreya.

Delphine pushed the tab back down, stopping the flow through the faucet above. "If this is too scary, we can fill the tub and leave you to wash. The shampoo and soap are here. You use that to clean your body and a little bit from the bottle to wash your hair."

Camilla nodded and took a step toward the tub. Lia moved out of the bathroom. I heard her footsteps moving down the hall. Sticking my head out between Dre and Kota, I called out to Dahlia. "Grab a pair of black leggings and one of my Disney sweatshirts, please." Lia nodded and disappeared up the stairs.

"Do you need help or do you think you can manage on your own?" Dea asked Camilla. She had shut the water off because the tub was filled with water.

The ghoul picked up the bottle and turned it upside down. Phi extended her hand slowly and took it, showing her how to open the cap. "After your hair is wet, you use a small amount in your palm and scrub it through your hair then rinse it out."

Dea grabbed a clean towel from under the sink. "Be sure to close your eyes though, because it can sting."

Camilla crouched down and stuck her hand in the water. She yanked it back instantly. "It's hot. And this is not done by magic? How is that possible?"

"There is a lot in this world that you won't understand and none of it is done with spells or witchcraft," I explained. "It is probably overwhelming to you, but we will help you adjust to how things are today."

"We will help you while we renovate the house. We can't stop working on Willowberry. We have a wedding to plan for in a few weeks." I appreciated Lia's reminder. It would be easy to get lost in what had happened today.

Dea set the towel on the counter. "We will leave you to bathe yourself. We'll be right outside the door if you need anything or you become frightened."

Lia passed a stack of clothing to me and I put them next to the towel. A thought occurred to me. "Do you know what underwear and a bra are?"

Her furrowed brow was all the answer we needed. Phi picked up the bra. "We don't wear shifts or corsets anymore. The bra replaces the latter and you put your arms through the hoops and buckle it in the back."

Phi demonstrated for her before she picked up the panties. "You put your legs through these holes and pull them up to your hips. These are pants and this is a top you pull over your head. It will likely feel odd at first. Hopefully, it will become comfortable with time. I'm not sure where we might find something from your time period."

Dreya gestured above our head. "We can look in the attic for any clothing that might be left there. Not sure if there is anything, but it will be our best bet."

Camilla picked up the articles of clothing and examined them. "I worry I cannot survive in this time. Nothing is familiar to me. I would be a burden to you ladies and that is not something I could tolerate."

My heart clenched for the woman and what she might have experienced in life to make her so uncertain. I wasn't sure there was anything we could say to reassure her. "You will not be a burden. Our plans to conduct tours of Willow-berry wouldn't be as authentic without you. You're vital to that part of our business succeeding. In fact, I would say Phoebe bringing you back is one of the best things to happen to us since we purchased the property."

Camilla's eyes went wide. "You own the plantation? Not the men that were with you? How is that possible? Women cannot own property. Nor can a slave."

Phi smiled at Camilla. "Remember there are no slaves in this country anymore and there haven't been for quite some time. Another of the things that have changed since your time is that women can vote and buy any home they can afford. They can even own businesses. The six of us own Six Twisted Sisters. It's our party planning company. Why don't you get clean? We will take things one hour at a time."

Our heads nodded at the same time. Dre ushered us out of the bathroom. "We will be right outside."

The second the door was shut, I chewed my lip and crossed to the end of the hall so I could give the ghoul some space and look out the window. My sisters followed behind me. The sight of Noah bending over a stack of wood on the ground caught my eye and made me wish I were closer to get a better look.

"Dealing with Camilla is going to be like having a toddler again," Dakota observed. "We should show her one of the Real Housewives franchises to give her a crash course in life today."

Reluctantly, I turned away from the luscious sight of Noah's rear end and faced my sisters. Dakota was right about needing to get her up to speed fast, but her method left a lot to be desired.

Dre scoffed and shook her head. "We don't want her to think petty issues such as boob jobs and new dresses are dire concerns for us today."

"That is not all they talk about," Dakota countered. "But I see your point. Television is the best method to provide visual aids to go along with explanations. If I had never seen a car, I wouldn't know what you were trying to describe to me."

I shivered as a cold draft of air, filled the hall. Running my hands over my arms, I rubbed to warm them up. "Do you guys feel that?"

Dreya's eyes narrowed on the spot near the closed bathroom door. "I think our resident specter is back."

Deandra pursed her lips and furrowed her brow as she took a step toward the ghost. "She's so unlike the woman in the pink floppy hat I saw as a kid. Mary Alice seems angry, which I've never experienced before."

"That's Camilla's mom. Is it wise to allow them to see one another? There's a history there. That woman allowed her daughter to be her servant. I'd harbor ill feelings if mom did that to me," Lia pointed out. "I'd rather not deal with some magical spat between the two."

Dakota sighed. "We are so far in over our heads, it's not even funny. Shit definitely went sideways on us."

Dre chuckled dryly. "That's an understatement, sis. However, it reminds me we should put some cortisone on these bites to keep them from itching so badly."

Phi lowered her hand from her face. She'd been scratching some bites on her cheek. "Do either of you have any here?"

Lia nodded at the same time I did. We'd both packed up our houses and moved them here. "We haven't unpacked it yet. It's upstairs. I'll grab it while you guys wait for Camilla."

I thanked Lia and wrapped my arms around my midsection. "I wish we'd been dreaming. This seems too crazy to believe. Noah and Lucas can turn into wolves and we have a ghoul living in our house." I had to say it all out loud again because my mind was still struggling with reality.

"Mama would tell us we were too gullible for believing these people," Dakota pointed out.

"Yeah, but mom had a habit of denying what was right in front of her. While at the same time she swears that she saw the ghost of her grandfather. I loved her dearly, but sometimes she could stick her head in the sand at times," Dea replied.

I had to agree with that assessment. Our mother was one of the strongest people I knew. She was brave and faced her cancer with grace and dignity. But she had ignored her health for too long and in the end, it put her in a position where the doctors could not cure her.

I rubbed the ache in my chest that always grew when I thought of our mom. "Not even mom could explain what just occurred. As much as I want to say it never happened, I can't. The proof that magic, and witches exist is taking a bath as we speak. Plus, we all saw claws and fur on Noah and Lucas. Then there's what happened with the bees."

Delphine paused in pulling her hair into a ponytail. "Do you think we have magic now? Phoebe and her boyfriend couldn't say for sure, but he was positive we were something more than normal humans."

"They called people mundies," Lia pointed out as she returned holding a couple of tubes of cortisone. "And the god Aidoneus said he thought we had Fae blood."

Dakota took a tube and Lia handed the other to me. The

itching subsided immediately when I rubbed the cream over my arm. "What does that even mean?"

Delphine took the tube from me and rubbed some on her face first. "I've tried to look some information up when he mentioned it. Searches brought up information about mythical creatures whose origins are often connected to Ireland, but can be found elsewhere, too. It mentioned brownies and pixies and other creatures, but we aren't two feet tall and we have no wings."

The bathroom door opened and Camilla walked out with the sports bra held up in her hand. She had managed to get the rest of the clothes on her body. "You were right, Dakota. I feel much better now that I am clean. However, this object is foreign to me and I could not figure out what it was used for. It's too tight for comfortable clothing."

I laughed along with my sisters. "That is a bra. An item developed to hold your breasts in place. Those things are necessary evils in life today. We can talk about that over lunch. Are you hungry?"

Camilla nodded her head as we joined her. "I am famished. Show me the kitchen and I shall make us a repast."

Lia shook her head from side to side. "That isn't necessary. We can handle the food. Phoebe mentioned you needed to eat meat. Let's see what we have in the fridge. We might need to go to the store."

We were all still in shock, but we didn't let it stop us from moving forward. Our mama didn't raise fools. Hard work would get us where we wanted to be. We would never allow anything to get in our way, either.

Not even the prospect of being some mix of human and Fae creature. We were made of sterner stuff than that. We'd all get past the shock and find information to teach us about the magical world.

After all, there was no going back to pretend it didn't

exist. It had been thrust upon us and now we had to deal with it, whether we were ready or not. This was nothing compared to when we lost our mother. This new world was nothing more than a new adventure we'd embarked upon. Like the time we drove across the country with a car full of kids, this was going to be something we would never forget.

CHAPTER 9

DAHLIA

*L*ucas's intense gray eyes seemed to look right through me and to my soul. "How are you doing?"

I blinked, trying to gather my thoughts as they strayed in every direction but the question that he'd asked me. I swallowed and tried to focus on Dani or Camilla, both of whom were out tending the beehives. The rest of my sisters had left.

It turned out Camilla built the beehives with the help of her father. The two of them tended them together and she was showing Dani the ins and outs of the structures. Apparently, the lavender honey was a new development.

Dani and the ghoul were out of sight. I turned back to Lucas and lost my train of thought once again. What had he asked? "Eh. As good as can be expected. It's unbelievable how much our lives have changed in one day."

Lucas cocked his head to one side. "So, you really had no idea the magical world existed? That my kind was out there?"

I shook my head from side to side. "Not even an inkling. I mean, everyone that grows up in New Orleans has a greater appreciation for stories and folklore. And, I admit some part of us does believe in the supernatural. However, I never imagined it was *real*. It's one thing to know ghosts are a thing and another to say sexy men turn into wolves."

Lucas's chuckle stroked me in all the right places and made me tingle. It was unnerving the effect he had on me. I ignored the arousal and focused on his words. "Sexy men, huh? Shifters come in all shapes and sizes I assure you."

I was a widow and a middle-aged woman. I should be beyond this shameless flirting. Nor should I be like a giggling teenager with her first crush. "That came out wrong. What I meant is that I had no idea magical spells and witches were a thing. Or Fae for that matter."

Lucas tucked a piece of my flyaway white-blonde hair behind my ear. I shivered and took one step closer before stopping myself. He was not coming onto me. He was reminding me I probably looked like a mess.

"Is that what the god told you that you were? Fae?" The fine lines around Lucas's eyes and mouth spoke of a life well-lived and filled with laughter.

I nodded my head, wondering why I was even entertaining anything romantic about the guy. He had an adult daughter which meant he was likely married. I took a step back and stuffed my hands in the back of my jeans.

"He said we were part Fae. Although, I have no idea what that means. I can't find any information that isn't fiction or supposition based on stories passed down in families. I'm not two feet tall and I don't have wings or pointed ears. He has to be wrong."

Lucas twisted his mouth to one side. "Not necessarily. Elves have pointed ears, but other Fae do not. They look like you or me. Like mundies, they come in a variety of shapes, sizes, and colors. It is entirely possible that there is some-thing to what he is saying."

"That can't be true. We aren't magical. We're likely cursed, but not Fae."

He narrowed his eyes on me. "What do you mean cursed? And, what's wrong with being magical? Our world might be violent and turbulent at times, but it is filled with adventure."

I held up my hands. "There is nothing wrong with it. Part of me wishes the bees surrounding us with the teal light and biting us, gave us something other than scabs throughout our bodies, while the rest wants nothing to do with magic. I don't know the first thing about the world, and neither do my sisters."

Lucas closed the distance between us. "I could be your guide and teach you everything I know."

I lifted one eyebrow. "Why would you do that? I can't imagine your wife would like that very much."

Lucas threw back his head and laughed. "I'm not married. Shifters don't marry. We get mated."

"Then why did you ask us to host your daughter's wedding? Was that a lie?" I crossed my arms over my chest and glared at him.

"We used the mundie term you are used to rather than calling it a mating ceremony. Initially, Noah and I assumed you knew what we were. Otherwise, you wouldn't have been able to find us. We don't advertise to everyone and we rarely work for mundies."

My head jerked back. "Our sister, Delphine found you when she did an online search. Why didn't you walk away when you discovered we had no clue about the magical world?"

Lucas shrugged his wide shoulders, the movement pulling his shirt tight over his biceps. "We believe fate brought us to you. And the moment I saw you, I knew I couldn't walk away. It's one reason I asked you to host Lilly's mating. I needed an excuse to keep seeing you."

I wanted to believe he was that interested in me, but I was no ignorant twenty-something anymore. "That was probably smart. Our brother-in-law can fix many things, but I'm certain we will need a general contractor for even more."

Lucas shook his head from side to side. "That's not what I was talking about. Although, I will help with anything you need."

It was on the tip of my tongue to ask what he meant, but I left the question unasked. I wasn't ready to hear his answer, either way. "Speaking of Lilly, we will need to talk to her soon, so we can get started on the personalized stuff."

"I'm not sure I understand. What do you mean?" I was grateful Lucas followed my lead and let it go.

"I engrave wine or champagne glasses, either stemmed or stemless on our laser engraver. And, I cut out designs for signs that we all paint or stain and put together. We've done money trees for weddings, as well. Once we know what the couple wants then we can start planning all of the details. We refused parties because we knew we were going to be busy here, so Lilly's mating is the only thing on the schedule aside from the renovations. But we still need as much time as you can give us to get things done."

"And the sooner the better," Dani added as she and Camilla approached. "It will be helpful to know what flowers she wants. I can put in an order if she knows or make time to take her to the mart so she can pick some out."

Lucas scrunched his face up. I should have known the expression would be attractive to him. He made everything sexy. "This is why I needed you. She talks about making her ceremony one to remember and I haven't the first clue."

I chuckled. "I'm sure her mom would have helped her."

Lucas shook his head from side to side. "That's not possible. She died many years ago. My mom is good at some things, but flowery, girly stuff isn't one of them. My sister is just as handicapped in that area."

Dani laughed. "We can give your daughter the wedding of her dreams."

I lifted a hand. "It's actually not called a wedding. Shifters have mating ceremonies."

Dani cocked her head and looked at Lucas then Noah as he joined us. "What's the difference?"

That was a good question. One I hadn't thought to ask because I was sidetracked by the fact that Phi shouldn't have come across their company during her search. Lucas shared a look with Noah then addressed Dani. "When a shifter mates, it's for life. There is no such thing as divorce, for one. Another difference is there is a magical component to the ceremony. We join two souls together rather than two lives. There are no vows of obedience. We ask the gods to bless the couple and unite them."

"If mating is for life, what happens when you lose a mate?" The question was out before I could sensor myself. It was insensitive and irrelevant.

Lucas's gray eyes focused on me, making me shift from side to side. "Every shifter has what we call our Fated One and we rarely survive their loss. Shifters with young children are typically the ones that will live on to raise their kids before they perish suddenly."

I sucked in a startled breath. "Are you going to die after Lilly is mated?"

Lucas's forehead furrowed and his eyes narrowed. "No, why would you ask, oh. No, Lilly's mother was not my Fated One."

"Well thank God for that," I blurted. My cheeks heated and I wanted to put some duct tape over my mouth. "I'm sure it would devastate Lilly to lose you."

Dani bumped my shoulder and opened her mouth but closed it when Noah spoke. "Most never find their Fated One. We can search for decades. It's like winning the lottery when we find her."

"How do you know when you find the one meant for you?" Camilla's voice had a slight waver, but it was a major improvement that she'd addressed the men. Dani and I spent last night talking to her and trying to get her to understand that she wasn't living under the thumb of an abusive master any longer. It was surprisingly difficult given that she hadn't been alive for centuries.

Noah smiled at my sister like she hung the moon, leaving me little doubt how he felt about her. "Your entire world comes to life. Every dark corner of your soul is illuminated and your outlook changes. It's like seeing for the first time in your life. There are no words to describe the way every fiber of your being yearns to be close to her." That was the most romantic description I'd ever heard from a guy.

Dani cleared her throat and looked away. I caught her eye and jerked my chin in Noah's direction. "It sounds as unreal as the existence of magic. I have a hard time believing there is anything so pure. Love is an avenue others use to control someone, nothing more."

My heart broke for my sister that she'd lived a life that left her with no faith in the existence of true love. That's what Noah was describing. I loved my late husband, but it was nothing like that description. I often wonder what my life would be like if he'd lived. I'd dated the guy I'd just broken up with for several years.

He had a low opinion of women and their characters. He thought all of them were manipulative liars that couldn't be trusted. He also talked to me like I was a child when I had done something he didn't like. And then there was the fact that he never spent any time with my family which was my biggest sticking point. My family meant the world to me. Damn, Dani was right.

It turned out that I was just as jaded as Dani. No wonder we got along so well. "Not everyone is Hugo, sis. I understand why you feel that way. Most days, I agree with you. The past twenty-four hours have shown us anything is possible. Maybe we can turn him into a toad."

Noah's face transformed into a scowl. "I would geld this Hugo for hurting you and destroying your belief in love if it would help heal you. No one should walk around feeling like that."

Dani faced the shifter and shrugged one shoulder. "It's in the past. I'm on a new adventure with my sisters and don't want to discuss my ex. It looks like you made quite a bit of progress today. Do we need to worry if it rains tonight?"

Noah shifted his focus to the roof, accepting the shift in topic. "There aren't any storms in the forecast. However, if it does rain, we have you covered. We laid the ice and water shield of polyethylene and rubberized asphalt to protect the areas that had the worst damage. The rest of the roof should be able to repel any rain."

Dani bobbed her head and lifted a hand. "We will see you tomorrow then."

With that, she turned and walked away. Camilla lingered for a second then joined her. I sighed and said my goodbyes and went back to the house to get back to work on painting and changing light fixtures.

Camilla and Dani were in the kitchen when I entered the back door. "Are you cooking dinner already?"

Dani was pulling items out of the fridge and slamming them down on the counter. She was agitated and I felt responsible. I shouldn't have called her out. "I'm sorry, Dani. I should have kept my mouth shut. It's just hard for me to see you in so much pain."

BRENDA TRIM

Dani whirled on me with her nostrils flared. Camilla paused with a hamburger patty lifted to her mouth. Dakota had grilled burgers that afternoon for lunch and had cooked two dozen extras for the ghoul.

"You're right, Lia. It wasn't your place to mention how awful Hugo was to me. Now, Noah will see me as nothing more than a washed-up, middle-aged mother of three. There is nothing attractive about that."

I pulled Dani into a hug and noticed Camilla slip from the room. "You are a beautiful person, inside and out. And I have absolutely no doubt that Noah sees that. His interest in you is genuine and your history shouldn't change that. If he doesn't accept your past then he isn't the one for you. For the record, that is not the case. He wanted to hurt Hugo for being cruel to you. That's not a guy who has lost interest."

Dani sighed and laid her head on my shoulder. Her response was cut off when a loud crash sounded out through the hall. We both raced from the room to find Camilla frozen in place with the bowl of patties in a heap on the ground at her feet. Hovering a few feet from her was her mother, Mary Alice Carlton.

"Cami, are you alright?" I'd begun shortening her name. Initially, she didn't care for it, but I thought it was growing on her.

The ghoul turned terror-filled eyes to us. Her mother moved closer. "My beautiful Camilla. How are you here? You died long ago."

Camilla was trembling as Dani and I closed the distance between us. I looked at my sister, asking her silently what we should do. Her response gave me no clue. I grabbed Cami's hand, wanting her to know we were there to support her.

"You don't have to talk to her, Camilla." I had no idea if my reassurance was heard because she continued staring at her mother.

After what seemed like forever, Cami broke her silence. "I am here because a powerful witch brought me back. I don't understand the mechanics because I never got a proper education in anything magical. All I can say is that her power coaxed me from the grave. And you? Why are you here?"

Camilla's lower lip trembled and I patted her back with my free hand. "You're doing great. She can't harm you anymore."

Mary Alice lowered her head and her form wavered. "I never wanted you to be harmed. It killed something inside when William took you from me. A little more died each day that he forced you to be my slave as you grew up. When he enlisted help to suppress you, I thought I would die. I was bedridden for months."

Cami's eyebrows scrunched together. "Master Carlton said you had a case of the vapors."

"I was helpless to change either of our situations and it nearly killed me. Plus, something was draining my magic. My mother claimed that marrying the wrong man and cursing his land stole my ability to perform spells and improve my position in life. There was nothing I could do." Mary Alice was clearly upset over what had happened. It tugged my heartstrings to see her trying to help her daughter understand.

Camilla didn't have the same problem. She lifted her chin and her face went blank. "You were never my mother. I was your slave and served your every whim. I was not privy to your inner thoughts or struggles. What's the purpose of telling me any of this now? You are dead and I am an undead creature."

The ghost extended her see-through hand toward Cami. "I sensed you lingering on the property and prayed we could mend our relationship before either of us moved on to the next life. I have roamed these halls for centuries, searching for a way to be freed or find you. Now you are here." Her apparition flickered.

Camilla smiled at Mary Alice then. "You should move on, Mary Alice. There is nothing for you here any longer. Willowberry belongs to the Smith sisters, not you. Your mere presence disrupts the balance."

Mary Alice's face fell and her form went in and out again, then vanished. I looked at Dani and Camilla. "Is she gone? Did you send her away?"

Cami bent to clean the mess she'd made. "She is still here. I'm sorry about the bowl. I will replace it when I have money of my own."

Dani's head swiveled around. "There is no need to replace anything. I can see how upsetting that encounter was for you. You go relax Cami. I will bring you a steak as soon as they are done."

Cami lifted eyes filled with tears. "When I was a girl, I would have been whipped for such a thing. I've never met kinder women in my life."

"We will never hurt you," I promised before Dani and I knelt next to the ghoul.

We silently helped her clean the mess and carry the big pieces to the kitchen. I couldn't imagine what she was feeling after that. Their encounter had been an emotional roller coaster for me and I wasn't involved in any way. It had to be a million times worse for Cami. One thing was certain, life at Willowberry was anything but boring and predictable.

CHAPTER 10

DANIELLE

*T*he sound of Camilla cleaning upstairs seemed louder than it should have in the quiet house. It was six in the morning and I was still on the night shift schedule. After over ten years of being a nurse in a hospital and working while others slept it wasn't an easy habit to break.

Or perhaps it was the myriad of thoughts racing through my brain that had kept me up all night. Either was possible. I'd been going full-tilt since we purchased the house and I should have passed out like Dahlia had the second her head hit the pillow. Instead, I remained awake all night.

Camilla had fallen asleep soon after Lia, but she'd woken up around four in the morning and said she needed to do some work to feel useful, so I sent her up to clean and prep the rooms we were going to be painting today.

Rolling over, I watched my sister as she slept fitfully. I wondered if she had nightmares about the death of her husband. For months after Leo died, Lia had woken up covered in a cold sweat with a scream on her lips. It had happened shortly before I left my first husband because he was abusive to me and I ended up staying with her until I got on my feet.

Now, after my second divorce, I was once again living with Dahlia. I rubbed my chest where it ached. I couldn't shake the feeling that I was a failure and somehow unlovable. At forty-two years old, I should be past those insecurities, yet I wasn't. That was the thought that kept creeping to the fore-front of my mind. It was as if it was on the over seventeen thousand square feet of television screen in Times Square, which meant there was no missing the message. I was trying to hide from myself.

I cringed and sat up on the air mattress. We hadn't yet adjusted to the house and moved into our rooms upstairs. The plastic was like sleeping inside a bouncy house while a dozen toddlers were having a party inside it. There was no way I was going to suggest moving into our rooms. I needed to be close to my sister right now.

I know what my sisters would say to me if they knew I was obsessing over the divorce from Hugo. I wished I could believe them, but they weren't impartial. They had to tell me it wasn't my fault.

Forget about Hugo, there's a sexy wolf shifter that wants to take you on a date. Shaking my head, I got up and moved to the kitchen. I needed a tall-boy while I banished those unwanted thoughts. I could not get involved with anyone else. There was something fundamentally wrong with me. Noah was too nice to burden with my crappy life.

I shivered from the cool morning air, wishing for the millionth time I liked coffee. It would be nice to have a warm drink to banish the chill. *That's too much to ask of a simple caffeinated beverage.*

Seemed my gray matter wasn't going to give me a rest today as it continued beating me up. I sighed and filled my tumbler. Lia had engraved it with the title Queen Bee below the image of the insect.

"You need to turn off your mind, Dani. I can feel your restlessness in my sleep."

I turned to give Lia a smile. "Sorry. Lots to do here. You know how it is."

Lia lifted an eyebrow as she poured herself an energy drink. "I know exactly how it is. I can't even begin to understand what you are going through, but I know you well enough to know you are beating yourself up over how things ended with Hugo. In some ways, both of you are responsible for what happened, but the onus is on him. There is nothing wrong with you. Love ebbs and flows. You both need to ride out the waves and both need to make an effort to remain connected during the lulls, not just one of you."

Tears blurred my vision as I sipped my Pepsi. "I have two failed marriages, Lia. That tells me it is *me* that carries the onus." I hadn't meant to admit that much out loud.

Lia scowled and shook her head from side to side. "You're not responsible for Mike being an asshole. You are not the one that grabbed that gun and you certainly did not point it at yourself. No matter what you said to him. He made the choice to try and control you through violence and threats. He is the one that gaslit and belittled you and called you names."

"Now, I have no doubt that toward the end you gave it right back. I can't see you keeping your mouth shut. However, that doesn't mean you are responsible for what he did. When an abused woman fights back with either her fists or words, it's usually in an attempt to change how she's being treated and give their abuser a taste of their own medicine. You did the right thing leaving him for you and your kids.

That took courage. Especially when you had no job, or real training to go out and get one."

A couple of tears slipped past my lower lids to roll down my cheeks. "I have said some pretty mean things to Hugo and Mike. Maybe it's just me."

Lia wrapped her arms around me, holding me close. "You can make better choices in what you say and how you react. I see that you regret your words and actions. I'd bet Willowberry that neither Mike nor Hugo can say the same thing. They blame you and have you convinced it was all your fault. They've taken enough from you, don't let them take your heart too. I know how easy it is to close yourself off and avoid any further heartache."

I stepped away from Lia and smirked knowingly at her. "The same goes for you. Now, are you ready to paint some bedrooms? Cami has been up and preparing the rooms in the east wing ready for us to begin."

Lia groaned as she put the lid on her drink and grabbed three yogurts from the fridge and handed one to me. "I can't wait. As soon as we have the walls painted, Steve can come in and put the new windows in and get rid of the broken ones."

We'd discovered about half of the panels didn't open in the house. Instead of trying to refurbish the frames, we decided to replace them with double-paned, energy-efficient glass that will lower our bills in the long run. We weren't able to replicate the leaded windows exactly, but the end result will be beautiful regardless.

I followed behind Lia, realizing I felt better after our talk. It shouldn't surprise me because she was a social worker. It was her job to help people. What struck me was that she laid out the facts then pointed out what I am responsible for, what I have said and done, and that I can do better in the future.

I've known I held some responsibility and didn't want to

be absolved of it. Knowing what I needed to work on was half the battle. And now that Lia knew, she would be there checking in and assisting me throughout my journey. *The others will be there for you, as well. Don't discount the importance of having your sisters by your side.*

I swear my internal voice sounded like my mom from time to time and just then it was her sweet intonation that I heard. Camilla stepped out of the room and smiled when she saw us. "I'm just finishing up with taping off the baseboards and ceiling in this section of the house."

My jaw dropped open. "Damn, you work fast. We didn't expect you to get so much done."

Lia handed the ghoul a yogurt and a spoon plus a bag of leftover chicken that Dakota's husband dropped off last night. I hadn't seen my sister grab the chicken. "We might be able to get this wing painted today with everything you've done. If we work in pairs, we can get three done at a time. You did the hardest part of painting."

I mixed the toppings into my yogurt and ate while we gathered the painting supplies we would need. "Do you want to cut in or roll the walls?"

Lia finished her breakfast and tossed the trash in an empty box. "I'll roll the walls first then if you need a break from the ladder or squatting, we can switch."

I nodded and shook the paint can to ensure the color was mixed just right. Lia spread our drop cloth over the hardwood floor. After pouring some into a small bucket and the tray for Lia, I climbed the ladder and started brushing the edge along the top. Camilla ate as she watched us.

"I can paint along the bottom of the walls. We didn't have tools like these back when I did this. These make the task much easier."

I gestured to the other brushes. "Feel free to pitch in after you finish eating. Or you can take a break. You've worked hard this morning already."

We got into a groove and before the sky was fully light outside the window, we had the room finished. Lia gathered the drop cloth and carried it to the next room. "You are a blessing, Cami. We will be done painting in no time with your help."

I nodded my head as I folded the ladder. "Lia's right. Wait until the others see how much we've gotten done up here."

Camilla's smile was brighter than the sun now blasting through the picture window. "It feels good to accomplish something and get paid. I never realized how it would make me work even harder."

The ghoul's comment was a poignant reminder that she was a slave that lived hundreds of years ago and suffered unspeakable abuse at the hands of the man who built this plantation.

"With the stories, you'll be able to tell to tour groups, you will get the biggest tips," Lia pointed out.

We'd heard some of her stories about life on the planta-tion. The biggest surprise was that William Henry Carlton worked as hard some days as the slaves out in the field. Life on a plantation required him to be out there with his servants. My favorite was hearing about crawfish boils held in the slave quarters. That's how I thought of the meals they often shared.

I could never have survived a life back then. I liked my conveniences too much. The reflection of the sun off some-thing outside blinded me for a second and made me throw up my arm. I lost hold of the brush in my hand and shouted as it fell to the ground.

"I got it," Lia assured me.

I clung to the second step of the ladder and lowered my hand. I had to blink a couple of times to clear the bright spots dancing in my line of sight. When my eyes cleared, my heart skipped several beats and my palms started sweating at what had seared my retinas.

Noah and Lucas were pulling into the parking lot. And right behind them was my second ex-husband, Hugo. "What is it?" Lia was wiping her hands on a rag as she approached the window. "Crap."

My reaction involved several swear words and a note to ask Phoebe about hexes I could use against Hugo. Tension strung my shoulders tight as a bow as I descended the stairs.

Lia put a hand on my shoulder. "Do you want me to send him away?"

I shook my head and ran a hand through my shoulder-length blonde hair. I hadn't brushed it yet that morning. There were tangles from tossing and turning all night. My body flushed as I imagined seeing Hugo with the rat's nest on top of my head and the tattered, stained, and smelly clothes below.

"I've got this. I have to face him sometime."

I left the room and heard Camilla asking Dahlia who Hugo was as he got out of his sports car. My stomach was twisted in knots as I exited the house and approached a man I had hoped to never see again.

No matter how hard I tried, I couldn't come up with a reason for his visit to the plantation. I was caught up in my head when Noah stepped into my path. My breath caught in my throat at the smile he threw my way. "Good morning, Sunshine. How was your evening?"

"Morning, Dimples. My night was uneventful." I couldn't resist giving him a nickname, as well. I'd been wanting to call him dimples from the moment I met him and it came out after hearing his nickname for me.

His laughter usually seeped into my body and did

naughty things to my insides. Today, I stiffened and glared at my ex who was approaching from behind. "Who is that?"

I looked up at the snarl I heard in Noah's voice. The hint of anger had my heart racing and made me cringe away from the shifter. I should have known better than to think he wasn't an asshat like Mike had been. An alpha like Noah would never tolerate a strong woman.

To my surprise, Noah's face showed concern and regret. "Sorry. I was reacting to the way he smells."

I stepped closer and lowered my voice. "He stinks? Like what?"

Noah wrinkled his nose. "He smells like dirty water and mold."

A laugh burst from me making Noah smile. Hugo reached us at that moment. "Hi, Dani. It's good to see you doing so well. I'm Hugo, her husband. Who are you?"

Noah lifted one eyebrow. "Don't you mean ex-husband?"

Hugo's forehead wrinkled and his mouth pursed. I stepped in between the two men. Noah focused on me, giving me a seductive smile. "Lucas and I will be on the roof if you need anything at all. I'll see you for lunch?"

My eyes widened for a second before I recovered. I suspected he was making it clear to Hugo he was interested and I was okay with that for now, so I nodded and thanked him.

When I turned back to Hugo, he had his arms crossed over his chest. I sighed and took a seat on a nearby bench. I didn't have the mental capacity to deal with him at the moment. "Why are you here Hugo?"

"Are you dating him?"

I stared at him without answering. When he didn't respond, I got up and started walking to the house. He would get the picture when I shut the door in his face. "Wait," he called out. "I'm sorry. I came to see you. I missed you, love. I realize the mistakes I made and want to talk to you about working on us."

It felt as if he had hit me over the head with a two-by-four. "What are you talking about? Why now? Did your girlfriend leave you already?"

Hugo rolled his eyes. "I saw the mistake I made and realized you are the one for me."

"Too little too late, Hugo." My stomach roiled like a bowl full of worms making me nauseated. Then again, it was probably Hugo making me sick.

"It's never too late, love. We can still make this work. All we have to do is try. I'm so proud of the move you made. Taking the step with your own venue took bravery. I know how difficult that must have been for you. You're risk-averse."

He'd never told me he was proud before. It was always him telling me to pick up more shifts because our credit cards were all maxed out or we needed to pay off one debt or another. "Thanks. My sisters and I are working very hard to make this successful. We already have two parties; one is scheduled this month."

His eyes got big and he looked around the plantation. "You've got a lot of work to do before then. Do you need some help?"

My lower jaw hit my chest. He wasn't Mr. Fixit. In fact, he couldn't even mow the lawn. "This is all construction work. We've got it under control. Phi found some great contractors to help."

"I might not be the best, but I can paint and help build furniture. Remember the bed we made together? That was one of the best projects. We were both covered in stain by the end of the day." His laughter made me smile. It was one of my favorite memories with him.

"It wouldn't come off either," I added. "We have all the

furniture we need. There are some great antiques in the attic that have been there since this place was built."

"Wow. You found a gem with this place. It's got to be worth over a million. You'll be making more money than me in no time."

I could see the wheels turning in his head as he talked about how we could capitalize with tours and a souvenir store. My anger rose higher the more he talked. He'd heard about the plantation and decided he wanted to cash in on the gold mine.

I thrust my hands on my hips. "You're right about all of that. My sisters and I will make more money than we can spend. Before we know it, the others will be able to leave their jobs as well. But you know what? You will never see one dime from this business."

"Why would you say that? Our relationship means more to me than money. You're the love of my life." He looked so earnest when he said that. It pulled at my heartstrings until I recalled the avarice on his face as he looked around and talked about all the ways to make money with Willowberry.

"Get lost and don't ever come back. Our divorce was the best thing I ever could have done. You've used me one too many times and I am not about to let you take from me or my sisters again. And, I don't believe for a second that you saw your mistakes and wanted to try again. My bet? Your girlfriend realized what an asshole you are and left you."

It felt good to tell him off. He opened his mouth then closed it. A second later I heard a loud thud and turned to see that Noah had jumped off the roof and was approaching us. Hugo's face turned red as he left as fast as his feet would carry him.

CHAPTER 11

DANIELLE

*N*oah's eyes bored into me as he looked me over from head to toe. "What happened, Sunshine? I heard raised voices and came as soon as I could." There was no doubt in my mind that he was concerned I'd been hurt by Hugo.

Noah wouldn't be able to see the injuries I suffered from Hugo. They weren't physical. I wiped my sweaty hands on my pants and pasted on a smile. "My ex-husband wanted a piece of Willowberry."

Noah's forehead crinkled as he looked at the parking lot where Hugo was backing out in his mid-life crisis mobile. "He owns part of this place?"

I shook my head vehemently. "No way in hell. He's always been focused on money and when he heard we had purchased a plantation, he came hoping I would take him back so he could get a piece of the action. All he saw when he arrived were dollar signs. My sisters and I have never looked at what we do in terms of money. We see an opportunity to give people priceless memories to share with their loved ones. Our main concern is being able to survive and have enough money to fix this place up and make it the best venue it can be. None of us is in this to become a millionaire."

A smile broke over Noah's face as he looked around the property. "You've already changed the feel of the place. I have no doubt you six will be so successful you'll have to either hire help or turn people away."

I cocked my head to the side. "What do you mean we've already changed the way the plantation feels?"

For me, I had noticed a distinct difference in the energy surrounding us. Initially, it was dark and troubled. Now there was a sense of hope and freedom that hadn't been present before.

"This land used to be foreboding and was filled with rage before. It would literally make my skin crawl whenever I came here."

"Then why did you agree to help us with the roof?" It made no sense why he would come here to do the job if that was what he experienced.

Noah looked away and shrugged his shoulders. "When your sister called, I could sense how desperate you guys were. I assumed you were supernaturals and have never been able to turn my back on those in need. Plus, my gut told me I had to be here."

"Your gut? Is that a fancy way of saying you wanted to see the women crazy enough to buy a lemon of a piece of property? You were probably well aware of the curse and how real it actually used to be."

Noah chuckled. "I have to admit the thought crossed my mind. Lucas's too. Supernaturals typically steered clear of this place because of the negative energy. I figured it took guts to take the risk and hope you could beat the curse. Of course, I didn't know you were six beautiful women."

"Lucky for us we aren't men. Otherwise, we might not have survived the first night here. But we don't have to worry about the curse anymore. Phoebe used the energy from it to do whatever she did to us and Camilla."

"How is the ghoul? Is she settling in? I imagine this must be difficult for her."

I scanned the second-story windows and saw her watching us. "She's been a huge help. She doesn't know anything about modern living and she had an encounter with her mother's ghost which would have set me off if I were her, and yet she is handling it extremely well. She compartmentalizes everything and moves forward. I don't think she knows what she wants in life yet, but she finds freedom exhilarating. She prepped almost a dozen rooms before six this morning, so we could start painting first thing."

"She'll fit right in with you and your sisters, then. I've never met a more determined and talented bunch in my life. This house is daunting, and yet not one of you has ever said you can't do it."

My chin lifted with his praise. He wasn't saying this because he wanted something from me. We had already hired him and agreed to host Lucas's daughter's wedding, or rather mating. He was simply telling me what he thought. And it meant more to me than anything.

"We learned that from our mom. She faced stage four breast cancer with courage and grace. She never once gave up and said she couldn't fight anymore. There were days I would see what she went through and I wanted to give up. But she kept her chin high and did what she needed to fight. She lived almost three years after her diagnosis and until the day she died, said she was going to beat it.

"I watched her discover her bones were so riddled with

cancer they told her she would never walk again, yet she did. In the end, when it was in her brain, they said she would have mood swings and be in constant pain. You know, she never once complained and when we asked, she always said, 'I'm okay' This plantation is nothing compared to that."

Noah's eyes softened and his smile was beautiful. "It all makes sense now. You definitely have her strength. I wish I could have known her. She would have made an amazing alpha."

I shook my head. "I don't have a tenth of her toughness. There is no way I could handle her symptoms without complaining a hundred times a day."

Noah's finger under my chin warmed the cold that had started seeping in when we talked about my mom. "You each carry a piece of her and have more resistance than you give yourself credit for. You've gone through changes, discovered the magical world exists, and haven't crumpled under the weight."

I had no words, so I nodded in response. His chuckle sent a thrill racing through my veins and made me shiver. "Before I forget, Lucas will be bringing Lilly soon so she can see the place and discuss what she wants. I have to get back to work, but I wanted to ask you if you would go out to dinner with me sometime."

I swallowed through a tight throat, trying to get some moisture down it so I could talk. "I haven't been on a date in over ten years. I would love to have dinner with you." I practically yelled the last part because I was busy wanting to kick myself over my admission. He didn't need to know how long it had been!

He smiled and brushed a finger along one of my cheeks. His green eyes bored into mine and his face closed the distance. I lifted my chin unsure if he was going to kiss me.

He didn't. The tension built between us as his breath brushed against my lips and his eyes held mine.

I was about to be reckless and close the remaining distance when he broke the silence. "Dinner in a couple of days. And lunch today." He smiled then turned and jogged to the ladder leaning against the side of the house.

I watched him climb on the roof and ogled him for several seconds until Dahlia came out of the house and dragged me back inside. "We need to finish the hall downstairs and the library before we go back to the second floor. I almost forgot about those last two sections before we got started this morning."

"Noah asked me out on a date." I gasped and covered my mouth while Lia started waggling her eyebrows.

"Oh my God, sis. I knew he was into you. I told you! Where are you going? And when? We need to get your sexy panties unpacked and clean your slinky blue dress. It makes your butt look good."

My cheeks turned red and I sighed. "Why did I agree to dinner? I can't go on a date."

Lia scowled at me. "Of course, you can. You're single and beautiful. There is nothing wrong with going out with a sexy guy."

"Let's focus on painting for now. We can talk about the date later." To my surprise, Lia let it go as we entered the library and started on the shelves that hadn't been finished. I was anxious and unsure. I needed to think it through before I talked it to death or I might change my mind.

* * *

DAKOTA SANK onto the couch and brought her feet up under her then grabbed the throw pillow I'd purchased for her to hold when she came over. She had come to love her curves and the extra weight she carried, but she was still more comfortable holding a pillow when lounging around to hide her extra belly fat.

Dakota ate some of the fried rice we had delivered for dinner. "What are you wearing on your date?"

My head swiveled around so I faced Kota, and I shrugged. "Lia said I should wear the blue slinky one, but I think that's too much for a first date."

Dreya was crouched next to me as we filled our plates with Chinese food. "That one makes you look like you have a great butt. I'd go with it."

Dea laughed. "Give him a preview of what he can expect."

I rolled my eyes. "That is not going to happen. I'm not even sure we will be going to dinner."

Delphine sat cross-legged at the end of the coffee table. "You need to get out there again and see there are good men. Besides, one date doesn't mean you have to sleep with him or jump into a serious relationship." She had covered her mouth while she chewed making it hard to hear her clearly.

Camilla lifted a bite of orange chicken and smelled it before popping it into her mouth. "Mmm. This is delicious. I've never tasted Chinese food before. I've heard you say you have children and are past childbearing years, so why would Noah want to date you?"

Cami was picking up the modern use of language and slang rather quickly. That was not the case with the rest of the social mores. Lia smiled at the ghoul. "People have married for love and not their ability to have children for a couple of centuries now. It's often a physical attraction that prompts someone to ask for a date. From there you assess each other based on shared interests and whether or not you enjoy each other's company."

Camilla's face pinched making her look like she'd bitten a sour lemon. "That seems so odd. Of course, if you can walk into a store to buy food and other necessities, children aren't as important as they used to be."

I nodded. "How much do you know about the magical world? I've wondered how things used to be for them. Noah mentioned shifters had their Fated One but does that apply to all magical creatures?"

Cami shrugged her shoulders. "I have little experience and knowledge about that part of my heritage. There were stories and we had voodoo priestesses visit the plantation, but the information was kept from us. Our owners didn't want us to know too much. They feared we would rebel or find a way to escape."

"I can't imagine how that must have been. No way would I tolerate some jerk telling me what to do or beating me because he didn't like the way I made his bed. Forget that shit. I'm glad you get a chance to have a better life now, Cami. You deserve to be happy after all you've been through." Dakota had come a long way from when we were young adults. She'd mellowed and lost the judgmental attitudes she used to have. Her growth has been inspiring.

"Were witches persecuted in your time like they were the century before?" Phi set her fork down and picked up an egg roll. "I've been researching witches and Fae online and most of the information talks about the behaviors that branded a person a witch during the Salem witch trials or the herbs and crystals used in ceremonies and rituals. I doubt it is accurate. And there is a surprising amount of information about the Fae. I lost count of how many types there are, but it seems like they could be separated into light and dark or Seelie and Unseelie. I wish we could sit with Phoebe and Aidoneus and ask all about this new world."

Dahlia adjusted her position so she sat higher on her knees. "Me too. I'm going to ask Noah and Lucas some questions. First, I'd like to learn about ghosts and how to exorcize them."

Dreya cleared her throat. "I know nothing about ghosts or vampires or whatever, but I can say I don't like you three living here alone which is why Steve and I are going to sell our house and renovate one of the slave's quarters turning it into our house. That is if everyone is alright with that plan."

Dre was always looking out for the rest of us and I appreciated her effort now. The fact that she was willing to make that sacrifice meant the world to me. And it told me she was just as invested as I was. I thought my sisters were but wasn't one hundred percent certain.

"That would be perfect," Dahlia blurted. "It would be nice to have someone close in case something happens here. It has been quiet since that night when we saw the person in black prowling around, but you never know."

Dakota sighed. "I can't live in a haunted house and I doubt Jeff will want to move onto the property. It's hard enough to think about sleeping here tonight knowing your mom is haunting the place Cami."

Dreya held up her hands. "You don't have to move here. I worry about three women being here alone and the houses are perfect for Steve and I. Besides, he is excited to live somewhere with such a rich history. Frankly, I think he's jealous of the ghosts and ghouls and shifters. He wants in on the action."

"You can tell your husband the houses aren't haunted," Cami interjected. "The spirits that live here can't move on because they are tied here."

"How can we help them move on into the light? There has to be a way to give them peace." Lia asked the questions that were on my mind. I'd been wondering how we could get Mary Alice to leave since I first saw her.

What about the money having tourists see an actual ghost could bring in? I meant what I said to Noah. I wanted enough money to survive and create the perfect events for people, giving them memories that would last a lifetime. It doesn't matter how big your house is or how many cars you have when you come to the end of your life, but how well you lived it.

My mother's life was rich and filled with priceless memories. Baking caramel corn every Christmas. Teaching us girls how to make perfect meringue. She had ten children and thirty-seven grandchildren, all of whom were with her when she passed away telling their favorite moments with her. You couldn't pay for that much love and devotion.

Camilla shrugged her shoulders as she chewed more orange chicken. I was glad Dea ordered extra servings. "Most are slaves that are tied to the other buildings. I am not sure how to get them to move on. I know one spell and it will only come in handy when I need to make a bed."

"We can ask Phoebe sometime. She said she would help us," Phi interjected. "But you gave me an idea, Dreya. We should spend some time and money renovating the other slave's houses into places we can rent to people visiting the area. It's a way to make money to support their upkeep and give us finished homes should anyone else decide they want to relocate on the property."

"That's brilliant, but after we finish with the main house, Dreya's house, and the kitchen." I refuse to have many events here with things under construction. Clients will expect us to have our shit together and offer a place that suits their purposes. *Then you're going to need to put on your big girl panties and move to the third floor.*

That was the downside to how I wanted things. I just wasn't ready to move out of the room with Lia. It was going to be even better with all six of us there tonight.

Phi nodded in agreement. "I'm making a list of priorities

for the money we received from Phoebe. The kitchen is at the top along with the new windows. Aside from a fresh coat of paint outside, the rest of the work on the main house can be done by us. And we made mad progress on it today thanks to Cami's prep work."

"I will get the west wing prepped so we can work on it tomorrow," the ghoul offered.

I smiled at her, so she knew I wasn't upset. "You don't have to work like that. It's alright to rest, even if you aren't sleeping."

She tilted her head to the side. "I don't understand."

Dakota blew out a breath. "Girl, you make me tired thinking about how hard you work. It means there is no reason for you to be up and working just because you are awake. You can lay there and give your body a rest."

Cami's eyes widened. "I will try, but I can't promise anything. It feels wrong to even think about lying there and doing nothing."

"I'll help you adjust to a more leisurely life. It's good for the soul. Speaking of relaxation, I wish I had a margarita." Dakota yelped as a glass appeared between her clasped hands. The shape of the container and the color of the drink made it clear she had just received what she wished for. "What the hell? Did I just get my wish?"

Lia's wide eyes mirrored mine. "That is exactly what happened. I wish I had a beignet."

We all waited but nothing happened. Delphine made a wish for the dishes to be cleaned. Again, nothing happened. I finally gestured to the drink. "Taste it, Kota. See if it is real."

She lifted the frosty libation to her lips and drank. "Wow, this is the best margarita I've ever had. It's making me crave chips and guacamole, though. I could mack on some guac right now."

As if she'd made a wish, a big bowl of tortilla chips and a

smaller one of mashed avocados appeared on the pillow she was hugging. Dreya whistled. "Damn, sis. Seems like you're the only one that got magical powers from that snafu the other day."

I wondered what the extent of her powers was. Could she wish for the main plantation house to be repaired? Or was that too much?

Dakota put the bowls on the coffee table. "If I got power, you guys have to have it, as well. We just need to find out what it is."

My heart raced in my chest and my thoughts started going a million miles an hour. "Do you guys think that Aidoneus was right?"

I listened as everyone seemed to talk at once while I digested the fact that not only did we discover the magical world existed, but at least one of us was given magical powers. I held my breath and forced my mind to go blank. I wasn't ready to learn I wasn't a normal woman anymore. After my encounter with Hugo then having Noah ask me out, I needed time to process.

CHAPTER 12

DAHLIA

I wiped the sweat that had trickled down my forehead to attack my eyes. Midlife had brought so many fun gifts that hit me while I wasn't looking. Peri-menopause was a tumultuous roller coaster of heavy, sporadic periods, occasional night sweats, and the pop-up hot flash every now and then. It was a preview of what was to come.

I can honestly say I wasn't sure if I was looking forward to hitting full-blown menopause or not. On the one hand, I was looking forward to not having a monthly cycle anymore. I could hardly fathom what it would be like when my uterus no longer went ten rounds with Mike Tyson.

On the other, I dreaded having more chin hair than my nephew, Declan. He was always trying to grow more than me. At the age of twelve, he hadn't yet hit puberty. I try not to react when he checks me out every time I see him. God bless him, he just doesn't understand it's not cool for his aunt to have more facial hair than he does.

"These buildings look like they were updated in the seventies and haven't been touched since then. I'm glad the electrical and plumbing aren't in dire need because the rest is in dismal shape." Steve had paused in tearing down a wall between the living room and the kitchen.

Dreya, Dani, Camilla, and I had been helping start renovations on the slave quarters they'd chosen to move into. Dre wanted to be close to the main house, so they were in the one where Camilla lived and died.

"It looks nothing like it did in my time. There were small rooms that were shared by four of us. There were no bathrooms in here. We had to bring in a barrel and heat the water for bathing. Or use the river. That's one thing I have come to love about your time. Running water that comes out hot and the indoor toilet." Camilla was painting a primer over the ceiling.

It was almost a shame to cover the stains. It'd been fun to play a game of Eye Spy with them. At Steve's request, Noah and Lucas had checked the roof and determined it needed to be replaced, as well.

I stood up from cleaning the baseboards and stretched. "I couldn't imagine having to bathe like that. Or trek outside to go to the bathroom in the middle of the night."

Dre chuckled. "You didn't mind when we were camping as kids."

Memories flooded me of time spent in a green canvas tent laughing with my parents and siblings. "Those were some fun times. Remember how mom always made hobo stew? We should build a fire and make some tonight. We can put extra beef in the one for Cami."

Dani poked her head out of the newly finished bathroom at the front of the hall. She had us working right up until the moment it was time for her to go. I don't know how she worked so close to a date that would have made me nervous, but Dani could go from painting a house and getting on a plane fifteen minutes later without missing a beat.

"Do it tomorrow night when I'll be here. I don't want to miss that. Or maybe I could skip the date with Noah and have hobo stew with you guys," Dani suggested with a smirk.

Dre shook her head back and forth. "No way are you skipping this. Noah seems like a great guy. You deserve to have some fun, sestra."

Dani snorted. "I've had enough of men and their way of helping. I have enough on my plate and don't need to take care of anyone else. I've raised my kids and cleaned up enough messes. It's probably best if I don't go."

I happened to agree with Dani with some of what she'd said. Men tended to take advantage of the women in their lives. The division of labor was rarely equal and when they got sick their entire world stopped and they became two-year-olds, whining about how bad they felt. However, hearing it made me see how much she'd been underappreciated in her life.

"Noah isn't your average man, Dani. He turns into a wolf and by his own admission, once he finds the woman meant for him, he would do anything for her." The idea intrigued me as much as it was foreign. "Not that I think you should jump into another serious relationship. Just go out and have a nice dinner with good company."

Dani smiled and her eyes took on a faraway, dreamy look. "It wouldn't be horrible. The view would be nice and he's taking me to Brennan's, so the food will be good, too."

I scoffed and shared a look with Dre. "The view would be good? He's gorgeous and has the hots for you."

Dre waved her hand toward herself. "Get out here and let us see what you're wearing. We need to approve."

Dani rolled her eyes and walked toward us. "Does this pass muster?" She was wearing her charcoal off-the-shoulder sweater dress. It stopped above her knees and she'd paired it with her knee-high black leather boots.

I whistled and waggled my eyebrows. "Bow chicka wow-wow. You look stunning. He won't be able to resist you."

Dani chewed on a thumb nail, smearing her gloss. "This isn't a good idea. I'm a middle-aged woman with stretch marks and a shriveled raisin for a heart. He deserves better."

I pointed a finger at her face. "Don't you dare wall your heart off. Love exists. The fact that mom and dad had ten kids and remained married until the day she died is proof enough of that."

Dre wrapped an arm around Dani. "Steve and I have been married over twenty-five years. That's another example."

I sighed when the nervous look didn't disappear from her face. "Look, all we are suggesting is that you have a fun night out and leave yourself open to possibility. Think sex toy that doesn't require batteries."

Dre started laughing while Dani was torn between amusement and embarrassment. Steve on the other hand had walked away with a shake of his head. Camilla was staring at us. "I don't understand any of you." The ghoul's reaction made us laugh harder.

* * *

DANIELLE

I wiped my sweaty palms down the sides of my sweater dress discreetly, hoping Noah didn't see the move. We were walking down Royal from the parking structure. My heart was beating faster than a hummingbird's wings.

I couldn't recall ever being so nervous. Not even as a teenager. Back then I was awkward and had no idea what I was doing. It was enough to make my knees knock, but not enough to make me want to throw up.

Noah titled his head and looked sideways at me. "Are you still upset about how your sisters were teasing you?"

I cringed and my cheeks heated to the boiling point. I could fry eggs on my cheeks. "Nothing a little trip off a steep cliff won't cure."

Noah chuckled. "It'd be better to pay them back. I'm not sure about Dreya but I think we can help Dahlia understand how you felt."

Surprised, I looked up to see his sexy smile looking down at me. My feet stopped and I swayed as he held my gaze. "Wh...what do you mean? How can we do that?"

Noah shrugged his shoulders. "Lucas may or may not have admitted to being drawn to your sister."

"No freaking way. Are you serious?" I wasn't surprised. I'd suspected the same thing. However, hearing it confirmed made me smile. Lia was widowed years ago and had been raising her kids alone ever since. They were all grown and gone and nothing stood in her way.

"I'd never lie to you, Sunshine. I've never seen Lucas like this about someone. I can convince him to ask your sister out and you can pepper her with talk of using him as a sex toy. Although, for the record, I would have no problem with you using me in *any* way you wanted."

Butterflies took flight in my stomach while my girly parts heated and my head swam. I reached out to catch myself. The second my hand made contact with the wall of an art store, Noah disappeared and I saw a couple standing there arguing about the money spent on their vacation and not being able to afford a painting one of them wanted.

What. The. Hell? I jerked my hand back so fast you'd think I'd been burned. The hiss I emitted followed that vein. When Noah's hands landed on my shoulders and I looked up,

I almost fell over. I reached out and balanced myself on his shoulders.

The street vanished for a second time and I saw him standing in a bathroom while Lucas told him he shouldn't be so nervous about taking me out. When my hands flew into the air that time, I smacked Noah in the face.

"Dani. What's wrong?"

His voice jarred me and grounded me at the same time. "I have no idea. Ever since Phoebe was at the plantation and released the magic in the land, things have changed. For me, it was just a feeling until just now."

A deep V formed between Noah's eyes as he wrapped an arm around my shoulders. "Tell me what just happened. You looked like you went somewhere else."

I took a deep breath and tried to put it into words. Before I replied, I tested a theory and went on my tiptoe then touched the bottom of a gas lamp toward the back where few people would touch it. For the third time in as many minutes, Noah and the people around me went away.

In its place, I saw a man in a dark blue uniform with a weathered face tightening the screws on the fixture. There was another guy standing below him talking about how putting in a gas lamp seemed to go against the city's plans to modernize the French Quarter.

My head was throbbing when Noah returned a few seconds later. "Why did you do that?"

I pulled in another breath and leaned against him. That had sucked every ounce of energy from my being. "I saw visions of people when I touched those things. I can't explain it. It shouldn't be possible and has never happened before."

I lifted my head, trying to keep my lower lip from trembling. I was suddenly terrified. He ran a hand across my jawbone. "Change of plans, Sunshine. I'd like to take you to a different restaurant."

"It'd be better if I went home. I need to figure out what's happening to me. And tell my sisters. They'll want to know; they will likely develop powers too." I ran a hand down my face. "Does this mean I'm a witch?"

Noah started walking and took me with him. "I can't answer that. You're not a mundie, anything more I'm not sure. You could be Fae or a witch."

I hesitated when he turned down an alley. He twined his fingers with mine and my racing mind settled along with my gut. My heart hadn't slowed and I was still breathless thanks to the look he was giving me. "I'm going to feed you and tell you what I know and give you a little information about the magical world."

That was the ticket to my soul, apparently because I followed beside him as we traveled down the alley. He entered a door that had a weathered name painted into the dingy window.

"Silver Hound?" I lifted an eyebrow in question.

"My buddy Jack owns the place. He's an alligator shifter." My jaw hit my chest as he opened the door and greeted the biggest guy I'd ever seen.

He had to be six and a half feet tall with muscles upon muscles bulging under his blue flannel shirt. He had pristine dark brown skin and warm black irises. "Noah, good to see you again. Who's this with you?"

Noah pulled me closer. "This is my, uh this is Dani. She and her five sisters bought the old Willowberry Plantation. They're party planners and are planning Lilly's mating ceremony."

Jack's eyes widened. "Is that right? We could use a good planner in this city. I'm always bombarded by requests to have my place for one event or another. I can't close down every time someone wants to throw a party. In fact, there's a certain siren I've been hesitant to send away. You never want to get on the bad side of one of them women."

Noah nodded. "They can be a nasty bunch. Very vindictive. You should send her to the Six Twisted Sisters."

Jack threw back his head and laughed as he turned to allow us past him. "That's some name. Catchy. I won't forget that one anytime soon." His amusement died and his face turned serious as we entered the restaurant. "I'd hate to see the curse destroy that."

"That's the thing. The new Pleiades, Phoebe Duedonne broke the curse," Noah explained.

"Well, I'll be. That's good to hear. Do you do events elsewhere? I'm coming up on my thirtieth anniversary and want to throw a big bash, but have no desire to plan it."

I smiled and nodded. "Willowberry is our first venue. We've always gone to clients and done their events."

"Well, I'll be in touch as well then. You enjoy your dinner." With that Jack left us and Noah escorted me to a table close to the back.

The place was so ordinary, it was disappointing. I was expecting something more than the nicely painted gray walls and black tables and chairs. I silently berated myself. It wasn't as if I would be taken inside a spaceship. It seemed ridiculous now.

But the furnishings were so modern and common. Noah held my chair and I looked around as he took a seat next to me. The guests were what told me there was more to the Silver Hound.

I saw a one-foot-tall man the same color as the rust-colored floor. As if that wasn't enough, there were tiny winged women hovering over the long wooden bar. A man with pointed ears was talking to them.

We're not in Kansas anymore Toto. Our surroundings melted away when Noah smiled at me. "I can see the questions churning through your mind. Let's start with you first then we can move to everything else."

I sat up straighter. "I thought you said you didn't know what I was."

He grabbed my hand and twined our fingers. It was the second time that night and it made me feel tingly all over. It was a simple gesture, yet intimate. "I haven't a clue about what you are, but I can tell you that you are psychometric."

One of my eyebrows crept up as my disbelief increased. "And that would be what exactly?"

"A psychometric sees what happened in the past when they touch an object. From what I've been told, there needs to be intense emotions attached to said object to trigger a vision, but I'm not certain that's right. You touched a wall and saw something."

My face wrinkled as I thought about what he was saying. "I won't be able to touch anything at Willowberry. Some nasty shit happened there and I have no desire to see it first-hand. The stories are bad enough."

Noah scooted closer to me. "All powers can be controlled. In time, you will be able to shut down visions. I'm sorry for upsetting you. That wasn't my intention. I thought you wanted to know."

I smiled up at him. "I do want to know. It's tough to process. It's so outside anything I've ever known."

The waitress stopped at our table. She looked a lot like a tree with skin rough like bark and long willowy limbs. I ordered some etouffee and Noah ordered a blackened steak.

"That was Nelairi, she's a wood nymph that lives in the trees of Jackson Square."

I found my body leaning toward him. "What are they at the bar? I'd guess the guy with the ears," I gestured above my own, "is an elf."

Noah nodded his head. "That is correct. The small creatures with him are pixies. And the guy with the rust-colored skin is a gnome. There's a brownie over there. All of them are light Fae that moved to this realm through the portal in England."

"How can that brownie even hold a mop?"

Noah chuckled. "The mundie sense of reality no longer applies. You should never underestimate a supernatural being based on their size."

"Noted. Is there a way to tell the difference between witches and shifters by looking at them?"

"Not by looking at them. The same applies to the Fae. Vampires typically have pale complexions and aren't terribly social. You want to steer clear of them. They've been stepping out recently and word is they killed a shifter in Maine."

My heart skipped a beat and an ache spread through my chest. "That's awful."

The waitress delivered our food then. When it arrived, Noah shifted gears and started asking about me. At first, I shifted in my seat and gave only the bare minimum. His genuine interest was obvious as he hung on my every word. It took me by surprise.

In my experience men were good at putting up a front and feigning interest in what you had to say. Rarely did that last very long. When they were certain they'd roped you in, things would change.

There would be no more romance. They would no longer bring you a cookie you liked or get you flowers. All attempts to get to know you were done. And they wouldn't watch the romcom with you. You were relegated to the other room while he watched some game or another.

When Noah asked if I preferred nuts in my carrot cake or not, it was obvious he was paying attention and cared. No one asked for such details unless it mattered. For the next hour, we talked about movies, TV shows, and music along with what I used to do before buying Willowberry.

The conversation never dulled and when we finally pulled into the parking lot at the plantation, I felt like I'd known Noah for months or longer. "I'm glad I listened to my sisters and went out tonight. I haven't ever been on a date like this."

I paused at the front of Noah's car, suddenly feeling very awkward. Noah put his hands on my hips, making me shiver in anticipation. "Does that mean we've reached the sex toy part of the evening?"

My throat went dry at the desire roughening his voice. It was unreal to me that Noah was interested in me at all. I'd been married twice, had more lines on my body than a road map and fifteen extra pounds. Alright, twenty.

My head floated from my body as I looked up at him, waiting for him to make a move. All he did was stare at me for several seconds. His eyes smoldered and his fingers flexed, squeezing my cushioned hips.

It jarred me and made me take a step back. Apparently, my retreat was the cue for Noah to close the distance. Between one second and the next, his mouth descended on mine.

There was a moment where I swear my heart pounded out of my ribcage while my head floated away. His lips were soft and insistent as they moved over mine in a heated kiss.

True to his alpha nature, Noah pushed his tongue between my lips to tangle with mine. I moaned and wrapped my arms around his neck. I'd been careful not to touch anything since my experiences on Royal. Thankfully, the shirt didn't elicit another vision and pull me from the heat of the kiss.

My toes curled in my boots and my girly parts throbbed with desire. This was no mere kiss. He was making love to my mouth and telling me how much he wanted me all at the same time.

I never wanted it to end, but I wasn't ready for more. I'd always let my hormones lead the way and it had gotten me nowhere. I needed to take things slow. A snail would beat me to the finish line slowly.

As if he sensed my need, Noah pulled away and pressed his forehead to mine. "Are you alright? I know this is all overwhelming and the last thing you need is me coming onto you. I've been dreaming of kissing you since the moment we met."

"I need to take things slow. You know some of what I've been through. It's important to me that I pour all of my energy into this business. I talked my sisters into taking this leap with me and I need to make it work." I hoped he didn't walk away because I couldn't jump right in with him.

He lifted my chin with one finger. "You don't need to take this on yourself. Lucas and I are here to support you, as well as your sisters. I can already tell you six have what it takes to make this work. I can't wait to see how it progresses. Your courage amazes me, Sunshine. I've never met anyone like you."

I took a deep breath and put distance between us before I threw caution to the wind. "You are a smooth talker, Dimples. I will see you bright and early."

Noah pressed his lips to mine in a brief kiss that made me horny all over again when I turned and headed for the house. I was in way over my head and didn't care. Life was complicated but good.

CHAPTER 13

DAHLIA

"*I* feel like that woman from the home makeover show. Too bad I don't have the millions to go with it." I chuckled and unlocked the wooden door. "I never imagined we would have a workshop in a renovated silo. It's shabby chic."

At one point someone had come in and added drywall and insulation between the metal siding and the inside which would provide better temperature control. Before the heat of the summer rolled around, we would need to have Lucas and Noah build a second floor to the place and install an HVAC system so the laser wasn't fried.

Dani lifted the blanket tent off the laser and set it aside. "I wouldn't want millions. It would be too stressful. I would always worry about not having money anymore and be afraid to spend too much."

A laugh escaped my mouth before I could censor myself. "You would have no problem adjusting your lifestyle and spending money by the fistful. Neither would I. Hell, I can think of three pieces of equipment we would add to this space off the top of my head. And if we lost it suddenly, we would survive. Our lives made us survivors."

Dani shrugged her shoulders. "You're right. It would be nice if we could buy a CNC machine, or a UV printer maybe. We could do some nice shit with them."

I high-fived my sister. "We would never leave this silo. A printer would make painting the signs a breeze. Oh well. Let's get started."

"What are we doing again?" Camilla was bent over the laser with a furrowed brow.

I lifted the lid, exposing the waffle shelf inside. "This machine will etch the design we create into the wine glasses."

She watched as I retrieved the rotary attachment from the shelf and plugged it into the slot on the right side of the laser. The ghoul jumped three feet into the air when I turned it on. It was easy to forget she came from a time when nothing like this existed. To her, the noise must have sounded terrifying.

I stopped to consider it from her point of view and had to admire how well she was dealing with things so far. She had stopped jumping when our cell phones rang or when a car pulled into the parking lot. The microwave was no longer something she steered clear of. She'd even heated up a piece of chicken in it an hour ago.

I lifted my hands. "Sorry, I should have warned you about the noise. It won't hurt you."

Dani wrapped an arm around Cami's shoulders. "Can you help me move a table from the barn into here? We will need a space to organize and work."

Cami nodded her head and walked around the laser without taking her eyes off the machine. "Why is everything so noisy in your time?"

I smiled as Dani walked her to the barn ten feet to our left to retrieve a plastic table while explaining the fans and other components are what make the sound. My head was starting to clear. We'd painted just about every room in the house and it was filled with more fumes than a Cheech and Chong movie.

I decided to get the welcome to our mating cut out while we waited. Steve had stacked our birch plywood next to Lacey. We had a habit of naming everything we owned and the laser was no different.

I unplugged the rotary and set it aside. Wood on the waffle panel, I turned on the computer and did a quick design with their names. Before I hit the print button that would send the image to the printer to be cut out, I added the silhouette of a wolf with its head back.

The wood was cutting when Dani and Camilla each returned carrying a white table. I took the one from the ghoul and unfolded it. I had one of the legs extended when dizziness sent me to my knees.

My vision swam and the smell of wood-burning on the laser filled my nostrils. The scent was overwhelming, making me think the silo was the problem because I'd encountered the smell a million times and was never affected.

Maybe the fans are blowing the exhaust into the circular building. I shook my head. No, that wasn't right. Steve had vented it out a hole he'd created in the side of the structure.

My vision wavered and the vision of the silo disappeared. My heart raced and my mind whirled as I tried to understand what I was seeing. There were five men breaking down the door of the barn.

"No!" My shout was followed by me taking a step in their direction. My feet seemed glued to the floor and I tripped over them. I threw my hands out and my wrists took the brunt of the impact.

The smell of wood burning on the laser filled my nose as I watched them splinter the barn door. Pieces flew in every direction and they made their way inside. One second, I was on the ground and the next I was standing in the barn where we'd stored most of the product for parties. We had another barn where we were keeping the products we engraved on the laser.

It was our barn and our supplies only it wasn't. At the moment we hadn't put together the shelving units or installed the hanging rods for the table cloths. Dani outlined plans to have the linens in one section with a washer, dryer, and rotary iron with steam.

The men snarled and growled like animals. One guy held up his hand and claws sprouted from the tips, making me think of Lucas and Noah. I cried out when they proceeded to slash through the table cloths, shredding them to pieces. All I could smell was wood being cut in the laser.

My heart raced faster and pounded harder. Once they'd destroyed thousands of dollars' worth of tablecloths, they moved onto the shelving unit where we would store the center pieces that we offered. They smashed the hurricanes first then moved on to bend the wrought iron candle holders.

I squeezed my eyes shut and rubbed my temples. What was going on? Why was I seeing these things? To my surprise when I opened them, Dani was squatting in front of me with a look of concern on her face.

"What just happened? You cried out a couple of times and fell down. It was like you were possessed."

I took a deep breath, noting the smell was fading somewhat. "I'm not sure really. One second, I was inhaling the smell of wood in the laser and the next I was watching as shifters destroyed our party stuff. We had it organized exactly as you outlined and they were ruining it."

Dani's brow furrowed. "Did you touch anything? Maybe it's like my psychometric power. You might be able to see things in the past, as well"

I wasn't touching anything when I saw the men. "That can't be right. What I was seeing was the future, unless there was someone else with our supplies that set the barn up precisely as you designed. And, I wasn't touching anything at that moment."

Dani, who had been leery of touching objects, reached out and pulled me into a hug. It was an awkward embrace given my position on the ground but I needed it at the moment. The experience had been disorienting, to say the least.

"I'll call Noah. He will know what to do. He might even be able to explain what just happened."

I waggled my eyebrows as I stood up. "I'm happy to be the excuse you use to give him a call. It's not every day you're kissed to within an inch of your life."

Dani rolled her eyes. "I never should have told you about that. Don't forget, I can tell him to let Lucas know you're interested. We already know he thinks about you."

My heart raced for an entirely different reason then. Ever since she had told me about what Noah said regarding Lucas's interest, I hadn't been able to think about anything else. It was why I suggested making some of the mating ceremony stuff rather than spending time building the shelves to organize stuff in the barn.

I wanted to impress him with my skill. Silly, I know. Especially since I was a grown-ass woman and not an insecure teenager with something to prove. It had taken decades for my mom's words to really sink into my brain.

My mother liked to tell us we had intelligence, beauty, and talent beyond what most possessed. When Bobby Denton broke my heart in the seventh grade, she told me his lack of interest wasn't a reflection on me. She also told me it was important to own who I was and love myself, including every flaw I thought I had. *If you don't love yourself, Lia, how can you expect anyone else to? It makes you hide what's inside which is a travesty because you have so much beauty in your soul.*

Emotion burned in my throat as I tried to banish thoughts of our mom from my mind while Dani called Noah. The shifter's deep voice echoed through the silo. "Noah, it's Dani. Sorry to call so late, but I didn't know who else to call."

"What's wrong? What happened?" Noah's tone changed. I could easily imagine he'd jumped out of bed and was racing to his car as he spoke. To say he had it bad for my sister was an understatement.

"It's Dahlia. Something just happened to her and I have no idea what it was or how to explain it."

"Lucas, it's Dahlia. Let's go." I winced as Noah shouted through the phone. "Is she awake? Breathing? Bleeding? What are we talking about here?"

Dani shot me wide eyes, realizing it might not have been the best idea to call him. "It's nothing like that."

Lucas's voice was far away but there was no mistaking his concern. "What the fuck happened to her? If even one hair on her head is hurt, I will skin the motherfucker alive that touched her."

I flushed hearing him defend me so vehemently. It was nice to have someone care so much. At the same time, I was confused as hell. I didn't know him at all.

Dani waved her hand rapidly. "She isn't physically hurt. She just had an episode."

Noah's sigh of relief was palpable. "She isn't hurt." I assumed he said that to Lucas. "We will be right there."

"I'm not sure that's necessary," I called out. "I'm shaken up but fine."

The sound of a truck starting then peeling out nearly

drowned out Lucas's reply. "We're coming over. I have to see you for myself."

Dani waggled her eyebrows at me this time. "Thank you both. There will come a day when we will know more and won't have to call."

"I hope not. I'll see you soon." Noah hung up after saying that, leaving Dani with her mouth hanging open.

The laser beeped, making me jump this time. "I think we opened a can of worms we shouldn't have. It's not really a big deal." I crossed to the laser and removed the cut images and words.

Dani joined me and handed them to Camilla who was chewing on her lower lip. "I've never seen more chaos as I have since coming back from the dead."

I rolled my eyes at the ghoul. "I find that hard to believe given your life story. It's plucked right out of a soap opera. Can you set those on the table you brought in?"

We were just finishing with the wood when pounding footsteps echoed outside the open silo door. Lucas was inside first and pulled me up into his arms. I gave a quick rundown of what happened and what I saw.

"What did these shifters look like?" Lucas had released me but not moved more than a couple of feet from me.

"The main guy had blonde hair and these odd blue eyes. It was almost like they were dull and lifeless. And there was another with red hair and green eyes. I don't remember much else."

"That has to be Lilly's ex. He isn't happy she found her Fated One. He thinks she belongs to him."

I gaped at Lucas. "How did he discover who we were and why did I see this? Is it the future? Or did he attack here before? I just don't understand what happened."

Lucas shook his head from side to side and ran a hand

down one of my arms. It was like he couldn't stop touching me.

Noah stood about an inch from Dani as he joined the conversation. "You said the smell of wood was extra pungent before this happened?" I nodded without saying a word. "That makes sense. Your family has psychic powers. I'd bet each one of you will develop some kind of power that originates in an area of the brain. You have visions of the future that are triggered by various scents."

My jaw dropped open. "You mean to say I have some magical smell-o-vision now?" I felt different. Not as worn out and tired and hoped magic had given me vigor and nothing else. Having Dani afraid to touch anything and Dakota wishing everything into existence was enough for one family.

Lucas laughed at that. "Something like that. And like your sister, you can learn to control it to an extent, so you don't have to live in fear of having an episode every second of the day."

I groaned. He had no idea who he was talking to. I would worry, regardless. "Why couldn't I have gotten Kota's power to wish for things? That would be nice and easy."

Lucas shook his head. "No, it wouldn't. All magic has a price. Some more than others. If your sister doesn't learn how to curb herself, she will not like the consequences. The universe likes balance. Some believe the Tainted were created because witches forgot they couldn't use their powers for personal gain."

"What's a Tainted?" Dani had her arms wrapped tightly around her torso.

"It's a witch that has turned to Dark magic by stealing power from another witch. She is no longer of the light. That's not a good thing. They have to keep killing witches and taking their power to survive." My stomach turned hearing Noah's description.

When my mind caught up, I wanted to run to Dakota's house right away. "I need to warn Dakota. She's probably wished for every Frenchie statue she's ever seen and then some. We cannot let her fall to the dark side. Where can we find a teacher to help us? We're flying blind here and that's going to bite us in the ass."

"It definitely will," Dani agreed. "Not to mention now we need to worry about our barn being broken into."

Noah wrapped an arm around Dani. "I promise you we will secure the building and ensure nothing happens to your property. And we will help you find someone to help you understand what is happening and how to manage it."

Lucas took several steps closer to me. His heat bathed my backside and made me want to curl up on his lap and close my eyes. The days of little sleep were catching up with me quickly.

My mind whirled as they talked about ways to secure the barn. I could see the future. It hit me like a ten-ton truck. The only thing keeping me on my feet was the feel of Lucas standing behind me and knowing this was only a blip in the road. It wasn't the worst thing to happen to me. In the face of losing my husband, a man I loved, suddenly and violently, being able to see the future didn't seem so bad.

CHAPTER 14

I sucked in a breath and girded myself for what was to come. "Kota, we need to talk about your power and how you use it."

Dakota whirled around with a stemless wine glass in her hand. "What do you mean how I use it?"

I withered under her stare. "Noah and Lucas were here last night and warned us about the cost of magic."

Dre came over and leaned one hip against the table. "I thought I saw them rush into the silo last night. What happened? And at what cost? I don't understand."

I looked to Lia who turned off the laser. "She's talking about the vision I had last night when I smelled the wood being cut in the laser. It seems I have magical smell-o-vision and can see the future when I smell something. We freaked out and Dani called Noah since he knew about her psychometric power. They told us that we needed to learn to control our powers and that magic comes at a cost.

139

There is a price for wishing on shit and seeing the future or the past. They aren't witches so they couldn't explain more."

Dakota's face lost all traces of color. "Why the hell didn't someone tell me sooner. I've redone my entire bedroom! Shit, shit, shit. You bitches had better pull me back to the light if I go sideways. You can't let me become a killer."

I had no idea how we were going to manage all of this but her power was easy to control. "You are fine right now, but all the wishing for Frenchies and pizza and new comforters stops now. You cannot magic anything else into existence."

Dakota threw her hands up in the air. "I can't help it sometimes. I was just thinking about how badly I wanted to change the colors in my bedroom and a new comforter appeared on the bed."

Well crap. Dakota spent her days thinking about how to redecorate her house and the plantation. This was going to be harder than I thought.

Dre patted Kota's shoulder. "Try your hardest not to wish for anything. And definitely no thinking about how much you want something. When you're hungry, grab some food and cut off further thoughts."

"I have no idea how I am going to manage this one." Dakota looked dejected and forlorn.

"Hello, Twisted Sisters," Lucas's voice echoed through the open silo door. "Please tell me you haven't been working on Lilly's mating stuff since last night."

Because I shifted my focus to my sister, I caught the way Lia lit up when the shifter entered the room. She stood straighter, her face glowed and she was smiling. It was a damn good sight to see.

Lia shrugged her shoulders. "We haven't been out here all night. We went in to rest at some point. But we have put together some ideas to run by you both. You must be Lilly.

I'm Dahlia and these five are my sisters. The woman trying to make her way out the door is Camilla."

Cami froze like a deer caught in the headlights. Lilly was beautiful with long brown hair and green eyes. The billowy top did nothing to hide the fact that she was very muscular.

Lilly extended her hand to Lia. "It's good to meet you. I can't believe my dad found a way to give me my dream mating. I have always wanted to have my ceremony on a plantation. I can't say why, but I am fascinated by their history."

Lia chuckled. "We all feel the same way about them which is why when Dani found the deal on this place, we snatched it up. Cami was actually alive when the place was first built and can tell you some stories that will have you on the edge of your seat. For now, why don't we show you the ideas we came up with and you can tell us your vision."

"I would love that." Lilly followed Lia to the tables where the rest of us were standing.

I held up what we'd started. "Lia wanted to use a wolf in the welcome sign given your heritage. And I used a color that will match any color scheme you choose. We've also done a sample wine tumbler for you to consider. This one says 'cheers' and includes your names. We can add the date. On another one, we put 'fated to be together.' We weren't sure how formal or informal you were going, so we left it at that. We can customize anything you want."

Lilly turned a huge smile to her dad. "I like the second one. The flourishes make it beautiful."

Delphine stepped forward. "We also need to talk about the location of your ceremony and reception. We have a large covered area between the house and the detached kitchen where we can set up tables if it rains. We don't have the houses on the back of the lot ready for that purpose yet."

Lucas put a hand on his daughter's back. "We're

outdoorsy people anyway. Let's look around the property and see what you think, sweetheart."

Lilly bobbed her head and headed for the door. Lia was right behind them "I'd like to show you my favorite place on the plantation. It's what made me fall in love with Willowberry."

We all filed out of the silo. It was my turn to freeze like a deer caught in the headlights when I practically ran right into Noah. "Noah." I sounded like one of those porn sex operators when I said his name.

Noah's smolder told me it affected him as much as his presence did me. It was nice to be on somewhat even footing with a guy. Not that we would ever be entirely equal. He was way out of my league and would likely lose interest in me at some point. I was going to enjoy every moment I had with him.

He picked up my hand and kissed the back of it. "Dani. You look good enough to eat this morning."

Dea's choked laughter made my cheeks turn pink. "Sorry. Don't let me interrupt." She hurried to catch up with Kota and Dre, guffawing at my expense.

"I will never hear the end of that one."

He chuckled and pressed me forward with a hand at the base of my spine. "I should be sorry, but I'm not. I will catch up with you later. I need to work on the barn."

I shook my head as I caught up to the group near the massive willow tree that Lia loved. I arrived just as Dre was telling them our plans to build a gazebo there. Lilly shot her father, puppy dog eyes. "I want to be mated right here. This tree is perfect. I love the look and feel. It would be even better if we had the gazebo."

Deandra walked closer to the tree and held her arms out at her sides. "You'll have to imagine the structure. We don't have the time or money to have it built right now, but we will make this spot look stunning. Imagine a wall of white silk topped with twinkling light, greenery, and balloons in your colors. It will be just as beautiful."

I held up my hand. "Or you can look at one of my favorites. There's a grove of oak trees that provides an intimate clearing perfect for ceremonies of every kind. It is stunning without the gazebo we have planned for the spot."

Lucas groaned and rolled his eyes. "Why do you have to give me that look? You know I can't say no to you. I'll build the gazebo so she has it for her ceremony."

Dahlia's eyes widened and her jaw went slack for a fraction of a second before she clamped it closed. "Really? You're already doing so much with the roof repairs on each of the structures. We can't ask you to do that."

Lucas smiled at my sister and she glowed in response. "You aren't asking me. Lilly is and I would do anything for her. She knows it, too. The gazebo shouldn't take long. I can ask one of the pack members to precut the wood to make construction faster."

"You're either the nicest father in history or trying to win brownie points with Dahlia. I can't decide which," Dakota said. Leave it to her to say what's on all of our minds. It was something I loved about her.

Lucas's cheeks turned ten shades of red, telling us precisely what his angle was. Lilly bounced on her toes as she looked from her dad to Lia. "Well, I will say he's the best dad in the world. He took care of me when my mom left us and made sure I understood it wasn't my fault. He's loved me so well that I haven't missed her presence in my life."

"That's quite the endorsement. We already knew he and Noah were stand-up guys. They helped us out of a jam before we became magical. Now, what are your colors?" Dakota asked.

"Dad told me about the witch and the magic and the bees.

Crazy stuff. You guys seem so sane for having just gone through a major transformation like that. Anyway, I was thinking about cinnamon and rose. I love pink and they complement each other so well. But I'm afraid it's too formal for what we have planned. Shifters don't wear big fancy dresses. It's usually casual and earthy."

This was my department. I already had a vision of what we could do. "So natural décor then. You can be fancy and earthy at the same time. This is your day. We can add cream and sage green to the mix to make it less casual and focus the pinks on the napkins and flowers. With a gazebo, we can weave twinkle lights and flowers throughout."

Dakota nodded her head. "No tulle or silk. They have colored burlap that will make great bows. We can use the wrought iron hurricane lanterns for the center pieces. They're rustic and earthy."

"Yes," I agreed. "With ranunculus and gardenias. Maybe even some gerbera daisies. And eucalyptus and lambs ear would be the perfect greenery."

Phi typed notes in her tablet as we talked then paused and looked up. "What about the setup? Do we need to arrange rows of chairs, or is it standing room only?"

"The pack surrounds the couple for the ceremony," Lucas explained.

Lia lifted one brow. "How many people are we talking about? The gazebo won't hold that many."

Lilly turned in a circle. "About two hundred with kids. We can build a bigger one so the closest can fit and the rest can circle us. It won't be that different from having it at Shadowtail."

Lucas had migrated closer to Lia as we talked. I wondered if either of them was aware of what he'd done. It was like watching two magnets. It was clear they were drawn to each other.

Lia nodded as she listened to Lilly. "Alright, now, what about food. Do you have a caterer, or thoughts on that? We have several we have worked with regularly. Our kitchen wouldn't have been ready, but Phi managed to get the appliances delivered later this week, so we are starting on that reno next."

"We typically barbecue and have a potluck for these events," Lucas admitted. "This will be the first mating ceremony not held on pack land. Do you have a barbecue?"

I nodded my head. "We have a Big John grill. We can have it pulled into the drive between the house and the kitchen. Let's look at the garden next to the kitchen. I think it will be the perfect spot for the party afterward."

We all headed to the garden near the kitchen. A silver glint caught my eye as we approached. My mouth went dry when I looked over and saw Noah on a ladder above the barn doors. He was reaching above his head and exposing the skin at the base of his back. The stretch made the jeans pull even tighter over his ass.

"Do you need some help, bro?" Lucas called out.

Noah shook his head. "Nah. I've got it. The cameras are up. Now I just need to connect it to the ones at the meeting house and we will be alerted if anyone approaches this barn. So, I wouldn't go running around naked at night, ladies."

My cheeks heated along with other parts when he looked directly at me. I tried to look away when he descended the ladder, but my head wouldn't move. "Damn, sis, you should take a picture. It'll last longer," Phi teased.

I rolled my eyes and glared at her. Dakota popped her head over Phi's shoulder. "She has no reason to look away from the beefcake. She's divorced and free to do what she wants."

"What I want is to sink into a hole and disappear. Or kiss

him. I can't decide which. He kisses like a god, so let's go with that." I sighed as I whispered my response to my sisters.

To my utter embarrassment, Noah turned a heated gaze my way. My sisters laughed as he walked toward me, remaining focused on my face. My world narrowed down to him as he approached. My sisters were saying something about googly eyes but I didn't hear it.

I had to crane my neck back to look up into his face. His thumb traced my lower lip as he looked into my eyes. I swear electricity pulsed between us. It sent my arousal skyrocketing and made me forget where we were as I waited for him to close the rest of the distance.

He held my gaze for a minute then dropped his hand and gestured to the garden a few feet away. "After you, Sunshine."

I took one shaky breath willing my body to calm the hell down. My sisters were uncharacteristically quiet as I joined the group. No one hid the fact that they had been watching the interaction between us.

Hard as it was, I ignored the tension stringing me tight as a bow, and showed Lilly the area I'd been thinking about for the party. I was only paying attention to about half of what was said. My mind kept wandering back to Noah and how he drove me wild. His attention made me feel feminine and sexy. Something I hadn't felt in far too long.

CHAPTER 15

DAHLIA

I gaped at the sexy shifter as he walked from the parking lot through the porte cochère with a load of lumber the size of a large man balanced on one shoulder. "How did your guy get this done so fast? We just talked about it yesterday?"

Lucas smiled at me, making my knees weak as he passed by me. "One thing you should know about the magical world is that things work very differently for our kind. We move faster and get shit done where mundies take five times as long on the same thing."

I shook my head and turned to grab some of the pieces. "Cocky much?"

I thought I'd mumbled it until Lucas called over his shoulder. "Is that a request, Flower?"

I choked on my spit and stumbled. My arms windmilled to stop my body from face planting on the asphalt of the parking lot. I was as graceful as an antelope running across the Savannah. I refused to look back and see the look of horror on his face. Not to mention I had no desire to show him how red my cheeks were at the moment.

Under the pile of individual pieces of wood, it seemed that there was a half hexagon. It would go fast if they'd already put together the base of the structure. I grabbed five one by fours or maybe they were two by fours because they weighed a ton.

My back groaned when I stood up with my arms wrapped around the wood. Lucas was already halfway back to the truck when I managed to make it through the porte cochère. "When does that faster part kick in because I'm still operating at a snail's pace."

I cringed at how out of breath I was while carrying a measly five boards. Lucas scowled. "You're no snail, Flower. You do more than most supernaturals I know. I've never met a more hard-working group of women and you are at the lead."

I tried to blow the hair out of my eye that had fallen into it, but it was matted to my face. I'm sure I painted the picture of a badass with that move. "We didn't have much growing up. Watching my mom work her tail off to support us even when she could hardly stand up taught me that I had to do what it took to get shit done."

"Your mother sounds like an extraordinary woman. I'd love to meet the woman that made you who you are today."

Emotion caught me off guard and it took a minute to gather myself. "That'll be impossible. She passed away in 2015. I've got to keep moving before I fall over."

I walked as fast as my feet would carry me. Dani and Deandra came toward me. "Do you need help, sister?" Dea asked.

"There's a trailer full of wood for the gazebo. You can help carry it over to the willow." I didn't bother hiding how much strain the bundle was putting on me when talking to them.

"We've got it," Noah called out. "You guys sort the pieces into piles of similar cuts so it's easier to pick what is needed."

Dani's face flushed as she stared at Noah across the lawn. "Is there a schematic we can use to help guide the process?"

"Sure is. Lucas has it with him." Noah was at the truck a couple of seconds later.

"Can one of you take a couple of boards? My arms are going to fall off." I practically dropped them all when Dea took two from me.

With my burden lighter, I was able to walk like a human being rather than The Hunchback of Notre Dame. "Look, mama's looking out for us." I jerked my chin at the bird perched quietly in the willow tree as we approached.

I swear our mom visited us in various forms from time to time. There was nothing distinct that I could point out as to why I thought she was inside this bird rather than any of the others. It was an instinct in my gut.

Deandra set the boards in a pile outside the area we had designated for the structure. "Hi, mama. We miss you. I know you're proud of us for making our dream a reality. Can you believe this place?"

Dani sighed. "She would tell us we spent way too much money on the place and were wasting it with so many projects."

Dea laughed. "She would be pissed about the kitchen remodel. She'd say there was nothing wrong with the appliances in there and that we didn't need warming drawers or anything like that."

Our mom was a simple woman, who had enjoyed far too few luxuries in life. I recalled the time when she bought herself bras from Victoria's Secret and how excited she was about it. To this day, I didn't take the little things for granted.

"She'd be proud of us for repurposing the furniture in the attic, though. Can you imagine what she'd have been able to do with a place like this? I always believed she would have made an excellent host for a bed and breakfast." A smile crossed my face as I pictured her turning Willowberry into an Inn rather than an event venue.

"Will you guys be offering the house as a place to stay overnight?" Lucas's voice warmed me.

I turned to find him far closer than expected. "It will be an option for those having an event here. However, we aren't going to be renting the rooms on a regular basis. That would be too much for Dani and I to manage on top of everything else. Besides, we wouldn't be able to offer tours if we did that."

Phi pointed to the long, low buildings behind the one Dre and Steve were turning into their home. "Eventually, we will get those buildings into livable condition, and rent them out. That's a long-term goal and one we will likely need your help with."

Noah nodded his head. "We will always help with anything you need. A place this big will need a handyman on-site to fix minor problems as they arise so they don't become big ones. Do you already have someone?"

Thank God for so many brothers and brothers-in-law. I doubt we could afford the upkeep otherwise. "Dreya's husband, Steve is in construction. He started dealing with mold and biological clean-up and gradually expanded. He's able to fix most things. He can even address some plumbing and electrical issues. However, roofing and stuff of that nature are beyond his abilities."

"Your family is a lot like the pack. We look out for each other, too." Noah's observation didn't surprise me. He paid attention to everything. Both of the shifters did.

Lucas chuckled. "I think your family might even be bigger

than our pack. Didn't you say your parents have thirty-seven grandkids?"

My chest puffed with pride. "Yes, I did. My parents were blessed. It's their legacy to us. We didn't get an inheritance or a house. We have a big family full of chaotic love and laughter."

"I can't wait to see a family event. You have to invite us when you have your grand opening with your family," Lucas said while looking right at me.

I smirked and waved him off in the direction of the truck. "We won't be ready for that or your daughter's mating unless you get a move on."

Lucas growled. The sound was low and animalistic and a total turn-on. "I like a woman who's bossy. Damn, Flower."

Noah socked him in the shoulder and they were laughing as they walked away. I shook my head and flushed when I noticed Dea and Dani were watching me with a smile on their faces.

"Looks like it's your turn to get some, sis," Dani teased.

I rolled my eyes. "Shut up. It's harmless flirting. Let's get this wood sorted."

Deandra burst out in her infectious laughter and said something about me *sorting* Lucas's wood alright. As ever our giggling fits ended up with one or more of us crawling to the bathroom before we peed ourselves.

We hadn't sorted anything when the guys returned because we were still in hysterics. The sight of them made us laugh even harder. After a few seconds, I managed to calm myself and began the task of sorting through the pieces we had. Dea was running across the lawn to the house to change her pants while Dani was hobbling her way to the bathroom.

Noah and Lucas dropped another load. "That's the last of it. I'll go remove the shingles from Dre and Steve's house while you guys get a start on this," Noah offered.

"Let's start by marking the corners so we can set the posts around the outside. This base here will be attached to it." Lucas gestured to the two pieces they'd just brought.

By now I was no longer shocked that he was able to carry the thing by himself. I'd seen enough to know he was built like a brick house. It had images of what he might look like dancing through my head. Like a kid with visions of sugar plums, I found my mouth watering and my feminine parts waking up and taking notice.

It had been years since I'd been interested in anyone like this. I'd begun to wonder if I was broken. After my hysterectomy, I welcomed the drop in sex drive. I didn't want to be with a guy, so it was perfect at the time. Later I worried I would never be turned on again or have another orgasm.

After meeting Lucas, I knew there was nothing wrong with me. Whether my mom was right and it just took the right guy. Or if I hadn't been ready before now didn't matter. I wanted to do a happy dance that I hadn't lost my sexuality when they ripped my insides out.

"I'll grab one of the four by fours, I assume they are designated for the posts to be set in the corners. Do you have a digital tape measure? I can go to the other side and we can mark the area."

Lucas's eyes darkened and he licked his lower lip. "You have got to stop this, Flower, or I will not be able to concentrate enough to build this damn thing."

I lifted one eyebrow as a smile spread across my face. "I take it you haven't been around many women that can work a chop saw or nail gun. Wait till you see me with my drum sander."

Lucas shook his head and pointed to an area behind me. "Get your sexy ass over there before you regret taunting a horny wolf."

I gasped and scurried in the direction he was pointing. I

hadn't expected him to be so honest, or graphic. My mind caught up with what he'd said when I paused and looked to him for feedback. All I could concentrate on for several seconds was the fact that he'd called me sexy.

His sigh filtered across the area telling me I'd missed what he'd been saying. "You're put out with me already? That doesn't bode well for us being partners on this project. Perhaps I should get Delphine to help you. She's just as handy. Deandra is good, but not as fluid as Phi and me. Dreya and Steve are busy in their house, or I would grab her."

Lucas narrowed his eyes and growled. This time the sound wasn't sensual. It was agitated with a hint of anger. "You and I are partners. There's no getting out of it now, Flower. Just try to pay attention, please. Move back slowly until I tell you, taking the post with you. The laser is using it as a guide, so hold it in the same position while you move."

I saluted him then shuffled back several feet until he told me I could stop. I set the post down and grabbed a post hole digger from the tools that were lying there. "Should I dig right here?"

Lucas was at my side in an instant and took the digger from me. "I've got it. Can you mix the quikrete? That way we can set this one and use it to do the other one."

"Sure can. I'll grab a couple of buckets of water and bring them over." I ran to the horse barn where we'd decided to store tools and grabbed a couple of large orange buckets.

I was filling them at the faucet located at the side of the structure when I caught sight of someone lurking at the edge of our property. My foot bounced as I kept an eye on our visitor. Anyone dressed in black and trying to hide behind trees was up to no good.

"C'mon, fill faster dammit." It seemed to take forever before it was done. I hurried back as fast as I could. "Lucas, there's someone stalking us."

Lucas lifted his head as he dropped a load of dirt out of the hole digger. "Where are they?"

"Along the eastside of our property. They're trying to remain hidden in the trees and are wearing black which is suspicious."

"Get that concrete mixed. I'll be right back."

I chewed my lower lip as I watched him take off then went about doing as he asked. I grabbed an empty bucket from beneath the full ones then dumped a bag of quikrete into it then added water. I'd forgotten something to stir with, so I grabbed a broken branch that was lying on the ground.

"Did you find out who it was?" I practically pounced on Lucas the second he was back.

He shook his head as he caught his breath. This was the first time I'd seen him break a sweat. "They took off before I got there. I chased them into the woods but came back because I didn't want to leave you alone. It was a necromancer, though. There's no mistaking their scent."

He'd stopped close enough to me that I caught a whiff of his cologne. The scent was woodsy and masculine. It was delicious and immediately overwhelmed my senses.

The world wavered and dizziness sent me to my knees. The sensation was familiar to me now and I tensed, waiting for the vision that was to follow. Lucas's scent filled my nostrils. Like last time it consumed my entire being.

My vision blurred and the grass disappeared. My heart raced as I looked around, trying to determine what I was supposed to see. I was no longer outside. Instead, I was in a house with gray walls. The furniture was dark brown and leather. That coupled with the minimal décor screamed bachelor pad.

Lucas was standing there and he was yelling at a woman with dirty blonde hair. She was rail-thin and looked sick. He was telling her she lost the right to attend her daughter's mating ceremony when she walked away all those years ago.

She told him she was sorry and that she knew she'd made mistakes but she was getting better. I wanted to scream, yeah right as she scratched the sores covering her arms. I'd worked with enough drug addicts to spot one a mile away.

Lucas opened the door and informed her she needed to leave. She crossed her arms over her chest and refused. Rage came over Lucas's face for a split second. It was a terrifying sight. The vision ended as he stalked toward the woman.

The house disappeared and was replaced by Lucas's face. "Are you alright, Flower? Did you have a vision?"

I sucked in a lungful of air and barely caught a whiff of his cologne this time. "That takes it out of me. Damn. I saw you arguing with a woman that looked like an addict. She wanted to attend Lilly's mating ceremony."

Lucas closed his eyes and ran a hand down his face. "I can't believe she comes back. Why would she torture Lilly like that?"

I put a hand on his shoulder offering any comfort I could. "I imagine she lives with a boatload of regret and doesn't want to die without being there for this important event."

Lucas snarled. "I don't give a shit. She doesn't deserve to be in her life."

"I completely understand. I wouldn't recommend allowing her to be involved. Addicts never come without the baggage that tends to blow up and cause problems at the worst time. Not to mention the fact that Lilly doesn't need that stress. This is her special day. The good news is that you can avoid her and the conversation by not being at home since you know she will return."

Lucas dropped his head. "I thought we would never see her again. Hell, I've had dreams that she died years ago with a needle in her arm. I hate that she will try to worm her way back into our lives. If all she'd done was the cheating, I could live with that and allow her to be there. The drugs made her another person, though. One I couldn't trust. Lilly almost drowned one night because she passed out while giving her a bath. If my mother hadn't been in the house, I would have lost Lilly. She's the only good thing to come out of that mess."

"I thought you told me shifters mated for life and never cheated. Did the drugs make her do it?"

Lucas jerked his head back and pursed his lips as if he'd sucked on a lemon. "She isn't my Fated One. Finding your other half is rare for a shifter, so many take a mate informally and build lives. That's what we did and in those cases the bond is different. Most would never dream of cheating on their mate, but not all."

"What would happen if you found the one that is meant for you?" I doubted I would ever understand the dynamics of shifter relationships.

"I would have been compelled to be with my Fated One and left. But I would have taken Lilly with me. I would never walk away from her for anything."

It seemed like they were playing with fire by building lives at all. Then again, if it was rare to find their mate they could die alone and the species would die out. My head hurt considering all the implications. Or perhaps it was from the vision.

"So you never found your Fated One?"

Lucas looked down and shifted in his crouched position. It was clear he was uncomfortable. "Not when I was with Lilly's mother. What about you? You said you were married before. What happened?"

I got to my knees then used his shoulder as a balance to get to my feet. "Yes, I was married." I crossed to the concrete happy to see it hadn't set yet. I removed the post and poured it into the hole.

Lucas inserted the post and held it in place with a level on top. I thought about not telling him what had happened to Leo, but decided against it. We'd been flirting and I had no idea if this would go anywhere, but I wouldn't even start a friendship by keeping secrets.

"Like me, Leo was a social worker. I worked with abused kids and their families and Leo worked with juvenile delinquents. He was amazing with the kids and everyone loved him. But he was a stickler for the rules."

Lucas let go of the post and I walked to the other side of the space. He set up the tape measure and a laser level and crossed to me. "He was killed by the kids he was helping one night. It was spring break and the kids wanted to listen to music and watch TV. The rule in their pod was that they had to be quiet every night for an hour. They could have headphones on, but no TV and no talking. They didn't like that and decided to kill him because of it."

Lucas dropped the post-hole digger halfway through digging the hole and reached for me. I held up my hands as tears built in my eyes. I always got choked up and my heart ached like an old bruise when I talked about Leo or thought about him.

"No, please. I need to get through this and won't if you hug me now." I picked up the hole digger and slammed it into the ground. The rhythmic motions of removing dirt were distracting enough I was able to keep my tears in check.

"I went through shit when he was killed, but I survived. I would have been dead along with him if I'd gone to the dorm to pick up our car. I usually did because he stayed overnight. I discovered later that the boys were planning on stabbing me when I arrived."

"I don't know what to say. I thought I'd had it hard and then I heard this. And you raised your three kids on your own after that?"

I nodded as I continued working. "They kept me going. That and my mom. In the beginning, she was with me all the time and helped a lot. My sisters were there as well, but they all had their own families and couldn't be there as often. It's a part of my past that shaped who I am today. I'm proud of the woman I am and I owe that in part to Leo's life and death."

"Can I hug you now?"

I looked up and saw the earnestness in Lucas's face. It was surprising to also see grief etched across his features. I wanted nothing more than to go to him and allow him to hold me tight like my mom used to when the ache in my chest threatened to kill me.

I smiled at him and handed him the post digger. "I'd rather build your daughter the gazebo of her dreams. We don't have time for me to fall apart."

Lucas either hadn't heard me or didn't care because he grabbed me up. The hug wasn't compassionate, it was full of passion and was followed by him pressing his lips to mine.

Electrical sparks flowed between us as he kissed me. The kiss was full of so many emotions, but one rang through. He had to have physical contact and show me how much he cared. The emotions were too much for me to detangle and determine what was going through him.

It was clear he was not frightened of my past, or intimidated by it. It took a big person to look past such a horrendous history and see the person I was and not some broken shell. All someone typically saw when they heard this story was what a tragic life I'd had and how much pain I must have experienced as a result. They didn't see the vibrant and alive woman.

When he broke away, my grief was still there but I was no longer mired in it. I was ready to move forward. *And get this project done, nothing more. Who's delusional now?* I shook my head and set those thoughts aside for another time. Right now we had a gazebo to build.

He pressed his forehead to mine for a second. "I couldn't help myself. You are an astonishing woman. You have thrived under horrible conditions. Leo was lucky to have your love. Any man would be."

I chuckled. "You're a very smart man. You might stand a chance after all."

"What does that mean?" He pulled away and looked like he was trying to solve an algebraic equation.

"We have work to do, Wolfy." I laughed when he scowled and picked up the post hole digger. We got to work on the gazebo near my favorite tree. Life was a complicated mess right now, but this adventure with my sisters was the perfect change for the middle of our lives. We were at the best part now.

CHAPTER 16

DANIELLE

*T*he smell of fresh-cut wood surrounded us as we worked on the new gazebo. "I've never seen a structure go up faster. Lucas and Noah sure do have their shit together."

Dakota handed me the end of the café lights we were stringing through the rafters at the top of the gazebo. We were using twinkle lights everywhere else. "It's a damn good thing they have the hots for you two because they have some talented friends. We might need them at some point."

I stood on tiptoe and wrapped the strand around the beam. "They'd actually started on this earlier in the week for their pack land. Noah said Lilly had wanted to have it for the ceremony but she was less than happy to have it where everyone else did. So, Lucas diverted it to us."

Lia's whiskey brown eyes narrowed. "Why wouldn't he tell me that?"

Dre scoffed. "The better question is how he pulled that one-off. He has to be someone important in the pack."

"I've been reading about shifters online. Maybe he's the alpha," Delphine suggested.

I shook my head. "I'm not sure we can trust the information on the internet. That's not the biggest thing to happen today. What about the necromancer that was hanging around the property, spying on us?"

Dahlia sighed and tucked the end of the lights she and Phi had been working on behind the pole. "It's been bugging me all afternoon. I've been giving it a lot of thought. My gut tells me that she knows Phoebe was here. And she might even be aware of Camilla. What I don't know is what she's up to."

Camilla turned in a circle, scanning the night around us. "Perhaps I shouldn't be out here. I can go inside and organize the library."

Deandra wrapped an arm around the ghoul. "There's no need to do that. There are six of us here. You'll be alright. What do we know about necromancers, anyway? They bring back the dead?"

Aside from Phoebe telling us she needed one to call Selene's soul from the other side, I had no idea. "She can't be working with Phoebe or she would have approached us directly."

"You're right. If Phoebe sent her, she would have talked to us. There was something about her presence that gave me the willies. I'd bet she is up to no good," Lia suggested.

"Do you think she's why Oscar got sick today?" I asked.

When we'd let them out earlier, Oscar had gone tearing off in the direction of where the necromancer had been. Zoe and Frida stayed close to us. Oscar refused to come when called, so Lucas had to go and get him. It wasn't long after that Oscar seemed lethargic and got sick.

Lia chewed her lower lip as she took another end of a

string of lights. She was on one ladder and I was on the other. "We need to learn more about this magical world. I wish there was a crash course we could take."

Dakota thrust one full hip out and waved an arm. "I wish..."

"No!" The five of us shouted at the same time. I took a breath. "Do not finish that sentence. The last thing we need is for it to push the balance over and fry our brains," Dreya added.

"We should ask around the French Quarter. Phoebe mentioned going to meet with the head witch. Perhaps she is someone that can help us." Lia's suggestion was sound.

I pulled out my phone and typed out a text to Phoebe. Movement in the distance caught my eye. I couldn't see what it was. Stuffing the phone in my back pocket without sending the message, I climbed down the ladder and walked to the side of the gazebo.

"What is it?" Dea asked, joining me.

I squinted. Damn, my night vision hadn't been the same since I turned forty. "I saw something." The flash of red eyes made me scream. "Get to the house, now."

Lia was still up the second ladder. Dakota and Delphine took off with Dreya and Deandra right behind them. Dahlia wobbled and almost fell from ten feet in the air. I grabbed the legs and steadied them so she could climb down the rungs.

Camilla stood next to us, shivering. The second Lia's feet hit the ground, I grabbed Cami's hand and we took off. I jumped down the four stairs leading up to the gazebo. The move wasn't my most graceful and I ended up pulling Camilla down with me.

Dahlia landed in a crouch next to us. "What the hell is that?"

The night was calm a few minutes ago. Nothing was

amiss as we strung lights in the new gazebo. Now we were running from a creature that I could only describe as a demonic dog.

I followed her gaze and wished I hadn't. It affirmed what I'd seen in the distance. The dog-like creature was coming in our direction at breakneck speed. It was black, had no fur, and had massive fangs that dripped a green liquid. It showing up after there was a necromancer on the premises couldn't be a coincidence. It had to be connected.

Lia tugged me up. The ground was slick and it took a second to untangle myself from Cami. We were running across the wet grass a second later. The sound of paws hitting the ground behind us made my heart gallop up my throat.

Dreya, Dakota, Delphine, and Deandra made it to the porch and stood in the open double doors watching as we raced toward them. Their eyes got big at the same time and they started shouting and jumping up and down and motioning to us with their hands.

Camilla was panting as she tried to keep up with us. "I can't keep running." The wind carried her words away and made her sound even more out of breath than she actually was.

I squeezed her hand and a second later it was yanked from my grip. I stopped and turned to help her continue. "Let go of her Cujo!" My demand went ignored.

The demon dog had its jaws wrapped around Cami's ankle and was gnawing like it hadn't eaten in a decade. Perhaps it had been a mistake to encourage running. Wasn't there something about racing away inciting canines to attack?

I dropped to my knees and grabbed Cami's hands, pulling her with me. Lia took one of her hands from me. "Grab anything that can be used as a weapon. If we can kill it, you can touch it and discover where it came from and what it is."

My jaw clenched as I pulled Camilla and her surprisingly heavy attacker. "You want me to touch that thing? No freaking way."

"We have to do something, Dani. And we can't unless we know what type of supernatural it is."

Lia's foot slipped out from under her and she landed hard on her rear end. "Dammit. Call Noah. He can help. This dog isn't going anywhere."

Keeping hold of Cami's wrist, I kicked out at the demonic creature and retrieved my phone. With the flick of my finger, I had it open and was clicking on the phone app. The ringing was a balm to my frayed nerves.

"Hello, Danielle. I didn't expect to hear from you tonight." Noah's voice was low and seductive. Under normal circumstances, I would have been all over that. I had bigger fish to fry at the moment.

"Noah, there's a demonic dog attacking Camilla, Lia, and me. We need help."

"I'll be right there." Whatever else Noah said was lost on me as the creature let go of Camilla and lunged for me.

I threw my arms out, tossing my phone in the process so I could catch myself and avoid a bruised coccyx. The thing got in my face and snarled. It smelled like dead fish and feces, utterly revolting. A drop of its green saliva dripped onto me, burning a spot on my neck. My hand flew up and it returned to Camilla and Dahlia who were helping the ghoul get up.

The canine clamped its jaws over Dahlia's shoulder and bit down. Blood dripped down her shoulder. I was on my feet and crawling her way. I kicked the dog when I got close enough and sent it flying.

"Run," I told them.

Lia and I held Camilla between us. We made it three feet

when something smacked into Cami's back and sent her flying onto the ground between us. It was perched on the ghoul, like a tick on a dog. The sewer smell of the creature permeated the area, making me nauseous.

"Steve's coming," Dreya shouted from the doorway. "He's bringing his gun."

Steve came running from the other side of the yard just then. I heard the cocking of a gun. "Get back, Lia, Dani. And stay down Camilla."

The ghoul wrapped her arms over the back of her head and stayed low to the ground. The dog's saliva dripped on the back of her skull, making her whimper. I was running and looking back right as the loud bang of a shotgun blast echoed from the shot Steve fired.

I couldn't tell if the pellets hit the canine or not because it seemed to sink into Cami. The ghoul convulsed like she was having a grand mal seizure. I paused in my frantic running and met Steve's wide eyes. "What just happened?"

I shrugged my shoulders. "Help her up before it comes back." Dahlia started to go back and help Steve, but I stopped her. "Get back to the house. You're hurt."

Steve and I lifted a limp Camilla between us and dragged her toward the house. She now smelled like death and rotting fecal matter. Noah arrived just as we made it up the front steps. "Where did the demon go? Is Camilla alright?"

I sucked in a breath. "It kinda sank into Cami after Steve shot it. I think it's dead."

Noah leaned forward and sniffed the ghoul. "Get inside the house now. It's not dead at all."

My heart skipped a beat at the tone of his voice. "What is it?"

Noah's green eyes met my brown ones. "Camilla has been possessed by a demon."

As if that was her cue to come back to life, Camilla's

head lifted and she keened an awful, mournful sound right before she kicked Steve in the knee. He dropped his hold on her and clutched his leg, leaving me holding her other side.

The ghoul was surprisingly strong and managed to yank me to her. Noah was there before she could do anything more to me and had tossed her into the grass below the porch.

My neck burned like hell and my vision wavered as I watched Noah tackle Camilla. I winced as he shoved her face into the ground. "Dahlia, call Lucas."

Lia was slumped on the porch at my feet. She was patting her pockets before her phone appeared in front of her face. Phi held it above her head. Dahlia grabbed it with thanks and thumbed it on.

I held my breath when Camilla roared and bucked Noah off her back. He flew into some hydrangea bushes that had been planted close to the house. They were fluffy white clouds I had planned to use in the centerpieces for Lilly's wedding. I'd have to rethink that plan.

Camilla tore through the garden and walked right through the tall pampas grass situated in one of the beds. Damn, the possessed ghoul was hitting all of my favorites. The ringing phone got the demon's attention.

It paused in the middle of the grass and looked back. All that was visible were the red eyes. It must have some strong powers to force that upon Camilla. Noah took advantage of the hesitation and jumped into the air from where he'd been on the ground.

The attempt should have fallen way short of its target. Instead, he flattened the rest of the plant and took Camilla down. The loud thud was followed by her skull bouncing off the dirt behind her.

"Lia." Lucas's voice was urgent and all business, unlike the way Noah had sounded. "I saw Noah tear out of here. What's wrong?"

"There's a demon here and it's inside Camilla." Lia's voice was shaky. I understood how she felt. This wasn't our life. We were supposed to be running a fun party planning business.

"Luc, I need you to get the moon sickness cage and bring it out here to Willowberry," Noah called out. "Now! We have to contain her or she will go on a killing spree. This isn't an imp possession."

My head snapped in Noah's direction. He hadn't said that before. *He was a bit busy trying to keep the demon-possessed ghoul from killing you.* I was just grateful he'd come to our rescue yet again.

"Shit. I bet that necromancer called a demon to the plantation earlier. I'll be right there. Keep it on the estate."

Steve approached Noah. "How can I help?" Dreya's husband was rubbing a spot on the back of his head. No doubt he'd hit it when he was thrown around.

Noah wrapped his arms and legs around Camilla and squeezed. The ghoul bucked in his hold and tried to head-butt him. We were damn lucky Delphine found these guys. If she hadn't, we would be screwed right now.

They were our best source of information about the magical world. The more I thought about our situation and everything that had happened the more certain I was that Noah and Lucas were meant to be a part of our journey.

You're jumping the gun there, Dani. It's not like he's declared you're his Fated One. Silently, I cursed my inner voice and reminded myself it was right. We might have gone on one date, but that meant little else. We might end up being close friends and nothing more.

Disappointment set an ache in my chest when I considered the option. I held tight to that recrimination. I was not going down the same path I had before. Friends were good enough. But we had to get in touch with the head witch and get our shit together.

Phoebe mentioned something about wards around the property. I had no idea what that meant, though I could guess. And I would bet whatever protections used to be in place were abolished when Phoebe let loose the power in the land.

The important thing at the moment was that we needed to discover what we were, who had what powers, and how we could learn to better control them.

Our survival depended on us getting our shit together. It was nice to know Noah and Lucas would be there, but that was no guarantee. We'd learned how fragile life was and how quickly everything could change. We needed to be able to protect our plantation and defend ourselves if necessary.

CHAPTER 17

DANIELLE

*D*reya crouched next to Dahlia and scanned her for injuries. I could see the bump forming on the back of her head from a few feet away. Her shoulder was far worse than that, though.

There were tears in the shoulder of her top and blood was seeping from the wounds, drenching her shirt. "Get me a first aid kit," Dreya called out.

Dakota nodded and took off into the house. Deandra joined Dreya and assisted. They were both registered nurses like me. Dre quit nursing a decade before where Dea still worked nights at the local hospital.

"That already looks infected," Dea observed. "Could it be necrotizing fasciitis? God only knows where that thing's mouth has been."

My stomach knotted. Deandra was right about that. The saliva had been green and the thing smelled like a sewer. "We have to get the wound cleaned. She could die if we don't." I crawled toward the stairs, wanting to get it off of Dahlia.

Dakota was back with Delphine right behind her carrying a bottle of vodka. She held it up and shook it. "Should we drench the wound first?"

My mind went utterly blank. Every lesson I learned in school and over fifteen years on the job flew out the window. I had no idea what to tell her. Thankfully, Deandra didn't have the same problem. "It's worth a shot. It will hurt like a bitch and can cause skin irritation. It might even slow down healing, but it is a damn good disinfectant."

Dreya nodded her head as she ripped the sleeve of Lia's shirt. "Dea is right. This will hurt worse than the bite, Dahlia, but it's our best shot. We don't have bottles of hydrogen peroxide in the house yet."

Lia was panting and sweating as she lay against Dre's torso. "We might want to buy a few cases of that and beta-dine. This magical world isn't all rainbows and unicorns."

Noah laughed then grunted. "It's probably not flesh-eating bacteria. You're not a mundie anymore, so it offers you some immunity from demon venom."

My head swung around and my eyes widened. "You mean to tell me that necrotizing fasciitis is caused by demons?"

Noah was on his back with Camilla on top of him. His legs were wrapped around hers and his arms pinned hers to her side. "That's exactly what I'm telling you. Many bacterial illnesses and infections are demonically born. Once here they tend to spread like wildfire."

The grunt Noah emitted next was followed by a wail from Camilla. From the sound, it was clear she was in great pain. One look at her snarling face and red eyes erased any sympathy I felt for the ghoul. The demon was fully in control now.

As soon as the thought crossed my mind Cami's face

crumpled and her eyes squeezed shut. "Is Camilla aware of what's happening to her?"

Noah twisted and pinned the ghoul under him then shot me a look. "Not based on what I've been told." Noah's gaze lifted above me and he sucked in a breath a second before Lia screamed bloody murder.

Lucas dropped a silver cage next to Noah and ran for the porch like he was on fire. "Flower!" The concern in his voice was palpable. He dropped to his knees in front of Dre and Lia.

I pushed myself to my feet and headed toward Noah who was once again struggling with Camilla. "What do I do? Where's the door?"

Noah cursed and put a hand around the back of Camilla's throat. "Lucas dropped it with the door face down. We need to lift it and get her inside."

Delphine handed the vodka to Dakota and joined me. We each grabbed a side and lifted. "This beast is heavier than my car."

"It's not that heavy, Sunshine. Try wrestling a pissed-off hellhound possessing a ghoul." Noah winked at me to let me know he was teasing.

I rolled my eyes and lifted. The cage went up thanks to Steve helping at the top. He pushed it up while we lifted it. Once it was upright, Steve opened the latch and turned to Noah.

Noah still had one arm under Camilla and lifted her with that hold. He ran toward us and threw her inside the small cage. It was tall enough for her to stand, but she couldn't lay down in it. Steve slammed the door the second Noah let go of the ghoul.

"Where's the padlock?" Noah asked Lucas.

Without looking away from the wound on Dahlia's shoulder, Lucas tossed the biggest padlock I'd ever seen. It was the size of his fist. Noah clamped it around the latch and blue sparks flew from the metal and continued over the entire surface.

"What was that?" Phi whispered.

Noah shrugged. "Magic sealing the lock shut. She can't get out of there until Lucas lets her out."

I braced myself on my knees to stop the dizziness I couldn't seem to shake. "Is that because he's the alpha of your pack?"

Phi spoke at the same time I did. "Does he have magic like a witch?"

Noah chuckled and ran a hand down my back, offering comfort. "Yes, he's the alpha and no we don't have magic. The local high witch trades favors for magical objects and potions."

I stood up at that. "Who is she? We need to talk to her. Perhaps she can tell us what we are and help us with our magic."

"Her name is Kaitlyn and we will definitely set up a time to meet with her, Sunshine. While she will be helpful with learning control, I'm not certain she will have all the answers you want."

Camilla let out a plaintiff wail and started yanking on the bars of the cage. Blue sparks flew from the metal everywhere she touched. The ghoul threw herself at the sides over and over again.

I winced and took a step closer. "How can we help her? The demon is going to hurt Camilla if it keeps this up."

Steve covered his ears. "If we lived close to anyone, they'd be calling the police. We will never get to sleep with this racket."

"There isn't much you can do until the demon is banished from the ghoul. You could call Phoebe and ask her to place a dampening spell around the cage," Noah suggested.

I sighed and turned to see how Lia was doing. I hesitated to call Phoebe. Her presence here is what started this mess. I wasn't so sure she could help. She seemed almost as green as us.

"I'll reach out to her." I winced as the cage rattled even more. Then I cringed when I caught sight of the blackened wounds around Dahlia's shoulder. "We might want to take her to the hospital. I don't think we're magical enough to fight off necrotizing fasciitis."

Dreya looked up from swabbing the holes. "Believe it or not, these are improving. There was an inch of blackness all around the cuts a few seconds ago."

Dahlia had her head on Dreya. She was panting and covered in sweat. Lucas brushed her sweaty white-blonde hair off her forehead and pressed a kiss there. "You are going to be just fine. If it doesn't improve soon I will take you to the pack healer and have her apply a tincture to the area."

Noah pursed his lips. "Or we could take her to Kip. She could heal this right up. Although, either way, you are going to be left with scars from the incident."

Lia grunted and hissed as she shifted her position. "Then my outsides will match my insides. Ah, shit."

Deandra had dropped the edge of her top and it hit one of the wounds. Black goop bubbled and hissed. Dea immediately dumped more alcohol on it. Dahlia's back arched and she screamed louder than the ghoul in the cage.

Lucas reached out and ripped the cotton from her body. The sweatshirt hung open, exposing her bra. "Get it off her. It's covered in demon venom and keeps reintroducing it to the injuries."

Dreya lifted Lia and I grabbed one sleeve while Dea snatched the other. I tugged it off her good shoulder then passed it behind her to Dea. Lucas took the fabric from Dea and gently pulled it off Dahlia's body.

I was certain Lia wouldn't want the sexy shifter to see her exposed and covered in sweat like this, but it was necessary. I nudged Phi. "Go grab her a top. A button-down."

Delphine raced through the open front doors and disappeared from sight. Noah stood next to me with his back to Lia and Lucas. That was nice of him to offer her some privacy.

My phone dinged when Phi returned and handed Dre the new shirt. It was lost somewhere in the yard. "Where the hell is it? I think that's the alarm."

Noah's head jerked around and he ran right to the thing. His curse could be heard as I hobbled to catch up. "Someone's breaking into the barn."

Lucas stood up and the two shared a look before they took off in the direction of the barn. I looked at my sisters. "What should we do?"

"Leave them to it," Steve suggested.

Lia rolled to the side and landed on her hands and knees. Her hiss of pain was audible as she pushed herself upright. "Nonsense. This is our plantation. We need to be there."

Dreya shrugged her shoulders and wrapped an arm around Dahlia's waist from her uninjured side. I'd taken a few steps when a wet cotton pad landed on my neck. It sent a sharp jolt of pain through me. I turned to see Deandra holding her hands up with a cotton pad, stained pink. "You have a burn there. I figured we should clean it."

"Oh, thanks." I took the cotton from her and pressed it over the wound. My hand shook as I held it in place. "How the hell did you not pass out when they dumped alcohol on you, Lia. This freaking hurts."

Dahlia grunted as we reached Steve's truck. I could see Lucas and Noah were almost to the barn. They weren't traveling down the dirt road leading to the barn but through the garden.

The structure wasn't that far from the house, but given our injuries, it would be faster for us to drive. Steve helped Dahlia in the cab. Dreya joined them and the rest of us got in the back.

I heard the snarls and howls before we even arrived. Steve's headlights bounced off amber eyes too low to be from a man. *Wolf.* They'd shifted into their animal forms. I'd never seen it before and it unnerved me.

I had no idea which of the five wolves were Lucas and Noah, but I hoped one of them was the gray that tackled a rangy-looking brown one. "Let's stay in the car."

My sisters nodded their agreement and we all sat watching avidly as the wolves fought. The gray one was the biggest and clearly the strongest. There was a black and white one that was nearly as big and powerful.

A white one snuck around the black and white one and bit its hind leg. The black and white wolf swiped a paw that was bigger than my hand across the gray and white wolf fighting it from the front then turned and grabbed the white one by the neck and tossed it.

The wolf hit the side of Steve's truck, making us scream. The sounds from inside the cab were muted, but just as startled. The whimper the white one let out sounded like it could be the last sound it made.

I peered over the side of the bed. Blood slowly soaked white fur as the wolf lay there panting. It made no move to get up and return to the fight. I found myself praying that it wasn't Noah. Something told me the large gray wolf was Lucas.

The gray wolf pinned the tan wolf down. A second later the air shimmered around it like asphalt on a hot day, between one blink and the next Lucas was standing there naked.

"Shift." His voice reverberated through me, making me

want to obey him. Damn, I was glad I wasn't into him. That was too much wolf for me.

The other four wolves all shifted a second later. To my relief, the black and white wolf turned out to be Noah. My entire body flushed as I took in his very naked body. He was built better than the airbrushed models in magazines.

It turned me on yet made me feel inadequate. This shifter was so far out of my league it wasn't even funny. *At least you got a scorching kiss out of him before it ended.* I told myself to stop being negative. Noah liked me. That was enough for now.

Dahlia climbed out of the truck and pointed to the guys. "They're the ones from my vision. Did they get inside?"

Lucas had a hold of one of them by the back of the neck. "No. Silver burns shifters, so they wouldn't be able to get past the lock on the outside."

"Who are they?" Dahlia was listing and white as a ghost. Wait, ghosts were a blue mist, not white. I'd have to amend that particular saying.

Lucas shook the guy hard enough to rattle his teeth. "This asshole thought he could ruin Lilly's mating by making it so she couldn't be mated here after all."

"Keep an eye on them. I'm going to get us clothes. Stay," Lucas told the three shifters.

Dahlia's gaze followed as Lucas ran toward the parking lot where his truck was parked. I climbed out of the back of the truck and put a hand on her back. She turned a tired smile my way. "You need to keep Noah around, sis. He's a good luck charm."

I snorted and shook my head. "*You* need to keep Lucas around. He's the one making us money already. Besides, I have a feeling you like what you see."

Lia's smile contained a bit more life then. "He is pretty

irresistible. Did you see him? And what about your wolf? He's something, too."

Noah winked at me. "Have you guys always lived such an adventurous life?"

Dakota laughed. "Our adventures typically involved almost causing a ten-car pile-up on the freeway thanks to an improperly tied Christmas tree or getting lost as we drove across the country. It's never been this exciting. But Dani's happy. She's got the soul of an adventurer. She's always planning trips that involve hikes and sixty-mile walks."

Noah caught the pair of navy-blue sweats that were thrown his way. I lamented that he had to cover up such perfection and was too busy plotting how I could get him alone and naked once again to hear what was said after that. Something about going on adventures together.

I was always the first one to plan something new for us sisters to do. And would have normally had plenty to say on the topic, but I was lost in my fantasy world at the moment. My imagination was made all the better by the sight of Noah in the buff. I didn't ever want to come back to the real world.

CHAPTER 18

DAHLIA

*T*he beep from Lacey signaled the last of the jars I'd
etched with the logo I'd designed for Lilly's
wedding were finished. It was simply because I wasn't
capable of doing much more than that. Thankfully she loved
the diamond shape with their initials in the center and a
sprig of wildflowers in the upper-righthand corner.

I turned off the machine and the exhaust fans and rubbed
my temples. "Is there anything else we can engrave? I'd rather
hear Lacey than Camilla's wailing."

Phi groaned as she put the last jar back inside the box.
"Tell me about it. It was a nice reprieve. Are we sure she
doesn't need more than two hundred jars?"

I chuckled and grabbed two of the last four boxes. "Lucas
said they only needed a hundred and fifty. I added the last
fifty because I was reluctant to stop so soon."

Phi snorted as we headed out of Lacey's silo. Balancing
the boxes on my hip, I locked the door. Lucas had promised

none of the shifters would bother our stuff again, but we had more than that to contend with. There was that necromancer that was snooping around.

"Do you think she needs more food?" Phi asked as we passed the cages.

We knew that as a ghoul Camilla needed a significant amount of meat and feeding her the past day and a half had been like feeding pigs. We tossed it inside the cage and turned away while she tore into the food. That part had been particularly difficult for Delphine since she was vegetarian.

"I just fed her," Dakota called out. She was surrounded by seven Frenchies, two of whom were mine. I got Oscar and Zoe a few years ago then Dani got Frida and Kota got Daisy, Willow, and Scout. "These guys were getting restless in the kitchen, so I brought them out to run around and go potty."

I bent and set the boxes on the ground. Oscar bounded over to me first followed by Frida and Willow. The rest followed suit and I was soon drowning in puppy love. "Has Ozzie tried to take off again?"

Dakota looked off in the direction he had run the other day and shook her head. "Not even once. He has stayed right next to me the entire time. Lucas established who was alpha and he hasn't pushed it once."

I scratched Oscar behind his bat ears. "That's cause he's a good little guy."

Phi joined in petting the puppies for a few seconds then all ten of us headed to the kitchen where Steve was busy hauling out the old appliances. It had the biggest island and a sink, both of which were necessary for filling jars of lavender honey.

The dogs raced to the other side of the room as far from Steve and his noise as possible and curled into a big ball of fur. We were using the counter where Steve had already removed the small dishwasher to hold the empty jars.

Dani was at the large island which was the one item we wouldn't be changing much in the space. The counter was a gray marble sitting atop a cabinet with finials at each corner and shelves on the shortest ends and storage on the longer sides. We would be painting it gray to match the rest of what Dani had planned.

"This is not as easy as YouTube makes it look." The scowl on Dani's face was comical. She had removed the frames from the hive and used the smoker when we went to etch the jars. She had plastic bins filled with honey and wax sitting in front of her.

Dakota snorted. "The smoker worked like a charm and it was easy to scrape the honey from the frame. It's removing the wax. The stuff is sticky as hell, but we will have enough beeswax to make candles."

Delphine brightened as she dipped her scoop into the golden syrup. "That's a great idea. There's a lot we can do with the wax, not just candles."

"I think we should talk to the head witch about selling it to a magic shop. It has magical properties and it would give us a way to develop relationships in the magical world. We're going to need them." I loved how we fed off of each other and all contributed ideas about how to make money, expand and diversify our business.

"If the past week is any indication, I would agree. We need to get her out here now. Camilla's driving us all nuts. I can't go another sleepless night," Dreya added when she came back in after helping Steve carry the stove out of the building.

Dani lifted one of the jars and held it up to the light. The honey inside was slightly opaque, but the piece of honeycomb was clear, and a nice touch. "Noah said he and Lucas called her last night. What do you think?"

Dakota nodded her head and held up a cinnamon-colored

ribbon. "The honeycomb is perfect. It's rustic and in style right now, but will also fit the shifters."

Dakota took the jar and it slipped from her hands. Dreya shouted and lunged forward with her hands outstretched. What happened next occurred so fast that I had to replay it in my head a couple of times.

Phi and I were closest to Kota and dove to catch the jar before it shattered and got honey everywhere. My head collided with Phi's and we crumpled to the ground. Dreya's hip hit the island at the same time. My arms flew up in the event the honey hit me in the head, but it never happened.

The jar was suspended mid-air and three of my sisters were staring at it wide-eyed. "Who is doing that?" I asked as I climbed to my feet.

Dreya gasped and her head shook rapidly from side to side. I would have continued to wonder who had done that if the jar hadn't dropped to the ground where Phi and I had been moments before. It shattered, sending honey everywhere.

Dre shifted wide eyes to each of us. "You have got to be freaking kidding me. I thought you three had gotten the freaky magical crap and I was left alone. Dammit."

"What's wrong, Dre?" Steve approached her and wrapped an arm around her shoulders.

Dakota started laughing. "Your wife is a witch, Steve. She just stopped that jar of honey from falling."

Steve's brow furrowed as he looked from the ground to Dakota. "Um, I hate to break it to you but it did hit the ground and shatter."

Kota rolled her eyes. "Yeah, after she stopped it for a second."

Dani nodded her head and picked up another jar. "Try it again, Dre." The honey left her hand before Dreya could reply.

For the second time, Dre's hands shot out and the jar froze. No one said anything for a tense second. I cleared my throat, not wanting to frighten Dreya. "Don't break your concentration. See if you can move it too, or if you can only catch things."

Dreya's body started shaking. "How the hell do I keep my concentration and try to move it? I'm not like you guys. I don't have powers."

"Yes, sister, you do. It's obvious by the floating jar," Dakota pointed out. "You can do it. Just think about what you want it to do. Magic seems to work based on intent. At least with me, it does."

Dreya and Dakota were close to each other and Kota finally managed to get through to her. Dreya's eyes narrowed and her lips pursed. She pointed to the jar and waved it to the side and down. The jar followed the slow movement and landed on the island.

Steve made a choking sound. "My wife really is a witch. Holy shit. After over twenty years, I thought you were done surprising me."

Dreya turned to face him and pressed her lips to his in a brief kiss. "That's the perk of being married to a Smith woman."

Phi had clapped her hands together. "This is so exciting. I wonder what power I will end up with. Try to lift my tablet and bring it to me."

"Are you sure? That's the lifeblood of this operation." Dreya was chewing on her lower lip. "If I break it and you lose all those contacts and the calendar, it would be devastating."

Delphine kept records for us. She was the most organized and best suited for the job. She never missed a thing. She nodded her head vigorously. "I'm positive. I've backed it up to the cloud, so nothing will be lost."

"Alright." Dreya repeated the process, focusing on the tablet with a pinched expression and a finger. A bead of sweat trickled from her hair and rolled down her temple.

The tablet lifted and rattled as it landed back in place. Dre took a deep breath and tried again. This time the tablet flew toward Delphine who squeaked and ducked. Dre sucked in a breath and her hands both flew up, palms out. The iPad stopped mid-flight and hovered in front of Phi.

"That'll come in handy when Dea is hanging balloon arches," Dani said.

"Why do you think we've each displayed our abilities at different times? Why did Dakota get hers right away while the rest of us have come into it later?" I'd been wondering that ever since I started having visions along with whether or not we were all magical.

Dani threw a scowl over her shoulder in the direction of Camilla who was screaming obscenities and rattling the cage. "That's a question for another time. Right now, I am calling Phoebe to find out when we are saving Cami."

Dani replaced her spoon with her cell. She typed out a message on the screen. "I hope she has a timeline for us. This is crazy."

I nodded. "But can they put a soul in Cami when she's possessed? It seems like the demon is occupying the spot where the soul goes."

Dani's phone pinged with Phoebe's response. When she fist-pumped the air, I guessed the news was good. "She's getting something called a Netherlight for the ritual and will be over tonight to do the spell."

"That's a relief," Dreya replied as she waved a finger and sent a jar sliding between Dakota and Dani.

"Knock, knock." The sound of Lucas's voice made me smile before I even laid eyes on him.

Dani waggled her brows at me before we turned to face

our visitors. I stifled an eye roll and smiled at Lucas and the beautiful woman that was with him. She was precisely the type I pictured him with. She had long black hair and brown eyes and perfect makeup. Were they dating? Lucas and I had never even gone out on a date, so it shouldn't bother me.

"Hello, Lucas. Who did you bring with you?" My palms were sweaty and my heart was racing. I wasn't sure if it was from his presence or hers.

"This is Kaitlyn, the head witch here in New Orleans. I promised I would bring her to you." His smile was wry, telling me he sensed my jealousy no matter how hard I tried to deny it. He introduced each of us to the head witch.

My heart leaped at that bit of news. "Oh, thank God. We could use your help. We need to know what we are now, but before we get into that, we have a ghoul that has been possessed and we need to kick the demon dog out of her, so Phoebe can restore her soul tonight."

One of Kaitlyn's perfectly plucked eyebrows rose to her hairline. "I take it the woman cursing and banging is your possessed ghoul."

I nodded my head. Kaitlyn smiled, showing her straight, white teeth. "I'm no expert on demonic possession, but I will give it a try. You will need a plan for how to deal with the hound once it's out."

Lucas unsheathed his claws. "Noah and I will be handling that one." He held a hand out to me and I accepted.

I inclined my head to Dani as he tugged me to the door. I didn't have to encourage my sisters to follow me. They were as curious as I was. Delphine caught up with Kaitlyn. "Can you sense what we are? Is there some witchy way of deter-mining these things?"

I glanced back at my sister and saw amusement cross the head witch's face. "Witches can have a sense of each other, but it is nothing definitive. I can feel your power. It seems to be coming from you collectively. I'll have to give it more thought."

Camilla spit through the bars, making me jump aside. I hoped Kaitlyn could do something. The head witch stopped close to the cage and scanned Cami. "*Somnus.*"

Camilla collapsed to the ground and began snoring. Dakota sighed loudly. "Thank you, Katy. That was beginning to make me eye the knives."

Kaitlyn chuckled. "It's a simple sleep spell. Have any of you tried to cast spells?"

We all looked at one another. Dreya shook her head first. The rest of us followed suit. Dani's hand was an inch from resting on the side of the cage when Noah's hand slid between her palm and the silver. "You don't want to see what shifters have suffered through in this thing."

"Noah." Dani's voice was breathy when she said his name.

"Why wouldn't she want to do that?" Kaitlyn looked between the couple.

"Because she's psychometric." Noah shrugged his shoulders as if it was no big deal when it was a very big freaking deal. At least for my sisters and me.

Kaitlyn's eyes went wide. "If you five are witches, you're from a rare and powerful line. Not many of us have extra abilities like that."

I held up my hand. "There are six of us. And we have four brothers."

Kaitlyn whistled. "There aren't many families that size. I would love to hear more about your family, but right now I want to try and force this demon out of your ghoul. Can you bring her out of the cage?" The head witch directed the last part to Noah and Lucas.

Lucas pulled on thick leather gloves then unlocked the padlock and opened the door. Noah picked Cami up and laid her gently on the grass next to us. My mouth went dry when the shifters unbuttoned their jeans and began to undress.

"Grab your gun, Steve," Lucas told him. "You might need it. The rest of you stand back."

The air around Lucas and Noah wavered and their bodies morphed into that of their wolves. Kaitlyn moved closer to Camilla. "Witch magic won't work on your ghoul. She's been overtaken by an evil entity that is hijacking her against her will. Phoebe told me about how she dealt with something similar with Selene, so I'm going to use her technique."

I wasn't certain what I was expecting when I imagined Kaitlyn doing magic, but it wasn't what we saw. The head witch kept a laser focus on Cami. "*Liberatio.*"

Camilla didn't so much as stir. It was far more impressive when she fell asleep instantly. Kaitlyn turned to us. "The demon has a strong hold on her. Care to join me in the next attempt?"

Dreya's shoulders were tight and she shook her head. Dani put her hands on Dre's shoulders. "C'mon, sis. Let's help her. It'll be a good test to see if we can do witchcraft. It might not work. Either way, we won't hurt anyone."

Dreya sighed and nodded. Dakota shifted her stance and jerked her chin toward Kaitlyn. "Wait a minute. What do we have to do? There's no blood sacrifice, right?"

I laughed as did Phi while Kaitlyn gasped and started shaking her head vigorously. "I don't work Blood magic. No good witch would. I'll teach you what you need to know later. Let's see if we can combine our power."

"Thank you for coming when Lucas asked. We aren't your problem, so we appreciate your help," I told her as I closed the distance.

Kaitlyn brought her arms together. "Join hands and picture the demon dog being pushed out of Camilla with everything in you. When I nod, chant the spell I used a moment ago."

We all nodded our agreement and I clasped Dani's hand on one side and Dakota's on the other. Immediately, I called up an image of the creature being pushed out of Camilla. Dakota held Delphine and Kaitlyn grabbed Dreya's and Phi's palms. Seemed fitting that she held the oldest and the baby of our group.

Kaitlyn nodded her head. "*Liberatio!*" My body tingled as a mild electrical current worked its way through me. The air crackled and my skin heated. Thankfully no smell accompanied the spell or I feared I would be pulled into a vision with the strength of the moment.

Camilla's back arched and she opened her mouth to scream only no sounds came out. The black mist lifted from her body and solidified into the shape of the dog. It made a screeching sound and leaped at Delphine. She shouted and dropped her hands.

The second she took off running, Noah came at the hound from one side and Lucas came from the other. The pair of shifters swiped at the demonic dog and tried to bite it. The creature managed to get through them and headed for the trees.

A loud bang echoed right before the demon yelped and fell forward as black blood burst from its hindquarters. I looked at Steve who had his gun still aimed at the thing. "Good shot," I told him. He smirked.

Lucas jumped on the dog's head and clamped his mouth around the skull while Noah ripped into its chest. With the thing injured, the two shifters made quick work of the hellhound. They ripped it to shreds and didn't stop until the thing was in foot-long pieces.

Kaitlyn walked closer to them as they shifted back to human form. "I'll cleanse you in a minute. Let me deal with this." She muttered something under her breath and amber fire shot from her hands and engulfed the dead creature.

I gasped and raced forward at the same moment she put her palm on Lucas's bare chest and muttered, *"purga venenum."*

Before she could help Noah, I pointed wildly at the fire. "You're going to burn our property to the ground. That's not the kind of help we wanted. We poured everything we have into this place."

"Relax, Dahlia. It's witch fire. It will not spread unless I direct it to." Kaitlyn's words calmed my racing heart.

"Oh. I didn't know." My cheeks heated and I wanted to crawl in a hole. I'd made a fool of myself in front of the gorgeous witch.

She patted my shoulder. "It's alright. You'll learn all about this world. And, I think it's safe to say you are definitely witches. But I don't think that's all you have in your heritage. That's something we will also look into for you."

I nodded and watched as she extinguished the fire with the wave of her hand. We were at least part witches. That was pretty freaking cool. Excitement fueled my steps as I walked back to Camilla and my sisters. It was nice to see her back to her old self.

CHAPTER 19

DANIELLE

The sight of the beautiful black woman heading toward my sisters and me set my teeth on edge. I couldn't pinpoint what it was about the woman in the lead, but something about her had my stomach churning and bile rising to the back of my throat.

"Who is that?" Deandra had barely spoken her question, but our visitors seemed to hear it nonetheless because they all turned their heads in our direction where before they'd been focused on Camilla.

Dreya walked forward a step. "Can we help you? This is private property and we aren't open for business."

The black woman in front smiled. "I've been invited for da ceremony dis evening. My mambos and I will be supporting my necromancer in da soul retrieval." She had a thick Creole accent that made her sound as exotic as she looked.

My heart started pounding against my rib cage. "You must be Marie Laveau."

"Dat is correct." Marie walked right past us muttering something under her breath while her mambos shook engraved sticks in their hands. She didn't bother with introductions and the air began to hum as they walked further onto our property.

I was too concerned with what she was doing to worry about learning names. Kaitlyn had told us to be wary of these people. I met Lia's gaze and nodded. She grabbed my hand then Dea's. When the six of us were connected, we enhanced the protections Kaitlyn had placed over our plantation earlier in the day.

"Augendae et muniendum." The second the chant left our lips a teal flash of light rose from the ground and disappeared a second later. Sparks flew when it encountered Marie and her entourage.

It must have done something because the look she gave us made me cringe. Dakota held her head high and I could practically read her mind. I knew she was a second away from asking the group to leave. Dahlia shook her head at Kota who sighed.

What our actions did was stop their progress any further onto our property. Despite the fact that Marie was a legend where we were from, we refused to allow her free reign on our land. Kaitlyn, Noah, and Lucas had warned us it would be dangerous to do so.

Without a word, Marie's mambos returned to the car while she spoke with a woman with brown hair and light blue eyes. I'd bet she was the necromancer and if the scowl on her face was any indication, she didn't seem too happy about whatever Marie was telling her.

We moved closer when the other women returned carrying torches and a wooden table. They set it up and

Marie pulled several items from a bag I hadn't noticed her carrying until that moment.

The crimson cloth was embroidered with symbols I'd seen associated with voodoo many times before. She set black candles on top along with what looked like incense. One of the mambos lit the cone that sat on a small silver plate and white smoke drifted up in a spiral.

The smell of orange, cinnamon, and clove permeated the air. The breeze didn't seem to affect the spiral of smoke. It continued its path up in a straight line. It made me slightly dizzy. Or perhaps it was the energy that was building around us. There was a distinctly darker feel to it than there had been with Kaitlyn or Phoebe.

Dahlia's gasp broke my focus and I turned my head in time to see her eyes roll back in her head before her knees gave out. I let go of her hand and wrapped my arm around her waist at the same time Deandra did the same.

Dreya, Delphine, and Dakota all closed ranks around us right before Marie Laveau asked what was wrong with her. Dakota narrowed her eyes at the voodoo queen. "Our sister is sensitive to strong scents and whatever you lit is making her sick. Nothing for you to worry about."

My heart was still racing and I swore it would give out at any second when the tension ratcheted up to a million. I remained focused on Dahlia as she was slumped between Dea and me. She was having one of her visions. The glassy, vacant expression in her eyes was the same as the only time I'd seen her have one.

It seemed like an hour that Lia was lost to whatever she was seeing, but was likely less than a minute or two. It was Marie's presence that made it seem so long. I swear I felt fingers probing the air around us, trying to reach into Dahlia. I tightened my hold, as did Dea. The others had to have felt it as well because they created a wall between our visitors and us.

I held back my relief when Dahlia blinked a few seconds later. "Are you alright, sestra?"

Lia straightened and nodded. "I'm alright."

"What happened? You looked like you were in a trance." Marie's voice was sharp and compelling as she cut Lia off. In fact, I almost opened my mouth to answer her.

I squeezed Dahlia's hand as she opened her mouth. Dea put her hand on Lia's shoulder. "We told you she's sensitive to certain scents."

Lia took a deep breath and squeezed me back. "Deandra's right. I'm what you might call allergic and that scent is particularly difficult for me to tolerate." She took a step back right as footsteps echoed across our property.

Marie's head swiveled in that direction and her eyes narrowed. Dahlia had already started walking toward Phoebe and her entourage. The haste to her steps told me the vision likely had something to do with the witch.

Dahlia was out of breath when she reached them. "Thank God you're here. These women showed up carrying a wooden folding table and a bunch of bags. We worried you weren't coming."

Dakota joined them next trying to keep an eye on our visitors. "Those bitches freak me out. They feel cold."

I gaped at Dakota. "Are you kidding? That's Marie Laveau. She's the Queen of New Orleans, sis. Regardless of how awful she feels, we can say we've actually met her in the flesh." Regardless of how they set me off, she was infamous. And I had a feeling we needed to have a healthy amount of respect for her or we would suffer.

Phoebe cocked an eyebrow. "You'd be wise not to invite her into your lives. She will use you for her own gain and will bespell your land again. Only this time it will serve her."

Dahlia nudged my shoulder with hers. Then her eyes went blank and she slumped against me again. Dakota helped me hold Lia and we shook her shoulder. Surely, she wasn't having another vision so soon.

"Lia! You with us?" I waved my hand in front of her face, hoping she was just tired.

Dakota snapped her fingers next to Dahlia's ear. "Girl, snap out of it. Shit. I think she's having another one of her visions. That smelly crap those necromancers lit is still affecting her. Dani, ask them to put it out. Unless it's necessary?"

Phoebe's complexion lost some color as she looked at Dahlia. "Did you always have powers? How have you six been feeling?"

I rubbed the back of my neck but before I could respond, Dahlia gasped and grabbed Phoebe's forearms. I almost peed myself when Aidoneus closed the distance and growled.

It was at that moment that the infamous Marie Laveau walked over. The energy that preceded her made my stomach churn even worse. "Is everything alright over here?"

The necromancer, who introduced herself as Temperance, and a couple of the mambos along with Deandra, Delphine, and Dreya were right behind her.

Phoebe dismissed the concern with a wave of her hand. "We're great. Your attempt to divert us didn't work. Continue preparing. I will be right over. Selene, why don't you and Aidoneus prepare the herbs and I will be right there."

Phoebe never let go of Lia's hand, even when she kissed her boyfriend on the lips. It seemed as if she was afraid of Marie taking Dahlia away before she could hear what my sister had to say.

I told my sisters to help. We couldn't leave the mambos unsupervised. That much was clear. Phoebe ignored Marie as she chanted a spell. "*Secretum*. Alright now tell me what happened."

Dahlia sucked in a breath and ran a hand down her face. "Well ever since the other day things have been happening to us. I get visions from various scents. I have no way to control it and never know when it's going to happen."

I needed to move this along. Whatever my sister saw had to be important for her to have two visions back-to-back. "What did you see, Dahlia?"

Dahlia was shaking. My heart clenched for my sister. I could tell the toll this was taking on her. "I saw this ceremony going all kinds of sideways. I didn't see much more than that before something yanked me out of the vision. When you arrived, I got another glimpse and saw Marie take over. She's going to insert someone other than Selene into her body."

Phoebe gripped Dahlia's shoulder. "I suspected she was up to no good. Thanks for the confirmation. Let's go get Camilla and Selene their souls."

My jaw went slack. "You mean you're still going through with this?"

Phoebe was serene when she nodded her head. "I am eager to get this done. But don't worry, I won't allow Marie to get her way. This is precisely the reason I said you couldn't trust her. She works for the loa who are untrustworthy gods."

Dakota scowled as she looked at the group. "I haven't trusted them since the moment they stepped on our property. It was all I could do to keep from wishing them away. That's my power. I get anything I wish for."

Phoebe's head jerked at that. She recovered quickly and I felt a pop. "It looks like you guys have done some work to the place. The gazebo is a wonderful addition. I bet you'll get countless weddings out there."

I wasn't sure what she'd done until then. She had to

194

have canceled her privacy spell because she'd shifted to a neutral topic we hadn't been discussing. My mind reeled as I tried to catch up with her shift. Given the scowl Marie was giving us, I knew she'd done it to move the process along and keep the voodoo queen from hexing us, or worse.

Dahlia didn't have the same trouble keeping up as I did. "I helped build it for the wedding we're having this weekend. There are a million fairy lights strung throughout the structure. It's hard to believe we're actually having our first event here. It helps that they're alright with the house not being finished. We will barely get the kitchen renovated in time for the caterers to use it."

"I can't wait to see pictures. I still want to talk to you about doing my daughter's birthday party." Phoebe's demeanor didn't fit her words and I wondered if the power set her teeth on edge like it did mine.

We'd reached the others and Phi stepped forward then. "I made a few notes about ideas. I plan on calling to get the budget and specifics from you."

Phoebe smiled at my sister. "That will give me a chance to talk to Nina about her thoughts."

Phoebe continued to the others. We watched Temperance do her thing with herbs and salt spread around her in a circle. Stella had prepared our herb mixture and sprinkled it in a circle that Phoebe would cast as soon as we had Selene's soul.

"I need the Netherlight to house the soul for transference." Temperance gestured to Selene who was holding a small box. I recalled Phoebe mentioning something about it in a text and assumed the light had to be inside the container.

The tension in the air hit defcon five when Selene opened the lid and Temperance retrieved the orb. The glass sphere in the necromancer's hand was the key to being able to secure their soul. Apparently, there was no other way to pull a spirit from the other side and shove it right into a person.

My pulse increased when the necromancer closed her eyes and started chanting a spell. The energy crackled around me. Unlike when Phoebe had released the magic of the land, this time it smelled acidic and like black licorice. When a dark light ignited the salt and herbs the scent shifted to one of charred herbs.

I was standing close to Phoebe and hoped she was ensuring Marie couldn't hijack our ritual when I saw her chant in Latin. As a nurse, I was familiar with the language, so I assumed her words were in that language, although I couldn't be certain. I wasn't about to ask her and draw attention to what she was obviously trying to hide.

Electricity sparked between Phoebe and Aidoneus when he twined their fingers together. It was a poignant reminder that he was a powerful god. He steadied Phoebe when her body jerked subtly. She was still a second later.

That didn't last long, though. I took a step in her direction when she started breathing heavily. When it turned choppy and her body shook minutely, I was worried she was being attacked magically. I had no idea how to help, but I felt like we needed to do something.

I looked at my sisters and inclined my head in Phoebe's direction. They caught on and within a second, we'd all joined hands. Camilla stuck close to Dreya and was holding her bicep in a death grip. I didn't blame her. Something serious was going on even if we couldn't see it.

"*Obstructionum,*" Phoebe chanted. The way her jaw clenched and the veins in the side of her neck stood out, whatever she was blocking was powerful.

A second later Temperance cried out and Selene stood frozen and shaking. Light burst from Phoebe and Aidon's clasped hands. It was actually leaving him and entering her.

What was it like to have a god feed you energy? It seemed good because Phoebe appeared to strain less.

Marie's mambos started dancing and chanting, making the acrid odor increase. Worried about Lia having a vision, I looked at my sister. Thankfully, she was with us. All of a sudden, Phoebe gasped and went white as a sheet. Unsure if it would help, I willed my energy to her to aid the process.

Phoebe's friend, Layla, shifted into a black wolf and lunged at the mambos. The chanting and dancing were replaced with screaming and running. The strain on Phoebe's face eased a fraction.

I was relieved to see Lucas and Noah join Layla in attacking the mambos. I realized Phoebe had surrounded herself with powerhouses. Not just Aidoneus or Layla, but Stella, too. Dreya, Dakota, and Deandra joined Stella to stalk across the area to Leveau. I was going to join them, but Camilla hovered close to me, Lia and Phi. I didn't want to leave her vulnerable.

"Your attempt to take over Selene isn't going to work, Ms. Leveau." Stella crossed her arms over her chest and glared at the powerful voodoo queen.

Marie shifted her gaze from the mambos that were being clawed by wolves to my sisters and Stella. My heart was in my throat as she opened her mouth to say something back. Stella beat her to it. "*Silentium.*"

Marie's mouth snapped closed at the same time the Netherlight flared a neon teal color. Phoebe let go of Aidoneus and moved to Selene who was standing in the circle that Stella had prepared a few minutes ago.

Dahlia shot me a look when Aidoneus made a promise to Phoebe without her having said a word. "I won't let anything happen, Queenie." As a god, he could probably read minds.

I shook my head at the fact that that wasn't the craziest thought I'd had all night. Phoebe took the orb from Temperance while Aidoneus drew symbols into the ground. I wondered what role they played in the process.

Phoebe held the orb over Selene's chest and held it there. *"Sanguine praedam et animam, ut nulla inter eos etiam petulans, Psyche Benedicat vos dicimus vinculo."*

Selene's head went back and her entire body vibrated the neon teal light that surrounded her. She was breathing like she'd run a marathon as her arms went out to her sides. I gaped as the teal light seeped beneath her skin.

When Selene opened her eyes, they were no longer hazel. They glowed the same teal as the light. "What the heck?" Phi whispered.

I shrugged my shoulders and opened my mouth, then closed it. Selene's face split into a smile and her eyes returned to their normal shade. "It had to be the magic working."

Emotion clogged my throat when I saw tears shine in Selene's hazel eyes. It was clear she was overcome by the process. What she said as she hugged Phoebe confirmed my suspicion. "Thank you is not enough to express my gratitude, Phoebe. You are the best Pleiades the world has ever known."

Phoebe released the ghoul. "I'm sorry it took so long. Let's get Camilla fixed up then we can go celebrate."

Camilla shook as I nudged her forward. She glanced from us to Marie then Phoebe. Phoebe had to have picked up on her nerves because she offered Cami reassurances. "It'll be alright. We have this process down now."

Phoebe held the orb in her open hand. *"Purgo."* I gasped when white light flashed like the flash of a camera. When the spots cleared, the sphere returned to the state it had been in before.

Phoebe gave it to Temperance who did the same thing as she had moments ago. I kept my eyes glued to Phoebe and Marie. The voodoo queen scowled at Phoebe who didn't seem to be under the same strain as the first time. That was a freaking relief. I hadn't done anything, but the process had exhausted me.

When a warm burnt orange color glowed brightly in the orb, Temperance handed it to Phoebe. That must be Camilla's soul. The color fits her perfectly. Aidoneus ran his finger over the symbols again while Phoebe added more herbs and salt and called out to the elements.

Phoebe held up Camilla's soul. "Are you ready?"

Camilla sucked in a deep breath and looked at my sisters and me. "Maybe I should let her kill me. I no longer belong in this world."

My heart skipped a beat for this poor woman. My sisters and I walked to the edge of the salt and herbs. I smiled at Camilla. She'd come to be part of the family over the past week. "I know it hasn't been long, but you've earned a place in this family. We would love for you to stay and be a part of the Six Twisted Sisters party planning business."

"You will make a great tour guide with your stories," Dakota added. "We love hearing about the history of this plantation."

Delphine nodded in agreement. "Besides, don't you want to be part of making better memories here?"

Camilla was on the verge of crying. "I thought you wanted me gone."

Dahlia laughed and waved a hand through the air. "I use bitch as a term of endearment. We don't want you to go anywhere."

Camilla joined in the laughter and met each of our gazes then faced Phoebe. "I'm ready."

Phoebe held the orb over Cami's chest and repeated what she'd done with Selene. My sisters and I clapped and whistled when the amber light sank into Camilla and her eyes did that freaky glowing color change. Dre hugged Cami first.

After we had each embraced her, I was surprised to see Marie Leveau and her mambos were gone.

"Will this get you into trouble with her? I can look into protection for you if that's the case. I know people." Phoebe was obviously upset she might have gotten the necromancer in trouble with the powerful voodoo queen.

Stella leaned toward Temperance. "By people, she means the God of the Underworld, Hades."

Temperance shrugged, seeming unconcerned. "She's pissed, but her hold over us is weakening. This might just be the impetus we need to get out from under her thumb. I'll have to see what the others say."

Phoebe practically jumped on the necromancer as she hugged her. It had taken Temperance by surprise and it took a moment for her to reciprocate. "If you need help gaining your independence, I will come back anytime," Phoebe promised.

"I'll hold you to that," Temperance replied.

We thanked Phoebe and her friends while the necromancer gathered her supplies together. It was nice to have Camilla free from worrying about possession again. So many things had happened in the past week, but it hadn't hampered the Six Twisted Sisters from preparing the best wedding possible. And now that this phase was over, we could focus fully on the ceremony and renovations.

CHAPTER 20

DAHLIA

"*S*hit." The curse flew from my mouth as the wire refused to cooperate with my sore fingers. We were finishing the last-minute decorations for Lilly and Jeremy's mating ceremony.

"Are those flowers attacking?" Lucas's deep voice made me shiver as I straightened from one of the posts around the gazebo.

"No, more like my fingers refuse to cooperate. If I could get these attached, I could finish setting up the chairs with Steve and Jeff." My mind went blank as I stared at Lucas's gorgeous face.

He smiled, making it even harder to recall what I should be doing instead of staring at him. "Noah and I can help with that. I'm afraid flowers are beyond me. This looks amazing, by the way. I've never seen so many decorations in one place before."

I threw my head back and laughed. "Wait until you see the

table settings. We pulled out the best dishes, chargers, and gold cutlery. Camilla even folded the napkins into hearts. Is Lilly doing alright? Does she need anything?"

Lucas's smile shifted to one of affection as he glanced toward the house. "She's doing great. I've never seen her happier. I'd better go help, but save a dance for me later."

All I could do was bob my head. Dani and Dea approached as I watched him walk away. I sighed and fanned myself. "That man is hot. And wants to dance with me later. What am I going to do?"

Dani lifted one eyebrow. "Does he know you've got the rhythm of an elephant?"

I chuckled, waiting for Deandra's infectious laughter, but it never came. Her jaw was on her chest and she was looking in the direction she'd been a minute ago installing the balloon arches.

I clasped her shoulder. "What is it?" Dreya was standing there talking to Phi. She'd been using her telekinesis to help Deandra before.

"We have some unexpected visitors," Dea replied.

My head swiveled left then right searching for Marie Laveau or one of her mambos. I was certain she would blame us for her failure the other night. Even though Kaitlyn promised our protections would keep those meaning us harm off the property, I was still worried.

"Is it Leveau? Where are they?"

Deandra was shaking like a leaf as she pointed to an area just beyond Dre's shoulder. "They're ghosts. Can't you see them?"

I scanned the area several times but saw nothing. "There's nothing there. We should be able to see them like we can Camilla's mother." Dani reiterated what I'd just said.

Dea gasped and her hands flew to her mouth. "There's more now. How come I can see them but you guys can't?"

Cars pulled into the parking lot, telling us we were running out of time and needed to get a move on it. "That's a question to address with Kaitlyn when we see her again. Right now, we need to attach these flowers and then light the candles on the tables."

Dea was shaken like she'd been as a kid and talking about the woman in the pink floppy hat. We made quick work of the gazebo and had it complete just as the sun was setting and Lilly made her way out of the house.

There was no wedding march preceding her. She wore a fitted green dress that made her green eyes stand out. The flowers woven through her hair were a beautiful touch that complimented her feminine appearance. It was easy to forget she turned into a wild animal seeing her dressed like this.

Lucas and Noah climbed the gazebo steps and watched as the pack embraced Lilly. Jeremy was right behind her. It surprised me to see him dressed in a charcoal gray suit. I'd expected dark jeans like Lucas was wearing. His white button-down was the most formal thing I'd ever seen him wear.

The couple joined about halfway across the lawn and continued their way towards the gazebo. Every member of the pack touched or embraced them as they went. That usually happens after the marriage ceremony.

My sisters and I stood on the side of the wrap-around porch close to the house and watched the proceedings in the distance. I wanted to move closer to hear what Lucas was saying but didn't dare.

It was clear this ceremony was vastly different from anything we had been involved in before. The pack members drifted closer and surrounded the gazebo in concentric circles. Lucas gestured to the sky above when Dakota nudged my side. "Let's get closer so we can hear what he's saying."

I chewed my lower lip and looked at my sisters who

resembled bobblehead dolls with their heads bobbing up and down. Sighing, I descended the stairs closest to us. "We need to be quiet and not interrupt the proceedings."

Six middle-aged women that had been up and down ladders decorating all day weren't stealthy in the least. The shifters at the back of the group looked in our direction before we made it very far.

I can't imagine what we looked like as we froze in place. I know I had to look like an idiot with my back bent and my back leg lifted to take the next step. An older woman with brown hair, streaked gray waved her hand to us, encouraging us to come closer.

To my embarrassment, Lucas had paused his speech and was holding his hands in our direction. "We owe a debt of gratitude to the talented Six Twisted Sisters for preparing such an elaborate mating ceremony on such short notice. Many of you know this has been a dream of Lilly's ever since she was five years old. I couldn't have given her this without their tireless effort."

My cheeks flushed as all eyes landed on us. Dani came up with the vision and was the first to shrink behind me so she couldn't be seen. Dakota and Dea lifted their hands into the air and smiled.

Lucas kept his gray eyes on mine for several seconds before turning to Lilly. His smile was bright and full of the love he had for his daughter. "I call on our ancestors to bestow their favor on this couple. May they celebrate and rejoice with us. I call to the goddess of the moon, Selene, and the god of the sun, Apollo, and ask that they bless this union. To be blessed with your Fated One is rare. The fact that Jeremy and Lilly found each other is a good omen for us all. *Deména mazí gia pánta kai pánta.* May your love last this life-time and into the next. Your souls will be bonded as one tonight. Never take that connection for granted. Love must be nurtured and honored on a daily basis. Now, let's eat, drink, and dance."

I don't know what came before that speech, but I loved how succinct it was. The shifters erupted in cheers. Jeremy lifted Lilly into his arms and kissed her passionately. There is no way I could do that in the presence of so many others. I admired that it didn't bother them in the least.

Dani tugged my arm. "We need to light the candles and turn on the safety lights in the porte cochère."

With one last look at Lucas, I followed my sisters and grabbed a lighter from where we'd stashed them earlier. It didn't take long for the seven of us to light the candles. Delphine plugged in the strings of lights and we stood back while men and women from the pack filed into the kitchen.

Music started playing from fifteen feet to our left at the entrance to the biggest part of our garden where we had a wide concrete patio that served as the perfect dance floor. It was surrounded by semi-private coves built into the flowers and shrubs.

Lilly and Jeremy came dancing across the lawn. Metal containers of drinks were carried out of the kitchen as one of the women lit the fire on the massive barbecue that we pulled behind Dreya and Steve's truck to parties where they wanted to grill a ton of food.

I went over and checked the display of wine glasses and made sure it was all arranged. I was shifting some of the plastic cups we had for kids to the correct shelf when someone stopped behind me.

"You make it difficult to think about anything but getting you naked." The deep voice reverberated through me, scaring the daylights out of me.

I yelped and straightened, knocking into the A-frame display. Glass rattled together and several tumbled from the shelf they'd been perched on. Lucas's reflexes were much faster than mine. He caught three before they fell to the ground, while I just managed to snag one.

"Lucas." My hand went to my chest where my heart was racing faster than the cars going around the track at the Indy five-hundred.

Lucas put a hand on my hip and closed the distance. I searched for a way to get out of this situation. Not that I didn't like him or want to talk to him. I just didn't trust myself to remain coherent. His presence still turned my mind to mush.

His intense gray eyes held mine. "Did I tell you before how beautiful you are tonight?"

My cheeks heated and I averted my gaze while I gathered my thoughts. Lilly was dancing a few feet away with Jeremy and several friends. Her joy was obvious. It was precisely what you hoped to see on a day like this.

"I'm flattered. Our uniforms are rather bland though. We found that the black hides any stains and usually remains clean throughout the event." *Ok, idiot. You should shut up now.*

He laughed while I clamped my lips together. "I should see if anyone in the kitchen needs anything."

He shook his head. "That's not necessary. The pack has it handled. You and your sisters have done enough. You've made my daughter's day. I love seeing her like this."

I was distracted from Lilly and the others when I saw Deandra and Dani were hurrying in our direction. My body stiffened and I stepped toward them. "What is it?"

Dani forced a smile to her face. "It's nothing major. Can you excuse us, Lucas? We need to have a sister's conversation."

Lucas hesitated for a second before nodding. "We will be dancing before the night is through."

My face was flaming as I smiled and nodded. Dani and Dea were teasing me before Lucas got five steps away. He looked back with one brow lifted. I shrugged my shoulders. "You'll get used to them, eventually."

His laughter was deeper than his voice. "I look forward to it."

I turned to my sisters. "What the hell?"

Dea's teasing and eye waggles stopped immediately. "There are ghosts everywhere. It's like the party was an open invitation for them to come out of hiding."

My heart skipped a beat and I shifted my gaze out over the crowd. I didn't see any blue figures floating around. "Do you think it's their ancestors? Lucas called to them. Perhaps it's normal for these types of things."

Deandra ran a hand down her face. "I wish Kaitlyn had a handbook we could consult. LIke Witching for Dummies, or something."

I giggled. "We'll learn fast enough. In the meantime, we need to celebrate our success. This is a stunning start to the Six Twisted Sister's venue at Willowberry Plantation."

Dani called out and told Kota, Dre, and Phi to join us. I ducked inside the kitchen, grabbed a bottle of champagne, and brought it out. We'd made extra glasses for the couple, so we used those to toast our first party.

"Excuse me." The small blonde woman cleared her throat as she approached. She was one of Lilly's friends. She'd arrived with her earlier and had been in the parlor helping her get ready, but I couldn't recall her name.

"How can we help you, Stasia?" Leave it to Phi to remember her name.

"I was wondering if you guys could help me throw my parents a fiftieth anniversary. They both love this setting and can't stop talking about what you guys pulled off in such a short time."

Phi's head was already nodding. She didn't have her tablet with her or she would be taking notes. "We would be happy to help. As long as it isn't in the next month. We are undergoing too many renovations to accommodate another party so soon."

Stasia held up her hands. "Oh, it's not for nine months, but I didn't want you guys to book up and not have space for us."

Dani's shoulders sagged and she smiled. "Perfect. Call us in the morning, we will reserve the date for you. Then we can get more details when you're ready." I loved my sister but she was not a patient person. She wanted everything now when it wasn't feasible.

Stasia jumped up and down in excitement, making her blonde curls bounce on her shoulders. "Yay. Thank you so much. I've been trying to think of something to recognize the time they've been together."

"We'll help make it a night to remember," Dani promised and shooed the girl away. "Now, go enjoy Lilly's party."

The woman practically bounced away. Dakota lifted her glass. "To Dani launching into our greatest adventure yet. She started the Six Twisted Sisters way back when and found Willowberry. I had my doubts that this would succeed this fast, but we're already in the black. I couldn't ask for better sisters. I love you guys."

We clinked glasses and took a drink. The alcohol was bitter. "Next time we toast with margaritas or pina coladas. I still don't care for champagne."

"I agree, sestra," Dani added. "I wonder what mom would think of us now."

Dreya took another sip of her drink. Apparently, she liked the stuff. "She'd be proud of us and what we're building."

Deandra's gaze was on the crowd and her head bobbed. "And she'd tell us it was about time, that she knew we had it in us all along."

Phi's phone dinged with a message. She pulled it out of

the pocket in her black slacks and her mouth dropped open. "Lucas just paid us. The full amount."

"What?" I searched the crowd and found him talking to a beautiful redhead. His eyes were trained on me though. "Why would he do that when we agreed to reduce the cost of replacing the roofs? We still have a dozen jobs for him to do."

Dani's shoulder bumped mine. "Because he wuvs you."

I rolled my eyes at the same time my heart swelled at the thought. It wasn't the case. We hadn't known each other long enough. "I am irresistible."

That launched my sisters into a round of teasing me about falling for the shifter. I laughed and took the ribbing without saying a word. I had no idea if anything would come of it, and at the moment I refused to analyze the situation.

My sisters and I accomplished one of the goals we'd set out on years ago and this moment needed to be properly commemorated. We had a second gig lined up and a referral for yet another. Life was looking up for the first time in years.

DOWNLOAD the next book in the Twisted Sisters Midlife Mayhem series, CADAVER ON CANAL STREET HERE! Then turn the page for another preview.

DOWNLOAD the first book in the Dame of the Midnight Relics series, SURPRISED BY A SUPERNATURAL START HERE! Then turn the page for a preview.

DOWNLOAD the first book in the Mystical Midlife in Maine series, Magical Makeover HERE! Then turn the page for another preview. Then turn the page for a preview.

. . .

DOWNLOAD the first book in the Midlife Magic series, MAGICAL NEW BEGINNINGS HERE! Then turn the page for a preview.

CLICK HERE to Download The Prime of my Magical Life, book 1 in the exciting new Supernatural Midlife Series. Then turn the page for a preview.

EXCERPT FROM CADAVER ON
CANAL STREET BOOK #2

DANIELLE

*T*here was an undeniable pep in my step as Lia and I walked down Canal Street. We were meeting with a new client that wanted us to throw her a birthday party. It was the siren Noah and Lucas had referred our way.

It was less than two months ago since Phoebe had released the magic in the land of the plantation my sisters and I had purchased as a venue for our party planning business. In doing so, she awakened our magical heritage and life hadn't been the same since then.

Initially, I'd worried I had made a mistake in pushing my sisters to invest in the rundown antebellum mansion and grounds. When the first ghost appeared and was quickly followed by a leaky roof and a ghoul, I was convinced we were doomed. It didn't take long to change that opinion.

Two sexy shifters came to our rescue, fixed our roofs, and became our first clients to book an event at Willowberry. Six Twisted Sisters still had existing parties, but none were at our venue. The mortgage on the place necessitated continued bookings, so we couldn't turn down anyone wanting a party, hence the reason we were walking around the French Quarter less than a week after Mardi Gras.

"God bless it, this place is a zoo." Lia was right about that. It was like watching a pinball game with drunk people stumbling down the sidewalk. And it would only get worse after night fell.

"The hassle will be worth it. We're being asked to throw a party for a siren. I wonder if she knows any mermaids." I didn't bother to hide what I was saying. New Orleans was known for its supernatural connections.

Mermaids and sirens sounded better than necromancers and voodoo gods. I hoped we didn't see Marie Laveau again anytime soon. She had tried to hijack the ritual to give our ghoul a soul.

When Phoebe had first brought Camilla back, I thought she was a zombie. She looked and acted like one. Discovering a ghoul was nothing like a zombie was one of the lessons we'd learned since being thrown in the deep end of the magical world.

Talk about trial by fire. Good thing I used to be on the transport team for the NICU department at the hospital. There you had to roll with it and learn as you went.

"We have our second client, so it already is worth it. What was the name of the bar, again?" Dahlia tucked her white-blonde hair behind one ear as she scanned the area.

"It's called Final Swallow. It's on Royal Street." I'd never seen or heard of it.

There were more bars in the French Quarter than there were ghosts and vampires. At least I hoped that was true. I honestly had no idea. It was something we grew up saying. Now, I wondered how accurate the claim was. I'd have to ask Noah.

Just thinking the sexy shifter's name made my thoughts turn gooey. It stunned me that he'd worked his way past the house of ice surrounding my heart. After two shitty marriages, I'd sworn off men and was focusing on myself.

That lasted all of two minutes. The first hot guy to bat his lashes at you and you caved. Sometimes I hated my inner snark. She was a real bitch sometimes.

Dahlia laughed and for a second, I thought I'd said that out loud. "A guy named that place. No way would a woman have anything to do with that double entendre. Still, they must have some potent stuff in the place."

I rolled my eyes at my sister, but couldn't stop the laughter. It died quickly when something occurred to me. "It's not a strip club, is it? I will kill Noah if he sent us to a titty bar." There were clubs where men and women took off their clothes throughout the Quarter, so it was possible.

Lia threw her hands in the air and shook her head. "How the hell should I know? What's the address? Royal isn't that big and we've been on it for a few blocks."

I stopped and pulled my phone out. The device unlocked but I couldn't press any of the buttons with my gloves on. I'd taken to wearing them all the time to avoid having visions of the past.

It was especially bad in the house. The third time I saw a slave get beaten, I was over the appeal of a plantation house. There were plenty of good times, as well. Being thrust into the past took a toll on me which was why Lia had ordered me the supple black, leather gloves. They were supposed to be touchscreen capable. That worked as well as my Uncle Rob who has never worked a day in his life.

Lia held out her hand. "Here, give me that."

I handed her the phone. It wasn't until her eyes widened that I realized she would see the previous message from Noah. "Wait, I'll get it."

"Nuh-uh. This is some juicy stuff. He wants to take you to dinner and show you how a goddess should be worshipped. Damn, sis, that sounds hot. At least he knows you're better than an average woman and deserve to be treated like royalty."

Heat scalded my cheeks and I wanted to crawl in a hole. I was afraid my sisters would think I was moving too fast. They were too nice to say anything to me, but they would think it.

"Shut up. He's trying to woo me. Of course, he's going to say stuff like that. It means nothing." I snatched my phone and looked at the address while not really seeing it.

Lia put her hands on my shoulders and made me focus on her. "That's not true and you know it. Neither Noah nor Lucas are the types of guys to snow a woman. They don't have to say that to get laid. They're gorgeous with the bodies of Greek gods. Noah really likes you. Anyone can see it in the way he looks at you. I know you're nervous after what you've been through, but you don't have to worry about this. Be open to possibility and let it happen naturally."

I sighed and nodded my head. "I'm going to need you to remind me of that a hundred more times. Let's get to the Final Swallow." I scanned the number of the business behind us. "Looks like we passed it already."

Dahlia let the topic go. It was why she and I were able to live with one another without coming to blows. She would never push me to talk about more than I wanted to. "That's odd. I didn't see it."

We turned back the way we'd come and were both looking at the addresses and names on storefronts. When we reached the address, I understood why we had passed it. It was located in a courtyard and hidden by a hedge.

"It's in there." I pointed to the space behind the hedge. It was fine now, but I imagined it would be scary at night with nothing more than a gas lantern to light your way.

New Orleans, and the French Quarter, in particular, were known for their courtyards. Most had cafes or small shops inside them. It was one of my favorite things about the area, aside from the Creole architecture. It provided privacy while still being in the middle of the hustle and bustle.

Dahlia walked through the space behind the hedge and I followed suit. The cement sidewalk gave way to a tiled patio that had a fountain as big as one of ours in the center. The surrounding building was two stories high and the stucco was painted a terracotta color. There were plants and trees everywhere. It was like walking into a paradise.

"It's in the corner there. And the only business here," I pointed out.

I stuck close to Dahlia as she opened the wood door. The bar was vastly different from the beautiful courtyard outside. The bartender aside, it looked like any bar I'd ever been inside. It was dimly lit with dark walls. There were tall bar tables with barstools closest to the long wooden bar. Bottles of alcohol stood at the ready in rows on shelves.

My gaze got stuck on the thing making the drinks. The devil was indeed in New Orleans and working at Final Swallow. The spade-tipped red tail waved over the creature's shoulder. His black eyes focused on me right then making me shiver.

"What can I get you, beautiful ladies?" The voice was deep, indicating it was a guy. He tilted his head and I followed the movement of his red horns.

Lia cleared her throat. "Um, we're here to meet with Nedasea. We're from the Six Twisted Sisters."

"You must be Danielle and Dahlia," a beautiful woman called out. It was the only thing that broke my gaze from the red-skinned demonic creature behind the bar. "Thank you for coming. I was so excited to hear about you guys. This birthday is particularly important for me and I wanted a big bash to mark the occasion, but I don't have the time or talent to make it what I really want."

I snapped out of my daze and plastered a smile on my face. "That's what we do best."

Nedasea tossed long teal hair over her shoulder and cocked a hip. "Before we get started, do you guys want Brezok to make you anything to drink?"

"I'd love a pina rita if it's not too much to ask." Lia took a seat at the empty table closest to Nedasea.

Brezok picked up a bottle without looking and tossed it in the air. "That's easy enough. I prefer tequila over rum, too."

Lia laughed. "It's not the tequila really, but the combination of lime juice, pineapple, and coconut that I'm addicted to."

Seeing Dahlia at ease helped me loosen up and forget about the demon serving us drinks. I sat next to her and ordered the same thing. I took a moment to look around the bar and noticed there was no stage for a band or dance floor. The place was filled with tables, most were wood and sat four people. The place had more customers than I anticipated. Thankfully, most looked human.

Nedasea sat down with the drinks and rubbed her hands together. "Alright, here's what I'm thinking. I'd like to do an underwater theme. Can you guys get some big shells and starfish? How about a boat? Oh, and do you have a pool?"

I laughed at her enthusiasm. It was infectious and my mind immediately started churning through various ideas. "We don't have a pool, but we have several large fountains. And the perfect location for your underwater theme. It's outside, so your guests can enjoy the fountains and garden."

"It's also shielded in the event of rain. It's between the

main house and the large kitchen your caterers can use," Lia added.

Nedasea's face fell. "You don't do the food?" There was a quality to her voice that made the back of my neck prickle. It highlighted that I knew next to nothing about her kind.

I immediately wondered if the myths were true about sirens luring men to their deaths. Could she enthrall us with her voice? Or would she eat us for dinner? Each thought was more ludicrous than the last. I wanted to ask the questions racing through my head but didn't dare.

I shook my head. "We focus on the decorations and creating precisely what you want. However, we work with many restaurants and can arrange the food. All you need to tell us is what you want to serve and your budget and we will make it happen."

The siren was back to clapping her hands. "That's wonderful. Now about the decorations. Do you think we can get a giant conch shell? And make it sparkle? They've been my favorite since I was a girl."

Dahlia set her glass down. "As long as you are okay with it not being the real thing, we can do that. We have two options. We can use our CNC machine to engrave it in an inch thick piece of plywood or I can cut one out on our laser out of quarter-inch birch. We would paint either and use glitter."

"What's the difference? I don't know what either of those things is or how it would look."

"Neither would be a true shell. Both would be flat-backed. The one done on the CNC machine would be heavier, and we can engrave ridges into it. The laser would be layered wood, have a slightly different look, and be thinner. I'll make some small ones and we can get together another time and I can show you what they look like."

Nedasea was all smiles. "That's perfect. Oh, I can't wait. I want this to be perfect. Elegant and fun. Wait, wait about alcohol? Are we allowed to serve it on the plantation?"

Her question caught me mid-sip. My eyes widened and I made a noise of appreciation. Demon or not, Brezok could make a mean drink. Speaking of, she'd asked about serving alcohol at her party. "We can't serve the drinks, but we can hire a bartender that comes with a license and insurance to do it for us. That covers the requirements and allows you to have alcohol."

Lia sat forward and clasped her hands around the stem of her glass. "One thing we have to consider is that we do not know any paranormal bartenders. All of our contacts are of the mundane variety."

Nedasea cocked her head and looked between us. "How do two witches who have a party business and only deal with mundies? And not have paranormal vendors?"

I sighed. This was a long story and I didn't want to get into it with the siren. It showed our vulnerability. There were too many in this room that could use it against us. "Most of our clients are mundies. However, we have been looking for a reliable magical resource. I have a call with Kaitlyn later to see if any of her witches are bonded and licensed."

"I'm available," Brezok called out across the bar. "I can have one of my employees fill in for me."

Nedasea rolled her eyes and scowled at the demon. "You just want to come and feed off the attention you'll get. There's a reason I haven't invited you, Brezok."

"I'll order extra Highland Park and be there early so I can set up my bar." The demon didn't seem to hear Nedasea say no to him.

To my surprise, she winked at me with a smile then sighed like she was put out. "You'd better be on your best behavior. No preening on my birthday, dammit."

Lia looked at the bartender. "What do you mean by him feeding on attention?"

Nedasea furrowed her brow and opened her mouth but Brezok cut her off. "I'm a fame demon. I survive on being a household name. Most of my kind wear glamours to look like mundies and work in Hollywood. It's a cop-out if you ask me. They don't have to work for their survival. It isn't hard to hide behind a pretty façade."

Nedasea laughed. "You're so full of shit, Brez. You never learned to cast an effective glamour. That's why you own a bar and feed from scraps."

We discussed the budget, food choices, and the number of guests she expected for the next half hour. It didn't take long to get comfortable with the fame demon and Nedasea. She knew what she wanted which made it easier for me.

I put thirty bucks on the table and stood. "We will be in touch. If you have any questions or want to share other ideas, you have our number."

Nedasea smiled and pulled me into a hug then Dahlia. "I do. You guys are so easy to work with. I can't wait to see the samples."

We took our leave and I was grinning from ear to ear as we made it to Royal Street. "We sounded like professionals in there. Even with a demon manning the bar that was less stressful than working in the NICU."

Lia bumped my shoulder as we walked. "We've been professionals since the first party we threw. You have an amazing ability to come up with a hundred little things that show the clients we pay attention to every small detail. That's something I couldn't do with decades of training."

I chuckled at my sister's comment. She didn't give herself enough credit. "You are more talented than you know, sis. You are the one that creates everything on the laser and CNC machine. None of us could do that."

Lia snorted. "I can only do that because you tell me what we are putting together. I'm a proud worker bee. I'm pretty excited to come up with some designs for a conch shell. That's one we haven't done yet."

I had an idea of how we can add that into the center-pieces. "I was thinking we could use the rustic metal lanterns with driftwood and we should cut out conch shells on the laser to include in a floral bouquet."

Lia shook her head. "See, that right there is why you're queen bee. Phi comes in as a close second. Kota, too. We have to use holographic glitter on them."

"What do you think about having the demon be the bartender?" I ignored the tourist that looked at me funny.

Dahlia turned left onto Canal and smiled sweetly as we left the guy staring at us. "It's not like we have a choice. We can't take the chance that all of her guests will look normal. The last thing we need is for someone to go screaming about us being freaks. It's unlikely most would believe what they were seeing. Humans have a way of explaining away things that make them uncomfortable. Still, I don't want to deal with that. I liked your idea of asking Kaitlyn, though. We should do that regardless so we can find one for next time."

"I don't know. Brezok will likely be happy to become our de facto bartender. I bet the attention he gets at the bar has greatly diminished given that he's so commonplace there."

I stopped when I realized Dahlia wasn't with me. Turning, I lunged when her knees gave out and she collapsed. Shit, shit, shit! She was having a vision. Now plenty of people stopped to stare at us.

I held her close and jostled her. "Dahlia. Are you okay?" I kept my tone moderate, not wanting to alarm a bystander.

"Do you need help? I can call an ambulance," a young woman about my oldest daughter's age asked me.

I shook my head, hoping she didn't see the sweat rolling

down my temples. "My sister had minor surgery not too long ago and she's overdone it. She's going to be alright. Thank you, though."

I said a silent prayer that Dahlia snapped out of it so we could get the hell out of there. We were drawing attention that I'd rather avoid.

DOWNLOAD the next book in the Twisted Sisters Midlife Mayhem series, CADAVER ON CANAL STREET HERE! Then turn the page for a preview of the first chapter in MAGICAL MAKEOVER, book one in the Mystical Midlife in Maine books.

EXCERPT FROM MAGICAL MAKEOVER BOOK #1 MYSTICAL MIDLIFE IN MAINE

"*W*hat do you mean that was an irritated ghost?" I gaped at my patient as she lay on her hospital bed and shrugged her shoulders. Surreptitiously, I checked to make sure I hadn't peed myself a little. Ever since I had my daughter, my bladder control went out the window with sleep.

How was this my life now? I'd gone from being charge nurse at a respected hospital in the triangle in North Carolina, married to one of the country's best cardiothoracic surgeons to divorced and living back home with my mother and grandmother.

Hattie Silva, my patient and current employer stared at me with a furrowed brow. She was a ninety-year-old woman suffering from cancer of the intestines and required full-time care. After being fired from the hospital, my ex-husband ran me out of North Carolina and had managed to ruin my reputation, leaving me no options for work outside of in-home nursing with a hospice organization.

"I mean precisely what I said. Evanora isn't happy about

you ignoring her. She's trying to get your attention. I struggle to hear her most days. I'm at the end of my life and running out of time." Hattie looked frail when she spoke like that.

She was older and suffering far more than was pleasant. It was difficult to watch her in so much pain, but when she talked like this it was easy to forget all of that and simply see her as crazy. I thought her doctors needed to add dementia to her diagnoses.

I reached up and grabbed the necklace Fiona had sent to me a few weeks ago. My best friend had moved to England after her grandmother had died and started a new life without me. At first, I kept busy with the kids and Miles, but when my ex informed me that he was leaving me for another woman and proceeded to tear my life apart like a wrecking ball, I missed Fiona more than ever.

We met in college and hit it off right away. We'd been in each others' weddings, got jobs at the same hospitals and did everything together. I was there when her twins were born because her husband Tim had gotten stuck in traffic. And she was there for me through both of mine. Miles had elected to continue surgeries both times saying it was too complicated for him to hand off.

My heart skipped a beat when the bluish image of a woman wearing a bonnet with a tall brim and a floor length dress that was cinched around the waist with big, poofy sleeves appeared in the spot where the remote control had fallen. Startled, I dropped the necklace and reached my hand toward the ghost. The image disappeared and I shivered with the chill in the air.

Great, now she was infecting me with her crazy. Ignoring what I thought I saw, I set the glass of water on the tray beside the bed and raised the head of her bed more. "There's no such thing as ghosts. Let's get you some lunch. I made some chicken soup today."

Hattie was so thin I could see her bones under her flesh. She felt very breakable when I shifted her body's position. She started coughing when she slumped forward to make it easier for me to arrange her support. As gently as possible, I laid her on the pillows and held the cup in front of her mouth then adjusted the oxygen flowing through her nasal cannulas.

After several seconds, she took a sip then sighed. "How is it you have an item of power, but you are ignorant as the day is long?"

This was a familiar argument. She would say something about me having some powerful object and being ignorant of everything important around me. "I like you too, Hattie. You ready for lunch?" At her nod, I left to get the food. The house was massive and most of the time I didn't notice the echo throughout the place, but I was jumpy after that conversation about spirits.

Rumors from my childhood popped into my head. Maybe they had been right after all. It would make sense for her to believe in ghosts if she really was a powerful witch. Although, I could see only brief glimpses of the power she must have once held. Whether or not that was true didn't matter.

She was ill and susceptible to being taken advantage of. I hadn't been hired to consider anything other than her health, but I would never sit by and allow someone to take her for a ride. Hattie was richer than God and had numerous companies to her name. All of which poachers were dying to get their hands on. *Not on my watch.*

Hurrying to the kitchen, I turned off the pot that had been simmering on low for the past half hour since I finished putting it together. I grabbed two bowls and paused when my gaze caught sight of the water beyond the window. The panoramic views of the Penobscot Bay were to die for and cost a fortune.

Hattie's house was called Nimaha. It reminded me of how Fiona had always called her grandmother's home Pymm's Pondside. Their generation must have named their houses or something. I'd heard several friends talking about names of their grandparents' homes. My generation had nothing as refined to lay claim to. We had crow's feet, liver spots and unwanted chin hair among other unpleasant signs of reaching middle age.

Wanting to shove aside thoughts that would only lead me to perseverate on how my life had gone to hell in a hand-basket at the most inopportune time in my life, I refocused on the coastline. There was nothing on the more than three hundred feet of shoreline. Hattie had a serene sanctuary here. The waves lapped lazily against the pebbled beach. It was so peaceful and remote. Nothing like the hustle and bustle of the big city hospital where I spent twenty years caring for patients. I watched for several seconds until my mind quieted and I was relaxed.

Turning away from the big window, I grabbed the rolls my grandmother had sent with me that morning and headed back through the five thousand square foot house. Thank-fully I didn't have to clean all of the bedrooms and bath-rooms, or care for the three acres and its outbuildings. The gardening alone had to be a beast to maintain, although I had yet to see a gardener come and tend to the multi-terraced back yard.

A hiss nearly made me drop the tray of soups I had been carrying. Shifting my hold on the tray, I scanned the area for the little heathen that I swore was trying to kill me. There she was.

"Don't scare me like that Tarja." The tabby cat stuck her

nose in the air as if she could understand me and continued past me and up the stairs. She had the most beautiful coat I'd ever seen on a cat. Multi-colored with the oranges and yellows being vibrant and shiny.

The second bowl on the tray was to feed Tarja. I wasn't used to treating a cat like a person, but she ate the same food I fed Hattie. I swear Hattie invented the term crazy cat lady. Tarja was her princess and the only thing Hattie was forceful about during the job interview. I should have known Hattie wasn't entirely together when she told me Tarja was to be fed meals with her and her litter box needed to be cleaned several times a day.

I could deal with Hattie's eccentricities and bed pan and dressing changes without any problems. It was cleaning animal feces from a box that made me gag. Yes, I was aware how little sense that made. But c'mon it was a container filled with excrement that had been sitting for hours.

Shrugging off that unpleasant thought, I continued climbing the stairs and stopped short when I saw a large creature through the port hole window on one of the landings. It was dark green and almost as tall as the closest tree. And it looked like the dragons Hollywood depicted in countless movies. Only I didn't see any wings on this one.

What the heck was that? I swear something new popped up every day in this place. My heart raced and I was nearly hyperventilating as I tried to figure out what the large beast was. My breaths fogged the glass, making me use the sleeve of my top to clear the glass. When I looked back out there was nothing there.

When another scan didn't come up with the dragon, I continued up the stairs and hurried into Hattie's room where I deposited the tray and rushed to the window. Her room faced the side of the house where I'd seen the dragon. I hoped I would catch sight of it. Something that big wouldn't be able to disappear into the forest surrounding her without leaving a trail.

"What are you in a tither about now?" Hattie snapped at me like this more often than not. It was how someone talked to their child when they'd had enough of their odd behaviors.

I turned to my patient and pushed the table with the tray of food over to the bed. "I thought I saw a dragon in your backyard. I'm losing my mind just as much as you are it seems. Must be the stress of the divorce."

Hattie laughed, the sound like dry leaves rattling over a sidewalk. "You aren't seeing things, my dear. That was Tsekani. Oh, that soup smells delicious."

I was too tired to let my surprise show over her having named this imaginary dragon. *Are you sure it's not real? You saw it for yourself.* I was positive it was a bad sign that my mind was trying to rationalize my hallucinations.

I set the bowl I had brought for me on the plate where the rolls were. "Here's your lunch, Tarja."

The cat approached and sniffed the soup then started lapping it up. "She says the bay leaves were a good addition to the soup. That's not something I've ever added to mine."

My head snapped up to meet Hattie's smile. "What?"

"Seriously. Where did you get that necklace from? I'm beginning to sense you aren't magical at all." Everything in me froze with her words, including my heart for several seconds.

"My best friend, Fiona had made it for me as a symbol of my new beginning. Why are you saying it's magical? There's no such thing." Right? I wanted to believe I was open minded, but the past month of working for Hattie Silva and hearing her bizarre comments had me questioning that. There was no way I could jump on board with her and believe in magic.

Although, I had to admit I was beginning to have my

doubts. I'd seen enough in the past four weeks to really wonder. Problem was that I'm a scientist and relied on what I could prove and see. And while I had seen more than a fair share of oddities there was nothing I could hold onto or examine all that closely.

"You wouldn't believe me if I told you. Can you push the tray closer? I'd like to taste the soup Tarja can't shut up about." I shook my head and moved the tray over her bed and adjusted it, so she was able to reach the food easily.

I picked up a roll and tore off chunks while staring out the window. She had windows facing the forest and another on the wall above her head that overlooked the water. I was focused on the gentle waves and the pebbled beach when a dog raced across the area, kicking up rocks as he went.

My feet carried me closer and I watched as he bared his teeth. He wasn't like any dog I'd ever seen. He was big and dark grey in coloring. "Do you have wolves in this area?"

The clatter of a spoon filled the room. "Of course, Layla moved here first, but several others have taken refuge here over the years." I wasn't surprised to discover she named the wolves prowling in her woods. She had named her house after all. Wild wolves wouldn't have been my first choice of companions, but she had enough property to safely offer a place to as many wild animals as she wanted.

Dark coughing made me turn away from the window. I expected it to be Hattie, but it was Tarja. If she hocked up a hairball, I wasn't cleaning it. "When does your maid come to clean the house anyway? I've never met her."

Hattie cocked her head to the side and looked at me. "Mythia comes after you leave. She doesn't care to be around mundies. Why?"

"Mundies? "I have no idea what that means, but I assure you I have done nothing to upset anyone. I haven't been here long enough to make any enemies. I was hoping to talk to

her about how she gets rid of hard water around the shower faucet. I have never been able to get mine so clean."

I thought moving home would offer me a few perks. Like not having to clean bathrooms anymore, but I'd been wrong. There was no way I could take advantage of my mother like Miles had me for so many decades. Despite working long hours seven days a week I always pulled my weight around the house.

After the hurt of his announcement settled in, I immediately began dreaming about what my life would be like without him. In my naivete I had dreamed of continuing my position at the hospital and staying in the house and hiring someone to do the cleaning.

Reality was an entirely different beast. After being fired I had spent weeks of job hunting before realizing I had no choice but to move home. Miles's little tart worked in human resources at the hospital and made sure I wasn't appealing to anyone interested in hiring me. I could have filed a suit for violating my rights, but after Miles had managed to fast track our divorce and screw me out of what I deserved I didn't bother. He had friends in high places.

"Oh, I know you haven't. I did my research before hiring you. Speaking of, how did you piss off Tara so thoroughly? She had nothing good to say about you when I called. And Mythia won't share her secrets with me, so she won't share anything with you."

My head started pounding and I clenched my jaw then balled my hands into fists. Miles got his little girlfriend to sabotage my only shot at a job in this area, too? "Tara is the jailbait that slept with my husband and blacklisted me at all the hospitals in North Carolina. My ex-husband didn't want to be reminded of what a jerk he is or that his girlfriend isn't much older than our son."

Hattie laughed so hard she started coughing. Tarja

jumped onto her lap and placed a paw on her chest. Their connection was more than obvious. The cat was always close and offering comfort when Hattie had bad moments. I shifted Hattie forward and rubbed circles on her back until she stopped coughing.

"I was right about that one it seems. When I saw the written record of your employment, it made no sense to me that you suddenly started making fatal mistakes after twenty years of pristine performance reviews. She did her best to convince me that you were stressed out and upset over your husband leaving you and could no longer be trusted with patients."

I gently set her against the pillows again and returned to the window. "I was upset that Miles left me like he did, but it never affected my ability to do my job. I can assure you I will not cause you harm in any way."

Hattie waved a hand dismissively. "Oh, I know that dear. What do you say we curse her with premature winkles? Or maybe make him impotent!"

That made me choke out a laugh as I turned away from the beach outside. "I would love nothing more, but that would make me like them, and I will never be so malicious. I believe that you reap what you sow. They will both get what's coming to them one day."

"You've got that right, dear. Fate gets her way, even if it takes years and several unexpected turns." I nodded my head in agreement as I gathered the lunch dishes from her tray.

* * *

I TURNED my Land Rover off and couldn't help but smile. Keeping the nice SUV along with half of the house when it sold were the only concessions the judge awarded me which was why I was forced to move back with my mom and grandmother.

I couldn't afford the house payments on the lake front house and no one would hire me. I couldn't buy a house on the money I would be given whether Miles sold or bought me out. We owed too much on the property.

Looking up at the house I had grown up in, I couldn't help but think about the differences between Hattie's house and the house I left back in North Carolina compared to this one.

My grandparents moved into this modest one-story Cape Cod style home almost seventy years ago. The yellow siding had been repainted half a dozen times and the windows were replaced with double-pained ones last summer. The kitchen had been updated fifteen years ago when my mom moved in with my grandmother but not much else had been done.

The wood floors were scuffed and scarred and the marks measuring my height were still in the doorway to the garage alongside my mother's. Unlocking the front door, I entered to the familiar smell of lemon polish and baking bread.

"I'm home," I called out as I set my keys in the dish on the table in the entrance. "Where is everyone?"

My mother poked her head out of the kitchen. "We're in here, just finishing up dinner. Did you eat with Ms. Silva?"

I headed down the hall and caught the door before it closed after my mother returned to the sink. "Hi, nana. How was your day?" I bent and kissed her cheek while she sat in a chair at the table. She was the same age as Hattie but in much better shape.

She patted my cheek and smiled up at me. "I made some rye bread for you to take to Hattie tomorrow and finished the book I was reading."

"And you got in a good nap," my mother interjected. "Anything new happen out at Nimaha today?"

Both enjoyed hearing about the events, saying the house had been haunted as long as they could remember. I shrugged my shoulders. "Hattie has given refuge to wild wolves living in the woods around her house and she has a dragon named Tsekani."

Grandma nodded her head. "She owns something like five acres, so she probably does think she is giving them a place to live. But a dragon? Is it dementia? Many of my friends have succumbed already."

My mother shut off the water and leaned against the counter drying her hands. "Good thing we have excellent genes, and you don't have to worry about that mom. You might want to start looking for another job soon, sweetie. Sounds like she's going downhill fast."

"Who's going downhill fast?" Nina asked as she entered the kitchen and approached me with her arms open.

"Ms. Silva," I replied and embraced my daughter. She looked a lot like me except her brown hair was longer than my short cut and she didn't have crow's feet around her brown eyes. I had always loved the fact that she looked so much like me. Until I was fairly certain that was the reason Tara didn't want Nina around anymore.

Nina released me and went to the fridge. "She's been cra-cra since the day you started there. You don't have to worry about finding another job." I could hear the panic in Nina's voice. She was by my side when I struggled to find a position and celebrated with me when Hattie hired me to take care of her.

"I am giving her gold star treatment to make sure she sticks around. Do you want me to make you a snack?"

Nina gave me a side smile and shook her head. "No, you sit down and rest your feet. You work too hard. I'll grab you some rocky road."

I sat next to nana and held back the emotion choking me.

I might not have the fancy house or the cushy job, but I had more love than Miles would ever know and that's all that mattered.

When my daughter asked my mom and grandmother what they wanted and proceeded to get them some vanilla ice cream along with a cookie, I realized Hattie didn't have this. She was all alone in the world and had no one to shower her with love and affection.

I made a silent vow to ignore the crazy and show her how much she was appreciated. She was cranky, and adored cats, but she was funny and made me laugh all the time. And there were times when she had these little nuggets of wisdom that were priceless. Like when she told me to stop complaining that my daughter was asking for a car of her own.

Hattie had just finished the cookies Nina had dropped off at the end of my first week on the job when I started complaining about her latest request. I would never forget the way Hattie had scowled at me as she said, *"Be grateful she doesn't want it to go joy riding. She wants to give you and your mother a break from taking her to and from practice, and a way to get to and from a job. Yeah, she told me how much she wanted to earn money to ease your burden. Most children her age are selfish critters with no care for anyone else, let alone how much their parents sacrifice to give them what they have."*

I blinked and shoved the memory aside when Nina kissed my cheek and placed the bowl in front of me. "Thank you, peanut. You're the best daughter ever born."

"Agreed." My mom and grandmother both spoke at the same time while enjoying their dessert. My midlife makeover wasn't what I had hoped it would be when I was twenty something, but I couldn't ask for more.

. . .

Download the first book in the Mystical Midlife in Maine series, Magical Makeover HERE! Then turn the page for another preview. Then turn the page for a preview of the first chapter in MAGICAL NEW BEGINNINGS, book one in the Midlife Witchery series.

EXCERPT FROM MAGICAL NEW BEGINNIGS BOOK #1 MIDLIFE WITCHERY

⚜

*E*mmie released me and wiped a tear from her eye as she looked around the grounds. "I can see why you don't want to leave here. This place is amazing, mom. Well, aside from the eerie cemetery and mausoleum. I always hated that when we came here as kids, and it isn't any better. Anyway, knowing how much you love it will make being so far from you completely worth it."

I squeezed my oldest daughter's hand and nodded my head in agreement. I never imagined I would feel this way when I came to England to say goodbye to my grandmother. "For the first time since your father died, I feel like I'm home here at Pymm's Pondside. The only downside is not being able to hop in a car and visit you and your brother and sister."

"We don't mind coming to you, mom. You've done more than enough for us. It's about time you have something just for you," Skylar, my youngest daughter told me as she jumped into the conversation. She was leaning against the white picket fence that surrounded the massive garden my grandmother kept in pristine condition. That was one thing I wasn't looking forward to maintaining. The knee that gave me more problems than my son ached at the mere idea of so much bending.

Greyson turned from the pond at the front of the property I'd just inherited and rolled his eyes at his twin. Skylar was my sensitive one, where Emmie was the responsible one of my three kids, and Greyson was hotheaded. "Stop sucking up. Mom isn't going to fly you out to England every time you're homesick."

My head started throbbing with the familiar argument. Emmie had been away at college for two years, but the twins just started. And being my sensitive one, Skylar came home nearly every weekend. The three-hour drive didn't faze her at all, where Greyson almost always remained on campus. By staying in England, I will be making it impossible for them to come home for a weekend visit.

I am a horrible mother because leaving my kids without their home base close by didn't make me change my mind. Every cell in my body screamed that I was supposed to be at Pymm's Pondside. No. It was where I *needed* to be. I've lived the past twenty-two years for someone else. Now was my time.

I wrapped one arm around Greyson and the other around Skylar. "What have I always told you, Grey? It's your job to take care of your sisters. They do enough for you. I expect you to make time for her as we all adjust to this new setup."

Greyson's head dipped, and he took a deep breath. "Sorry, mom. You're right. I won't get lost in myself."

"I won't let you," Emmie added. "I never thought I'd be happy to move back in with you nutjobs, but I'm excited."

Dust billowed into the air as the car I arranged to take them to the airport turned down my dirt drive. Emotion clogged my throat, and my eyes burned with tears. I'd lost so much in my life, and it felt like I was losing them now, too. "I'm going to miss you guys."

Skylar squeezed me tighter. "We will miss you, too, but this isn't forever. You never know. We might decide to move here after college."

I released the twins and embraced Emmie next. "Now, remember you guys are closing on your house before the term begins. The agent will be contacting you, Emmie, to set up the date and time, but all three of you need to be there."

The second I stepped foot onto the property, I called a real estate agent in Salisbury and arranged to sell my house. I swear the gods are on my side because it sold before the week was out. Emmie was all too happy to find a place for her to move into with the twins. In no time, the three found the home they wanted. Thanks to the money from my house's sale, I put in an offer for the kids on the two-story they selected.

"I've got it handled, mom. Don't worry about us. We will be back next summer."

"If you need anything, call me." I hugged them each once more then sent them on their way.

Turning around, I took in my new home. Pymm's Pond-side was the name for the white cottage. When I visited as a kid, I thought it was neat that they named their houses here. But to call it a 'cottage' was misleading. The thing was nearly as big as my house in Salisbury, but it had charm coming out of the eaves.

The brown roof reminded me of a thatch design. Every angle was rounded, creating a soft, inviting look to the five-bedroom home. The brown shutters on the windows matched the roof, and the ivy growing up one side was straight out of a fairytale. I'd always thought that, and now it was mine.

I even owned a cemetery. I never thought I'd say that in

my life. And the craziest part was that it made me feel closer to the family I'd never known. I turned my head to the left and glanced at the headstones. Towards the back of the place were a couple of mausoleums. Yeah, it's super creepy but also pretty neat. I mean, there was a graveyard a hundred feet from where I slept. Good thing I have always loved them, or I wouldn't have been able to stay in the house.

Turning away from the cemetery, I glanced at the garden I had spent days wondering if I should remove. Not only did I cringe at the thought of so much bending, but I didn't have a green thumb. I wasn't as bad as Violet, my best friend, but plants didn't flourish under my care. And I'm starting a new life now. I admit that I have no desire to weed the damn thing. I was reluctant to pull the plants up. They're a part of the place's charm.

I headed to the pond and smiled as I looked at the large watering hole. I've seen deer, rabbits, and miniature bears drinking late at night or in the early morning. At least I thought they were tiny bears. They looked odd and had large floppy ears, and I swear they understood when I cooed at them. I was excited to have animals so close. And with woods surrounding the entire property, I hoped to see more. The area was lush, thanks to the rainy weather in Northern England.

Opening the small gate in the fence around the garden, I searched for some basil to add to my tomato sandwich for lunch. There were so many herbs and plants, and I knew what maybe a third of them were. Rosemary and mint were the most obvious. The rest I would learn in time if I don't lose it all to weeds.

I found what I was looking for in the far corner closest to the cemetery. My gaze shifted to the fresh grave. My vision blurred when I read my grandmother's name. A pinging started up in my head. That was the only way I could describe it.

Something was hitting the walls of my skull, almost like a bee trapped under a cloche. I've never experienced it before in my life. The stress of the past month must be getting to me.

I took a deep breath and thought about my grandma. Isidora Shakleton was unforgettable and an integral part of the town. Most of the residents of Cottlehill Wilds showed up for her service.

The pinging was gone by the time I turned away and walked back to the house. The inside was just as cozy as it appeared on the outside. The back door went right into the kitchen, where I dumped the basil before heading through the small living room and up the stairs to my bedroom.

The patchwork quilt my grandmother made was still on her bed. I had my clothes and a few of my favorite keepsakes shipped to me. The rest was going to the kids.

I need a new comforter. And sheets. Badly. I made plans to head into the city to pick up a cozy Down quilt and maybe a new mattress. I swear there were more lumps in the thing than there were on my butt and thighs. And that was saying something.

Being my age, it was shocking if you didn't carry an extra fifteen or twenty pounds. I know I certainly had the extra cushion. Along with aches and pains, I thought as I bent to pick up the towels Skylar left on the wood floor.

That was one thing I will not miss. The kids, much like my late husband, never picked up after themselves. And boy, did that get on my last damn nerve. I spent my entire life caring for others—both at work and at home. I swear being a caretaker was woven into my DNA.

After graduating with my bachelor's degree in nursing, I worked full-time in the ICU at a local hospital for twenty years then took care of Tim at the end. Perhaps that was what was so inviting about my grandmother's house. I didn't need to take care of anyone here.

After washing the toothpaste from the sink, I turned and yelped. "What the fuck?" My mouth got away from me when I noticed the towels back on the ground. What the hell was going on? I just picked them up and put them in the laundry basket.

I headed into the other bedrooms and stripped the beds before straightening the covers over the mattresses. By the time I returned to the room where Greyson had slept, the sheets were no longer neatly folded. Instead, I tripped over the tangled mess.

Pausing, I thrust my hands on my hips and glanced around. Was someone there messing with me? I didn't find anything else out of the ordinary, so I picked up the pile, added it to the basket, and then carried my load downstairs.

When I entered the tiny room at the back of the kitchen where the washer and dryer were, I stopped short when I noticed the soap tipped over on its side. "Alright, grandma, if you're haunting the place to scare me, there's no need. I'm not going to make too many changes."

It felt almost as if the house sighed around me. Shaking my head at my idiocy, I put a load on then entered the kitchen. The sight of the scuffed wooden stool sitting at the butcherblock island reminded me of all the days I used to sit there as a kid and listen to my grandmother tell me stories about Fae and witches.

I envied her creativity. I could never come up with the elaborate ones she did. She wove tales about portals, fairies, dragons, and gnomes. When I became a mom and my kids started asking for stories, I used my favorites from the ones she told me.

Skylar's favorite was one about a pixie that sought asylum

with a witch. A vicious beast had been hunting her. She was on the edge of her seat when it came to the part about the pixie barely evading the creature when she came up against a barrier. She pounded her tiny hands on the barrier, begging for help. The witch helped and provided the pixie with some woods to live in, and the fairy gave the witch fresh flowers in return.

Emmie's favorite was about a gnome family escaping from some barghests. While Greyson preferred stories about dragon shifters that needed to get away from the vile king that created them to ravage and kill.

I was making a sandwich while my mind traveled down memory lane when movement outside the window caught my eye. I sucked in a breath and immediately started choking on my food. Smashing the food in my hand, I raced for the back door and burst through.

I was still coughing when I dashed down the steps. After a couple more hacks, I managed to clear my throat. "Can I help you?" It still felt like food was stuck down the wrong pipe.

The woman paused with her hand on an herb in the garden and looked up at me. She looked like she was in her late twenties, maybe early thirties, and had stunning red hair. My hands smoothed down my pink t-shirt when I took in her crop top and flat stomach.

She lifted one hand and smiled. "Oh, hi. You must be Fiona, Isidora's granddaughter. I'm Aislinn. I thought you'd be on a plane home by now. I saw the car leave hours ago."

I crossed my arms over my chest, smearing mayonnaise over my left boob. I was a hot freakin' mess, but I didn't care at the moment. I have no idea how my grandmother did things, but I didn't want people wandering on my property whenever they wanted.

"This is my property, and I have decided to stay. Listen, I'm not sure what arrangement you had with my grandmother, but I would like a heads up before you go prowling around stealing my stuff."

Aislinn's eye bugged out of her head, and her hand dropped to her side. "I apologize. Like I said, I figured you'd be gone. I just needed some thistle for a potion, and Isidora has always allowed me to grab the few ingredients I need in exchange for helping with upkeep in here."

That brought a smile to my lips. My hands dropped, and pieces of tomato fell from between the bread. "In that case, you are more than welcome. Honestly, I was thinking about getting rid of the garden. I swear I have a black thumb. Besides, I have no idea what all this is or what it is for."

Aislinn chuckled and cut a couple of sprigs of the plant she'd been holding. "If you're Isidora's kin, you'll be able to keep things alive, but I am happy to help. Gardening has become my therapy since my husband left me a year ago. Is your husband not staying with you?"

I shook my head from side to side as a lump formed in my throat. Anytime I talked about Tim, I was close to losing my shit. Enough time had passed that I should be beyond this by now. But I knew better than anyone that there was no such thing as closure. Grief was a roller coaster that would catch you off guard when you least expected it. The loss of someone you love never stopped hurting, no matter how much time passed.

"My husband passed away a few years ago. Cancer." I preempted the inevitable questions about what killed him. "My kids went back home to college. They will visit, but they won't be living with me."

"I'm so sorry about your husband. You're starting over. That's good. It'll help to create a life that is separate from him. That way, the grief won't suck you under every time you turn around."

My jaw dropped open at the young woman's insight. I

would never have expected her to be so wise. "Honestly, I never thought about that. I had the hardest time letting him go. Despite how much it hurt to eat at our favorite restaurant and go to our park, I ignored it because it felt like a betrayal to do anything else. It wasn't until I got here and felt this sense of belonging that I started giving more thought to my desire to create a new life for myself."

Aislinn exited through the gate and stopped by my side. She was at least three inches shorter than my five-foot-five frame and skinny as a rail, but she exuded this green aura. I must be thinking that because she enjoys gardening.

"As a Shakleton, you belong here. I need to get home to make this potion, but if you ever need anything, I work at Phoenix Feathers. You should come in some time for a drink. On me."

I extended my clean hand and shook hers. "Thank you. I will be in touch, I'm sure."

I watched her walk away. I missed where she turned off my driveway because standing on the other side of the path was a man. He was muscular and intimidating. I wouldn't say he was gorgeous. He was too scary for that, although his beauty was undeniable.

I lifted my hand and waved at him. "Hi. I'm Fiona. I just moved into my grandmother's house." The guy didn't say a word as he stood with his feet braced apart and his arms crossed over his chest while he narrowed his brown eyes at me.

I waited a few minutes before realizing he was not going to introduce himself. Swallowing hard, I turned back to my house. By the time I got inside the kitchen, he was gone. Maybe I would ask Aislinn who the attractive yet angry man was.

Pymm's Pondside was turning out to be a pain in the butt in so many ways. I wanted to scream when I turned back to the kitchen to see silverware strewn over the island. It felt like the place was haunted. Well, too bad. This was my house, and I wasn't leaving.

I lost my Grams, quit my job, sold my house, and moved to another country. I couldn't exactly pick up where I left off. That life was in the wind now.

Download the first book in the Midlife Magic series, Magical New Beginnings HERE! Then turn the page for a preview of the first chapter of SURPRISED BY A SUPER-NATURAL START, book one in the Dame of the Midnight Relics.

EXCERPT FROM SURPRISED BY A SUPERNATURAL START

*"W*e're going to the pool, Keyboard King. You've got to stop that or we are never leaving this room," I told my husband.

Arjun looked at me in the mirror with that crooked smile. It won my heart twenty-one years ago and got me every time. "Are you sure you're set on visiting the pool, Firebird? This is the first vacation we've taken just the two of us in five years."

Turning on my stool, I smiled up at my husband. "You know I picked this resort for the pool, babe. I want to get some vitamin D and rehydrate while the sun is up. I promise to make it up to you tonight."

Arjun pulled me to my feet and wrapped his arms around me. My body ignited the second his lips touched mine. With a moan, I wrapped my arms around his neck and went to my tiptoes. His hands caressed my back as his tongue slipped into my mouth. I allowed him to get the both of us worked up, but not too far gone.

Pushing his chest, I broke away. "That's why we haven't

seen anything in Belize yet. I want to go to the pool and take a trip out to Shark Ray Alley and the ruins and..."

Arjun stopped me with a finger to the lips. "Alright, I get it. I'll book the next excursion for the Hol Chan Marine Reserve & Shark Ray Alley while you get us drinks by the pool."

"Deal." I grabbed the neon pink wrap that my girls had helped me pick out and checked myself in the mirror one more time.

I was not sure about wearing the bikini. It wasn't the triangle top that Maisy thought I would look great in but the bandeau that Amelia picked out for me. I had an extra fifteen pounds, stretch marks from carrying my three babies, and saggy boobs. Life had been good to me. My body, not so much.

"You look hot, Firebird. There is nothing to be self-conscious about. You're fit and strong. For God's sake, you carry men, women and children out of burning buildings. That extra weight you think you have is all in your head. You're perfect."

I preened and fluffed my short bob. "It's about time you noticed. It's only taken two decades."

Arjun grabbed his towel and snapped it at my backside. I yelped and jumped away from him with a laugh. Grabbing my pool bag, I danced out the door then paused and looked back. "You coming?"

"Right behind you."

My toes sank into the sand as we walked out the door of our cabana. Lifting my head to the sun, I inhaled the crisp ocean breeze. Ambergris Caye was a beautiful little island off the coast of Belize. Arjun twined his fingers with mine and we headed to the pool.

"Do you think Maisy and Amelia are getting to school on time?" I asked as we walked. Our girls were great kids who got good grades and trained hard for their cheer leading team. They were the opposite of me. I was as far from a rah-rah girl as you could get. As a firefighter, I was more comfortable getting down and dirty. And I was a plumber on my off days.

Arjun snorted as we walked up the stairs and found two lounge chairs. "There's not a chance in hell. They're going to have at least three make-up hours when we get back. And we'll have to detox them from eating cheeseburgers every day. I'll be right back. I'm going to see about that tour."

Nodding, I signaled a bartender. I ordered two Mai Tais and two Diet Cokes. The formulation for the soda was different in South America and I couldn't decide it I liked it or not. I kicked off my shoes and laid back on the chair. The heat of the sun felt good and reminded me I needed to put sunblock on. I was no longer twenty and able to withstand the UV rays without issue. Fine lines were no joke when you hit forty.

Yeah, I was a vain person and I wasn't apologetic about it. There was nothing wrong with having pride in yourself and wanting to look good. There were some things I couldn't do much about. I had a few burns on my back and arms but that came with the job.

"Good news, Firebird. There's a tour leaving in ten minutes. You ready to head out to see some sharks and stingrays?"

I sat up, dropping the bottle of sunblock in the process. "Damn, I was looking forward to laying around the pool. Someone kept me up last night."

Arjun grabbed my hand and pulled me to my feet. "Too bad. You wanted to do this one. We're going."

"Okay, okay. I'm going to go and change into my one piece. I don't want these ties coming undone while we are swimming with the fishies. Will you get us some of that pineapple and mango to take with us?"

Arjun pressed a kiss to my lips. "Anything for my gorgeous wife."

I grabbed the key from my bag and hurried back across the beach to our bungalow. I threw off my coverup and then the bikini. The one piece was on the table where I'd been getting ready earlier. I squeezed my body into it and got excited about this excursion. It looked like it was going to be a blast. I debated removing my makeup then dismissed the idea. There wasn't enough time and my mascara was waterproof.

Arjun was waiting for me at the end of the dock. He grabbed my hand and pulled me down to the boat. It was so nice to see him relaxed and having fun. Between his high-stress job in computer programming, the house, and the kids we rarely had time for fun. And never like this.

I hate to admit that I was a total cliché and after turning forty, I had a mini-midlife crisis. I didn't go out and buy a sports car, but have been evaluating what I want from life. I love being a fire fighter but wasn't sure it was my passion anymore. It just felt like something was missing. I hadn't figured it all out yet. But the one thing I insisted on was taking a vacation just Arjun and I once a year. We didn't make it happen last year which I made sure didn't happen again.

We climbed on board the boat and took a seat while the guide went over the rules for the trip. The captain left the dock when the last person sat down. I enjoyed the fresh fruit during the boat ride. After the captain anchored the boat, everyone got ready and jumped in the ocean.

My eyes were wide and my heart racing as I got my first sight of the world under the water. There were sea turtles, nurse sharks, stingrays, moray eels, and various colorful fish.

And then there was the stunning coral reef ecosystem. Belize was home to the second-largest barrier reef system in the world, after the Great Barrier Reef in Australia. It was why I selected Ambergris Caye to visit. I'd done research and picked out the brain coral then I found some elkhorn and staghorn coral. My favorite was the fire coral.

I turned to smile at Arjun and a scream left me. Floating next to me was a young woman of about seventeen years old with long, light blonde hair. Her silver eyes were glaring daggers at me while her white dress floated around her body. The style was familiar but I couldn't place it. I was too busy trying to figure out why she was pissed off at me and why she was down there without any snorkeling gear. She waved her hand and bright silvery light practically blinded me. My hand shot up to shield my eyes and I dropped to land on something soft. I held my breath because my snorkel had to be below the water now.

When the glow faded, I dropped my arm and gaped at what I was looking at. I was in the water but not. A bubble surrounded me and inside was the woman, me, and a nurse shark that was swimming next to me.

I lifted the mask and mouthpiece off my face. "What the hell is going on? Who are you and how did you do that? Whatever it was, you need to undo it. That shark is going to die."

The woman growled and flicked her fingers. Electricity tingled across my body and the shark was no longer in the bubble with us. "You're a hard woman to find Nylah Gilbert. I am the goddess Artemis and I am here to make you the Relic Keeper."

My jaw dropped open as I stared at her. "Did you hit your head?"

Artemis, if that's who she was, crossed her arms over her chest and glared at me. "You're standing in a magical sphere that no one can see and you're asking if I hit my head? I don't have time for this. We need to go so I can bring your latent DNA to the fore. It's not going to be pleasant."

I had no idea what the hell this crazy lady was talking about. It felt like my mind had fractured. Maybe I'd passed out and I was drowning. I extended my hand, hoping not to feel anything. I shrieked when my palm hit something that felt solid. Arjun swam by then and was turning in a circle. The way his eyes were scanning frantically, I knew he wasn't enjoying the wild life. I pounded on the sphere and started shouting his name.

"Would you stop that? It's not necessary. He can't see you."

I whirled and glared at Artemis. "Let me out of here you crazy ass bitch. My husband is worried and looking for me. You have no right to put me in whatever this is. I'm not going anywhere with you."

Artemis took a step toward me. "I do not have the patience for this. I have a mission for you. You need to get past your disbelief and get on board. Now." She snapped her fingers and the denial and rationalizing that was running through my head slowed until it vanished entirely.

In that second, I knew without a shadow of a doubt that things that go bump in the might actually existed. The panic I expected to feel never arrived. "What did you do to me?"

Artemis rolled her eyes. "I sped things along. Humans go through too much drama when confronted with the super-natural world. I don't have time to watch you process what I am telling you."

"Right, because you need to make me a Relic Keeper. I hate to break it to you, but I am not going to cooperate. I have no idea who you really are, but I want out of here. Now!" I put all my anger and frustration into my request.

Artemis cursed and said something under her breath and

a second later, I was sucking in water and kicking my way to the surface. I devolved into a coughing fit as I sucked in air the second that I broke the surface. My lungs burned from the salt water and my eyes were watering. I screamed when someone grabbed my arms.

"Are you alright, Firebird?"

Shaking my head, I continued coughing. When my lungs stopped spasming, I opened my mouth to tell him what had happened but stopped. "My mouth piece filled with water. I'm good now."

I put my mask back on and ducked back down, this time looking for the blonde girl in the dress. I searched everywhere, but didn't see her. Had I just imagined that? It felt unreal and my instinct was to deny she had ever been there. Except, thanks to whatever she'd done I knew vampires and witches and shifters existed. I wasn't into fantasy books or movies. It was all I could do to watch Harry Potter with my kids. This was not something I could have come up with in my wildest dreams.

I was shaken to my core and on edge. I jumped when Arjun twined his fingers with mine. He gave me a look and I had to point to a sea turtle to distract him. I spent the longest hour of my life looking at fish and petting nurse sharks and stingrays with Arjun until we finally climbed out of the water.

"Are you sure you're alright? I thought you would have enjoyed that more."

I smiled up at Arjun. "I'm okay. That truly was an amazing experience. I could seriously live here."

Arjun let it go and we rode back to the shore in silence with me tucked into his side. We ordered food to be delivered then headed to our room. I stripped out of my bathing suit and turned on the shower. Before I could get under the hot stream, Arjun stopped me. "Talk to me. Are you really

251

upset you didn't get to lay by the pool? I thought you'd want to go right away since you've been looking forward to that the most."

I nodded then ducked under the water and started talking. I told him everything that happened from the second Artemis appeared next to me. He felt the back of my head and looked into my eyes. "Did you hit your head when you dove into the water?"

Rinsing my hair, I shut off the faucet and growled at him. "No, I didn't hit my damn head. You should know I'd never come up with something this far-fetched." I wrapped myself in one of the resort's fluffy towels.

The knock at the door interrupted our conversation. Arjun answered it and carried our tray of food to the bed. "I don't know what to think of this, Firebird. It's completely insane, you know that, right?"

A bright light filled the room and that same electricity filled the air. Arjun jumped up and put himself between me and Artemis. "She...she just...how the fuck?"

Artemis sighed and snapped her fingers. Arjun's face went slack. "Supernaturals are real. I'm a goddess and I'm here to make your wife the Relic Keeper she was always meant to be."

"What?" Arjun and I blurted at the same time.

"Nylah has witchcraft in her lineage some generations back. Her line's powers lie specifically with the Relic Keepers. We are in need of one of her kind to protect Objects of Power from falling into the wrong hands. Now, can I get on with enhancing her DNA, please?"

Arjun looked back at me as I sank into his back. "No. You can't. Get out of our room."

Artemis grew in size so she towered over us by several feet. "Let me be clear. I am going to bring your weak DNA forward and you are going to become the Relic Keeper. My huntresses refuse to continue recovering artifacts for me unless we have you."

I swallowed the fear down and told my heart to slow down before I passed out. "Why don't you ask another Relic Keeper? I'm sure you're wrong about me. There is nothing magical about me."

"The Relic Keeper line was hunted down and killed for their power which made anyone with a modicum of Relic Keeper power go into hiding. Over the years your magical DNA had been diluted. This is what you were meant to be. The Fates would not have brought me to you if you weren't supposed to go down this path."

I was shaking my head back and forth when Artemis barked at me, "Enough of this. I wanted you to be on board because it makes this process easier. But I don't need it."

I was gaping at her when she shot me in the chest with a bolt of silver lightning. I fell back on the bed, my towel falling open as my back arched and I screamed. Any noise I was making cut off as I couldn't catch my breath. Every cell in my body felt like it was on fire. Agony consumed me entirely. There wasn't any part of me that didn't hurt. Having my legs chopped off with painful slowness would be preferrable to what I was experiencing at that moment.

It was as if something was growing inside each one until it made me feel like I was going to explode. I glanced down to make sure my skin hadn't split open. There was a silver glow worm traveling beneath my skin. It felt as if it was electrocuting every cell as it went, making the pain even worse. The part of my brain able to process was awed at the tiny red fireworks that exploded every few centimeters beneath the surface. It looked like the worm was shitting red as it traveled. The worst part was it felt as if my insides were rearranging themselves.

Arjun's hands roamed up and down my torso as he

shouted at the goddess. I was shaking my head telling him that threatening that woman was not a good idea. She could kill him with a snap of her fingers. My vision blurred and my mouth went dry yet I couldn't say anything. There was no doubt Artemis was a goddess. Whatever she did to me was not normal.

After what seemed like an hour, the pain subsided and I fell back to the bed. "What..did...you do?"

Artemis was back to just under six feet and glaring at the two of us. "I told you what I was going to do. You're welcome." She pulled a stone tablet from nowhere and dropped it on the bed. "That's the Stone of Transmutation. The first artifact you need to protect. You will want to cast a protection charm over that and keep it away from those you love or it will alter them in ways that will kill them. And you should build your vault before long. It's the only way you can ensure the relics under your care cannot be detected. We will have new Objects of Power for you soon."

I opened my mouth and the goddess disappeared. Arjun reached out to grab the tablet that looked like it was thousands of years old and had letters etched into the surface. "No!" I shouted at Arjun instinctually. Blue light shot from my hands and wrapped around the stone tablet until it was completely encased in it.

My shocked gaze lifted to Arjun who was looking at me with horror in his eyes. "What the hell are you now?"

My heart cracked in half when his expression turned to one of disgust. Arjun had been my best friend and partner for over twenty years. One visit from an insane goddess and I was going to lose him. There was no hint of the desire for me he'd had there only hours before. With one flick of a finger, Artemis had turned me into a Relic Keeper. That wasn't what was upsetting me. There was truth to her words that I was meant for this role. It was the fact that my husband was backing away from me with fear and revulsion. It didn't feel like there was a way we could get through this like we had every problem we'd ever encountered. I wanted to rip Artemis a new one for taking the one person I had always been able to count on.

DOWNLOAD the first book in the Dame of the Midnight Relics series, SURPRISED BY A SUPERNATURAL START HERE! Then turn the page for a preview of The Prime of My Magical Life, book one in the Shrouded Nation series.

GLOSSARY OF SMITH FAMILY

$\mathcal{D}$ean – Oldest brother and oldest child
Dawson – Second oldest brother and second child

Dominic – Third oldest brother and fifth child

Dagen – Youngest brother and eighth child

Sawyer – Dreya & Steve's oldest son

Spencer - Dreya & Steve's second son

Sean - Dreya & Steve's third son

Scarlett - Dreya & Steve's daughter and youngest child

Braxton – Jeff and Dakota's son and youngest child

Kora - Jeff and Dakota's third daughter and third child

Annabelle - Jeff and Dakota's first daughter and oldest child

Mia - Jeff and Dakota's second daughter and second child

Tegan – Dahlia & Leo's youngest daughter and last child

Eli – Dahlia & Leo's son and second child

Mackenna - Dahlia & Leo's oldest daughter and oldest child

Ashton – Danielle & Mike's son, one of the twins

Ava - Danielle & Mike's second daughter, one of the twins

Genevive - Danielle & Mike's oldest daughter and oldest child

Mason – Deandra & Maleko's oldest son

Maverick - Deandra & Maleko's second son

Mateo - Deandra & Maleko's third son

Matiu - Deandra & Maleko's youngest son

Justin – Delphine & Tucker's son and youngest child

Rachel - Delphine & Tucker's daughter and oldest child

Stephanie – Dagen's wife

Rory – Dagen & Stephanie's oldest son and oldest child

Addilyn - Dagen & Stephanie's daughter and youngest child

Zak - Dagen & Stephanie's second son and second child

Tracy – Dominic's wife

Tom – Dominic & Tracy's oldest son and oldest child

Terrance - Dominic & Tracy's youngest son and youngest child

Madeline - Dominic & Tracy's oldest daughter and second child

Maisy - Dominic & Tracy's second daughter and third child

Brianna – Dawson's ex-wife

Cassandra – Dawson & Brianna's oldest daughter and oldest child

Lilly - Dawson & Brianna's second daughter and second child; one of twins

Celeste - Dawson & Brianna's third daughter and second child; one of twins

Liam - Dawson & Brianna's son and youngest child

Nancy – Dean's ex-wife

Gracie – Dean & Nancy's youngest daughter and youngest child

Nicole – Dean and Nancy's oldest daughter and oldest child

AUTHORS' NOTE

Reviews are like hugs. Sometimes awkward. Always welcome! It would mean the world to me if you can take five minutes and let others know how much you enjoyed my work.

Don't forget to visit my website: www.brendatrim.com and sign up for my newsletter, which is jam-packed with exciting news and monthly giveaways. Also, be sure to visit and like my Facebook page https://www.facebook.com/AuthorBrendaTrim to see my daily posts.

Never allow waiting to become a habit. Live your dreams and take risks. Life is happening now.

DREAM BIG!

XOXO,

Brenda

OTHER WORKS BY BRENDA TRIM

The Dark Warrior Alliance
Dream Warrior (Dark Warrior Alliance, Book 1)
Mystik Warrior (Dark Warrior Alliance, Book 2)
Pema's Storm (Dark Warrior Alliance, Book 3)
Isis' Betrayal (Dark Warrior Alliance, Book 4)
Deviant Warrior (Dark Warrior Alliance, Book 5)
Suvi's Revenge (Dark Warrior Alliance, Book 6)
Mistletoe & Mayhem (Dark Warrior Alliance, Novella)
Scarred Warrior (Dark Warrior Alliance, Book 7)
Heat in the Bayou (Dark Warrior Alliance, Novella, Book 7.5)
Hellbound Warrior (Dark Warrior Alliance, Book 8)
Isobel (Dark Warrior Alliance, Book 9)
Rogue Warrior (Dark Warrior Alliance, Book 10)
Shattered Warrior (Dark Warrior Alliance, Book 11)
King of Khoth (Dark Warrior Alliance, Book 12)
Ice Warrior (Dark Warrior Alliance, Book 13)
Fire Warrior (Dark Warrior Alliance, Book 14)
Ramiel (Dark Warrior Alliance, Book 15)
Rivaled Warrior (Dark Warrior Alliance, Book 16)

Dragon Knight of Khoth (Dark Warrior Alliance, Book 17)
Ayil (Dark Warrior Alliance, Book 18)
Guild Master (Dark Alliance Book 19)
Maven Warrior (Dark Alliance Book 20)
Sentinel of Khoth (Dark Alliance Book 21)
Araton (Dark Warrior Alliance Book 22)
Cambion Lord (Dark Warrior Alliance Book 23)
Omega (Dark Warrior Alliance Book 24)
Dragon Lothario on Khoth

Dark Warrior Alliance Boxsets:
Dark Warrior Alliance Boxset Books 1-4
Dark Warrior Alliance Boxset Books 5-8
Dark Warrior Alliance Boxset Books 9-12
Dark Warrior Alliance Boxset Books 13-16
Dark Warrior Alliance Boxset Books 17-20

Hollow Rock Shifters:
Captivity, Hollow Rock Shifters Book 1
Safe Haven, Hollow Rock Shifters Book 2
Alpha, Hollow Rock Shifters Book 3
Ravin, Hollow Rock Shifters Book 4
Impeached, Hollow Rock Shifters Book 5
Anarchy, Hollow Rock Shifters Book 6
Allies, Hollow Rock Shifters Book 7
Sovereignty, Hollow Rock Shifters Book 8

Midlife Witchery:
Magical New Beginnings Book 1
Mind Over Magical Matters
Magical Twist
My Magical Life to Live
Forged in Magical Fire

Like a Fine Magical Wine
Magical Yule Tidings
Magical Complications
Magical Delivery
Magical Moxie

Mystical Midlife in Maine
Magical Makeover
Laugh Lines & Lost Things
Hellmouths & Hot Flashes
Holidays with Hades
Saggy But Witty in Crescent City
Nasty Curses & Big Purses

Twisted Sisters' Midlife Maelstrom:
Packing Serious Magical Mojo
Cadaver on Canal Street

Bramble's Edge Academy:
Unearthing the Fae King
Masking the Fae King
Revealing the Fae King

Midnight Doms:
Her Vampire Bad Boy
Her Vampire Suspect
All Souls Night

Printed in Dunstable, United Kingdom